I0664070

BUYER BEWARE

Diana Rittenhouse Mystery 5/5

Kate Merrill

This is a work of fiction. Names, characters, places, and incidents are either the product of the author's imagination or are used fictitiously, and any resemblance to actual persons living or dead, business establishments, events or locales, is entirely coincidental.

BUYER BEWARE

COPYRIGHT @ 2017 by Kathleen E. Merrill

All rights are reserved. No part of this book may be used or reproduced in any manner whatsoever without written permission of the author or Merlin-Janus Studio, Inc. except in the case of brief quotations embodied in critical articles or reviews.

Cover art: Kate Merrill

Merlin-Janus Studio, Inc.
Mooresville, NC

Publishing History
First Edition 2017
Second Edition 2022
Print ISBN: 0692757680

Published in the United States of America

CAVEAT EMPTOR

A Latin phrase meaning "Let the buyer beware."
In a caveat emptor state like North Carolina,
sellers do not have to disclose any facts
about their property
to the buyer.

ONE

April Fool...

The silly season was at hand. Ever since last Saturday, April Fools' Day, amorous squirrels had been darting under car tires, bluebirds were chasing hungry snakes away from their newly laid eggs and most foolish of all—many couples in Diana's lovesick circle of friends were choosing that particular spring to tie the knot.

Everyone, that is, but Diana Rittenhouse and Matthew Troutman, her longtime lover.

After five years in a committed relationship and six months of living together at Matthew's house on Lake Norman, they had now reached a crossroads. The road Diana had expected to travel involved selling her beloved condo, which she'd owned ever since moving from Philly to North Carolina, and then making their love official by accepting Matthew's ring. Problem was, Diana had still hadn't seen that ring.

She jerked hard on the steering wheel of her aging Ford Crown Victoria, "Queen Vic," narrowly missing one of the aforementioned amorous squirrels. She made a right on River Highway then glanced at the digital clock on her dash: 10:15 AM. She had precisely fifteen minutes to get to her appointment with the sewer inspection guy, and who would want to be late for such a romantic rendezvous?

And who would want to be a real estate broker in the middle of a recession? Only yesterday she'd gone to list a foreclosure in a rough neighborhood in old Mooresville. When she'd pulled into the rutted driveway, between two dilapidated mill houses, the one on the left being her prospective listing, an enraged pit bull in the yard next door flung his teeth against the chain link fence only inches from her leg, spraying saliva on her pants.

She'd ducked through the unlocked door of the foreclosed property into a kitchen littered with dirty broken dishes and gang graffiti on the walls. It smelled like a urinal. Sweeping her flashlight beam around the trashed space, she'd decided the place should be condemned, not merely foreclosed.

Adding insult to injury, two young men from the house next door had been waiting to greet her when she returned to her car. Stripped to the waist, their upper torsos covered in tattoos, they'd spat and cursed in Spanish. They'd gesturing with their fists, middle fingers folded in, index and pinkie fingers stuck out like the horns of the devil. She'd counted herself lucky not to understand that language. She'd been even luckier to escape from the driveway seconds before the punks released the dog intent upon eating her tires.

And although today was a glorious spring day, Diana was becoming more depressed with every passing minute. Yet the breeze blew fresh and cool when she turned south on Williamson Road. She crossed the bridge bathed in sunlight from a clear blue sky. It dazzled the dancing water, making the day near perfect except for the fact that she was scheduled to spend much of it watching a gang of unlucky men excavating an ancient, stinking, sludgy vault of sewage—not her idea of fun.

So much for the glamorous life of a Realtor.

2

She sighed and steered into one of the older original waterfront neighborhoods, where the modest cottages and ranchers commanded some of the best views of the lake. Compared to the prestigious new subdivisions, with their golf courses, yacht clubs and multi-million dollar McMansions, these humble homes were more affordable for folks still treading water in the shrinking middle class, like Diana and Liz, her best friend in all the world, who was currently Diana's Buyer/Client. These older homes were also plagued by lead-based paint, asbestos and questionable sewer systems, like this "diamond-in-the-rough" Liz was poised to purchase—a real estate agent's nightmare. But Diana loved Liz, so she had agreed to represent her.

So much for the power of love.

As Diana drove up to the rough diamond in question, 16 Blueberry Lane, she noticed a big silver tanker truck was already parked by the side of the road. It bore her pal Moby's logo—an environment-friendly green snake coiled to pump hazardous waste. Four guys stood around in the overgrown yard. They were knee-deep in weeds, scratching their heads, while Moby himself waddled towards her car. By the time Diana located her clipboard, Suprakey and her always elusive cellphone, the man was huffing at her window. She climbed from Queen Vic and shook his massive, sweaty paw.

"Good to see you, Mrs. Rittenhouse." Moby's huge grin in his round flushed face revealed a surprisingly perfect set of glittering white teeth. "I haven't seen you in a good long while. You're not hiring my competition, are you?"

"Course not." She smiled back, then frowned at the yard, where hopefully a functioning drainage system lurked beneath the ground. "I just haven't had a problem like this in a good long while."

"Tell me about it." He rolled his tiny blue eyes under his blond crew cut. "The Health Department didn't even have a septic permit for this address. Looks like we'll have to dig it up."

Shit. Diana seldom spoke that word aloud, but today she thought it loud and clear. Without a proper permit, the bank wouldn't approve Liz's mortgage, the deed would be clouded and they'd never make the closing date only three weeks away.

She ran fingers through her short white hair and rolled her blue eyes back at him. "How do these things happen, Moby? This house has been here since the early seventies and we just now have this problem?"

He shrugged his fleshy shoulders. He was very big and very white, thus his nickname. "Well, ma'am, I figure this system is what they call *grandfathered.* Likely the original owner built the place and put in the septic himself. Back when Duke Power dammed up the Catawba River and created Lake Norman they didn't much care about the environment. It's only been the past few decades they got worried about pollution, lucky for me."

"Lucky for everyone," Diana said. Sewage waste leaching into Lake Norman, which was now relatively pristine, would be disastrous for Realtors and all citizens who depended on its beauty and purity. "I'm sorry we need to deal with this, Moby, but better now than later."

"Who's the buyer?"

They glanced at the charming little cottage with a peaked roof and screened porches on both sides—road and lake. The place was painted aqua blue, like the water on a sunny day, with peeling white trim.

"Actually, my partner Liz McCorkle is buying it. I'm sure you've met her."

Moby offered a low wolf- whistle of appreciation. "Oh yeah, I've met her. How could I forget a gal like Liz?"

Right. Liz always made a big impression on men—big boobs, big red hair, and a big friendly personality to complete the package. Liz was a man magnet, partly innocent on her part. Diana was relieved that the days of Liz's fatal attractions were soon coming to an end. "I hate to break it to you, Moby, but Liz is getting married next month. This cottage will be their honeymoon home."

"No kidding?" His smile sagged and his shoulders drooped. "So who's the lucky guy?"

"She's marrying her childhood sweetheart, Danny Capelli."

"No way! I know the dude. Used to be a house painter, right? Now he's a general contractor. Capelli hired me to lay out the septic system for that new development at the Pointe."

"So you approve?"

"Helluva nice guy," Moby freely admitted.

Diana approved, too. Of all the men Liz had dated over the years—most had been train wrecks—Danny was the prize, the brass ring. And although Danny had never possessed the wealth and drive Liz claimed she wanted in a man, he was the steadfast love of her life. Unfortunately, it took Liz turning thirty-five to realize Danny was the one all along.

"Capelli's doing all right for himself now," Moby continued. He nodded at the house, which had been built at second-story level and was perched on free standing mooring posts, like a beach shack. "He's just the man to deal with this fixer-upper. Likely he'll create a basement and double his square footage."

"Maybe so." But Diana's mind had wandered to the four workers now stomping through the yard, probing at the ground with spikes.

"I don't get it," Moby said. "Liz McCorkle's a real estate lady. She works in your office, doesn't she, Mrs. Rittenhouse? How come she's not handling her own purchase?"

"Yes, she works in my office. In fact, we're officially a team. Let's just say I'm doing this deal as a wedding present." Diana watched as a scrawny worker located a rusted ventilator pipe buried in the weeds.

"Found it, boss!" he hollered. "Looks like the tank's down here. Should we start digging?"

"Yeah, go ahead!"

As a young Hispanic worker backed a miniature backhoe down a ramp from a platform mounted behind the silver tanker, Diana mused about the circumstances that had really caused her to represent Liz. Her partner had made a stupid mistake, an oversight, really. But somehow, while Liz and Danny were vacationing on the Outer Banks, deciding to get hitched, Liz had neglected to deposit a buyer's earnest money check into the company's escrow account. She'd left the client's check under their Broker-In-Charge's computer but forgot to tell him it was there. The North Carolina Real Estate Commission got wind of her rookie mistake and suspended Liz's license. Hopefully the Commission would forgive Liz after her hearing, but for now she was unemployed.

"So, where's the big shot inspector?" Moby glanced at his wristwatch. "Wasn't he supposed to be here at 10:30?"

Diana chuckled. "Maybe he's waiting until you've done the dirty work."

"Sounds about right." With that, Moby tied a loose shoestring on one monster running shoe, then lumbered across the field, where the hoe had begun scraping the skin off the rocky bones of the yard.

Diana made her way up a dirt path littered with crunchy brown pecan shells. The roots from the pecan tree had gnarled the surface while shade from its leaves bathed the path in dappled light. As she climbed the rickety stairs, brushing cobwebs off her face, she tried to remember when the house had last been shown. Although it had been on the market for almost a year, not unusual in these depressed economic times, it had attracted little interest. It took special buyers, with an imagination like Liz's and skills like Danny's, to see past the neglect to the gem this property would become with a little TLC. So likely Liz had been the last visitor, before her vacation, and Diana had never seen the inside at all.

She experienced a little thrill of excitement as she entered a secret code on the keyboard of her Suprakey and heard the soft buzzing of its activated infrared beam. Next she pointed the beam at the lockbox receiver and opened it. Applying pressure to the bottom of the metal box, she released the latch and a tiny tray slid out. The tray contained, of all things, an old fashioned skeleton key to 16 Blueberry Lane.

Good Lord, technology had changed so much, but some things never did. During her thirty years as a real estate agent—first in Main Line Philadelphia, more recently in North Carolina—she'd seen it all. Lockboxes once opened with traditional keys, then combo locks and now laser beams. Listings used to be laboriously published in cumbersome binders the size phone books, now they were entered into cyberspace in a matter of minutes for all the world to see. But she hadn't seen a skeleton key like this one since her grandmother's farm! What never changed was the thrill of seeing a property for the very first time, a sense of breaking and entering someone else's private space, the snooping and discovery. When that property was destined to soon belong to a friend, the anticipation was sweetened by the prospect of someday sharing wine, dinner and laughter within those walls.

Diana took a deep breath, twisted the key, and when the door creaked open she stepped inside.

TWO

Conjuring the spirits…

The space was chilly because the heat was turned off. It smelled faintly of must, aged wood and old ashes from the large brick fireplace on the north wall. The high-peaked ceiling featured seasoned pine boards and beams directly under the roof, while the window-wall, at the east end the great room, opened to the front porch and a breath-taking view of the lake. This main room housed an old fashioned kitchen where Diana had entered. The kitchen was hung with a bank of shellacked handmade cabinets and included a double porcelain farm sink set in a dented metal frame and outdated appliances. An oaken table and chairs established a dining area in the south third of the room, and beyond that, a narrow hallway led to three small bedrooms and a tiny bath.

All the modest rooms had spectacular views of the water because 16 Blueberry Lane was situated on a peninsula. The land across the road was too narrow to build on, so the cottage had unrestricted vistas front and back. Liz and Danny would have sunrise on the wide sheltered cove where their dock was located and dramatic sunsets on the Main Channel across the way. So although the dwelling was basic, it had "good bones" as Diana's mother used to say. With a little makeup, it would shine.

The real estate lobe of Diana's brain booted up a calculation multiplying the going rate times the number of linear feet of waterfront. She realized the worth of the land alone far exceeded the asking price, which made the place an excellent investment for her friends. Had wealthy buyers zeroed in on this lot they would have considered this house a teardown, and the neighborhood would have included yet another mini-mansion. But Liz and Danny, with limited financial means, would enlarge and restore, making the property charming and homey, the way Diana's sentimental heart believed it should be.

She glanced out the window to where the men were digging and hoped the deal would work out for her dear friends. In a transaction like this involving an older house with issues, anything could go wrong. It might appraise too low to support the mortgage, or possibly the septic permit would not allow a three bedroom home on the lot. Hopefully, all the officials involved would see the "good bones" and Liz and Danny would get their honeymoon nest.

First impressions complete, Diana began conjuring the spirits of the previous owners. In this case they'd left few clues— no family photos on the mantel, no curtains or bedspreads to imply either a male or a female influence. Thanks heavens she'd found no rotten food in the harvest gold refrigerator. Aside from the dining set, the only furniture left behind was a pair of faded wicker rockers on the screened porch, and they told no tales.

Before she could snoop farther, she was startled by a sharp rapping at the roadside door. When she spun around, she saw a stork-like gentleman with thick glasses perched on his beaky nose staring through the glass. His nametag said "Iredell County Environmental Health Department." From his official and officious attitude, she would have placed him without the tag. She quickly opened the door, reached into the pocket of her khakis and handed him a business card.

"Sorry I am late," he said. "My name is Ryman Meeks." He frowned at her card.

"I'm Diana Rittenhouse, Lakeside Realty. Would you like to see inside?" she offered.

"How many bedrooms?" He swiveled his narrow face on a stalk-like neck to peer within but did not cross the threshold.

"Three bedrooms," she answered.

"Hum, we will see about that. This house was built on low-lying land not much above the 760 Line. Could be the place will not perk for three."

Diana swallowed hard and tried to think positive. In lake lingo, the 760 Line referred to 760 feet above sea level, which was the height of the surface of Lake Norman at "full pool." Duke Power owned the lake and generous setbacks surrounding it. Property owners could not build within those perimeters, and often land only marginally higher than the lake surface lacked a sufficient water table to provide well water or a septic field large enough to serve an average house.

"You understand, Mrs. Rittenhouse, that without a septic permit *no one* should be living here. It is illegal."

"I do understand."

"It is against the law," the unpleasant man reiterated.

"Yes, I know." Good lord, the house had been occupied for forty years and so far no one had been arrested. "Why don't we go outside and see what the men have found?"

He grunted something Diana took as agreement, then held the door so she could pass in front of him and lead the way down the pecan-strewn path. As they entered the weedy yard, Diana felt his creepy presence close on her heels. Mr. Meeks walked like a stork, lifting his knees, taking slow precise steps, and she felt his breath puff against her neck with each footfall.

11

"Ryman, my man!" Moby stood upright, using a shovel like a cane. "How's it hangin', Mr. Meeks?"

Apparently the men knew one another, which was not surprising. It was surprising that Moby was using a hand shovel instead of playing supervisor while his guy worked the backhoe.

"I am well, Mr. Kerns," Meeks said. "How are you coming with this project?"

"It's slow goin', Ryman. We got down as far as the tank lid then had to back off. Some of these old concrete vaults will crumble if we accidentally bump 'em with the blade, so I'm goin' in close the old fashioned way."

"Yes, I see that." Ryman Meeks folded forward and peeked over the edge into the pit.

In the meantime, Diana noticed the Hispanic man driving the backhoe was digging a large perimeter hole encircling the tank about ten feet out. The other two workers were bringing more shovels, apparently planning to approach the ancient vault from the outside-in. She gave the air a tentative sniff. Nope. So far no obnoxious sewer odor, only the loamy smell of earth. She wondered if it would seem unprofessional if she walked down to the dock and waited until it was over. She could sit on the wooden swing in the gazebo and watch the waves, breath the fresh air until they needed her, right?

Wrong.

Moby nudged her elbow. "Take a look, Mrs. Rittenhouse, and you'll see why we earn every penny of our fee." He guided her to the edge of the abyss. "See all those roots? Helluva mess. We'll go in easy. Like the doctors say, 'First do no harm.' Our competitors wouldn't go to all that trouble."

Diana was curious. She'd always avoided getting up close and personal with sewer systems but inquiring minds should want to know. When she looked into the pit, she saw the thick roots Moby had mentioned, crumbling red clay and a rough concrete box that looked like the burial vaults she'd seen being transported by semi-trailers on the highway. She knew the basics of how the system worked, saw the pipe partially exposed that carried the waste from the house to the tank. Then somehow, after fermenting and decomposing in the tank, the neutralized sewage spread into the big drainage field beyond—but that was where her knowledge ended.

"This looks to be in decent shape, considering the age," Moby said. "They don't build 'em like they used to."

"So the system is good to go?" Diana asked hopefully.

"We do not yet know that yet, Mrs. Rittenhouse." Mr. Meeks's frown deepened. "This tank has not been used in months, maybe years. Take the lid off, Mr. Kerns."

"Yessir." Moby and three assistants eased into the space opened by the backhoe and gently inserted their shovel blades into the crack separating lid from box.

The Hispanic man abandoned the machine, picked up a shovel and walked out into the grass. "I'll take a look at the field, boss."

"Go for it, Lou," Moby hollered.

Diana had seen enough. She glanced wistfully at the gazebo, then heard a loud sucking sound. Suddenly the air was filled with a disgusting stench like the smell of portable potties at a public event. A collective gag went up from the crew and Diana felt sick to her stomach.

She walked rapidly away towards the guy with the shovel, who was now upwind from the pit. Yuck! Maybe it was the lack of food—she'd only had one peanut butter cracker on the road and no breakfast—so she was definitely queasy.

"Does it always smell this bad?" she asked the man.

"Oh, si, senora. Sometimes it is much worse." He performed overhead and side stretches to limber up. "You get used to it."

"Not me," she muttered as she stared unhappily at the shallow pathway Lou had dug into the drainage field. He was looking for the distribution lines that ran below the ground. At the bottom of the rubble tunnel, she spotted something out of place. "What is that down there? Did someone lose his shoe?"

Lou wandered stiffly to her side and looked to where she was pointing. "Looks like a shoe. I will go see..." Before Diana knew what was happening, the man scrambled down like a monkey. Seconds later, he had twisted the object from the rooted ground and held it aloft like a door prize. "Si, you are right, lady. It is an old shoe!"

Suddenly he tossed it up at her. Reflexively, she caught it. It was unusually heavy. "I don't want this filthy thing!" she shouted down at him.

He grinned up at her, his white teeth dazzling in the noonday sun. "No, you must keep it, is good luck. Empty it out."

"Why?"

"There is money rolled up inside," Lou insisted as he scrambled up to join her. "Check it out, lady." He handed her a short stubby stick. "You look, or I will. Finders- keepers."

The man was daring her, so Diana was determined to prove him wrong. When she shoved the stick under the rotted leather shoe tongue, she encountered resistance, so throwing caution to the wind she dropped the stick and began exploring with her fingers. She picked away the shoestrings, which broke like dry spaghetti, then pulled at the thing wedged inside.

Something cracked, then gave way. When she pulled her hand out the object she clutched bore no resemblance to anything she recognized. They both stared. "What is it?"

"I do not know." Lou plucked at it with his fingernails. He took a large cloth handkerchief from his coveralls and spread it on the grass. "Put it here, please."

Together they carefully clawed away the packed dirt until a complex pattern of interconnected twigs emerged. The powdery twigs became a network of five beaded flanges roped to a more solid flat, which in turn connected to a small, bony ball.

"Jesus Christ!" Diana gasped.

"Madre de Dios!" Lou cursed reverently. "It is a man's foot!"

Diana abruptly dropped the gruesome discovery as bile rose to the back of her throat. The bony little ball was a human heel. "Or it could be a woman's foot," she absurdly croaked.

The sun shimmered dizzily off the lake, and Diana felt faint. She was vaguely aware that Moby, Meeks, and the others had abandoned their project and were running in their direction.

"Question is…" Lou gasped. "Where is the rest of him?"

THREE

A stressful situation…

"What's happening?" Moby demanded as he approached the handkerchief spread on the ground. When he squatted for a closer look his shirttail pulled loose and Diana was treated to a glimpse of his flabby white backside.

She backed away, sat down on an old tree stump, dropped her head between her knees and waited for the dizziness to pass. In the meantime, all six men were talking at once. The result was an odd disorienting mix of Spanish, the African American worker's excited patter, which sounded like rap music, and Moby's whale-like bellowing.

"Is that what I think it is?" Ryman Meeks squawked.

When Diana looked up the two youngest workers, a towhead and a boy with a ponytail, were poking at the skeletal remains with the toes of their boots.

"This is way gross!" the blond kid said.

"Don't touch it!" Moby shouted.

"You reckon there's a body down there?" the guy with a ponytail wondered. "Can I dig it up?"

Diana reflexively wiped her muddy fingers on her trousers and realized with a fresh wave of nausea that she had handled the rotted foot. "Hey you guys, leave it alone!" she hollered. "You need to call the police."

"The cops?" Moby leveraged himself upright and frowned. "Nothin' like this ever happened before."

The man named Lou, who had actually brought the shoe up from the hole, stared at the treetops and crossed himself. Diana recalled the muffled crack when Lou twisted the shoe from the ground and fancied it was the sound of an ankle breaking away from a shinbone.

Mr. Meeks gripped his cellphone in trembling hands. "I am calling 911. All you men stand aside until they get here."

The African American and the two kids huddled together, laughing and nervously shoving one another. Lou wandered away into a grove of young willows near the shore while Moby hissed and growled at Meeks.

"I'm the boss, these are my men."

Meeks tucked his cell back on its belt clip "The sheriff is on his way. In the meantime, I am in charge." He puffed out his bird chest and hugged it with his skinny arms.

Diana sighed in helpless exasperation. What was it about a crisis that brought out the testosterone in some men? Clearly this was a stressful situation, but it made her want to cry, not fight. She stood up, grateful that her trembling knees still worked, and started walking towards the lake.

"Where do you think you're going?" Meeks called at her back. "You cannot leave. You found it and the police will have questions."

She pointed at the gazebo. "I'm not going far. Leave me alone."

Thankfully, no one tried to stop her. Weeds clawed at her sandals, but the brisk breeze off the lake blew away the stench of sewage and cleared her head. Unfortunately, no matter what the police uncovered, this changed everything. What would this disaster mean for Liz and Danny? She couldn't begin to speculate.

Next she heard a rustling near the beach and saw Lou leaving the willow grove and crossing into the neighbor's yard. When he looked over his shoulder and saw her watching, he broke into a run He was heading for the intersection leading off the peninsula as sirens wailed in the distance.

Well, Lou's strange behavior was none of her business, but she was glad the sheriff was fast to respond. Fact was, she wasn't thinking all that clearly yet. She walked shakily onto the pier and down the ramp to the floating dock, where she got down on her knees and dangled her filthy hands in the water. She rubbed them together, swirling them in the lake until the last mud from the grave washed away.

The lake was surprisingly cold for April.

Drying her hands on her khakis, she moved back up to the gazebo at the top of the ramp. A splinter from the wooden picnic bench pricked her rump and lodged in the seat of her pants. She picked it loose and sat elsewhere.

The sheriff's patrol car arrived while she was staring at the white-capped waves, so she tore her gaze away from the lake when the siren died with a shrill burping sound. Why wasn't she surprised when the tall officer who ducked from the unit, a Native American with hair black as a raven's wing, proved to be none other than Sheriff Wayne Bearfoot?

She knew the man well. They had history.

But the history they shared was dramatic, involving too many curtain calls with law enforcement. In the five short years she'd lived in North Carolina she'd been cast center stage at murder investigations, fraud, blackmail and even a kidnapping.

So much for the quiet, uneventful life of a real estate broker.

Wayne Bearfoot was always in the wings when Diana flirted with the dark side, so in spite of mutual affection, they'd come to regard one another warily. She watched the sheriff stride across the lot to the exposed drainage field, where everyone was talking and gesturing. He reached into his pocket, removed one of the sterile glove sets he habitually carried and snapped the rubber fingers over his big hands. Next he picked up the foot, which at that distance looked as innocent as a limp shredded rag.

Diana shuddered. When she caught Bearfoot's eye, he smiled. He already knew she was there—not because Mr. Meeks showed him her business card—but because he recognized her car, too often spotted at crime scenes. Indeed he'd likely expected her to be there, because trouble followed her like a yo-yo on a string. It bounced back in her face when she least expected it.

The sheriff waved, then held up one finger, meaning he would get to her testimony in due time. He then radioed for backup and started barking orders to the workers on hand. Clearly neither Moby nor Meeks was in charge anymore. Bearfoot had astutely realized he had a backhoe, shovels and eager laborers at his beck and call, so he'd brought more glove sets from his patrol car. He instructed those assembled in the art of forensic digging, the proper handling of evidence and then put them to work.

Diana was amazed. Although the Hispanic, Lou, had successfully disappeared down the road unseen by Bearfoot, the black guy, blond kid, ponytail, and even Moby considered themselves deputized and took to digging up the field with focused seriousness. Only Ryman Meeks remained agitated. His authority usurped, he followed on Bearfoot's heels like a newly hatched duckling, quacking and flapping his wings. Finally

Bearfoot handed the man a roll of yellow crime tape, so Meeks began tapping pegs and stringing yellow ribbon around the entire perimeter of the yard.

She was impressed with how the sheriff unobtrusively questioned the men one by one, and when a loud cry went up from the male chorus of diggers, she knew they'd found their corpse. Her heart sank.

She looked away to where a small boat called a Sailfish was gliding just offshore. It was now Friday afternoon, with folks getting home early from work for a happy weekend on the lake. Happy for some, not for others. She wondered how Liz and Danny would react to the news of a body buried on their land. Would legal red tape tie up their settlement? While she brooded, an ambulance, the county coroner and two more police units arrived. Neighbors drifted from their houses to find out what all the commotion was about and cars filled with curiosity-seekers congregated at the mouth of the dead end street. Most were turned away by a deputy stationed there.

"What a mess, Diana." Bearfoot had managed to sneak up on her. For a big man, he moved like a cat. "And here you are in the middle of the mess."

"So what else is new?" She smiled up at him.

"Is it true Liz and Danny are buying this place?"

She nodded unhappily. 'Yes, it was to be their honeymoon house. You know they're finally getting married, right?"

"Yeah, my wife and I got an invite to the wedding."

Everyone in her circle of friends knew Wayne Bearfoot. In fact, Wayne had introduced Diana to her beloved Matthew. That introduction had taken place at the graveside of a murder victim who'd just happened to be Diana's very first real estate client in North Carolina.

"So, what did you find in the hole?" she asked.

Bearfoot shook his head. "We found bones, Diana. The skeleton is intact and by the size of it, I'd say it was an adult male. Aside from another shoe like the one you found, all his clothes have rotted away. No telling how long he's been in the ground, but decades would be my guess. The coroner might be able to nail the time of death down within a year or two."

"Don't you need to call in a team of forensic experts in suits and booties to compete this dig?" she asked.

"Like in the movies?" He chuckled.

"I guess."

"Our little department doesn't have the luxury of hiring those sorts of teams, but I promise we'll take good care of the remains, Diana."

She was almost afraid to ask. "Any signs of foul play?"

Bearfoot slid in beside her on the bench, got a splinter in his backside, cursed, and then stood up again. "Ouch! Can't seem to catch a break today, Diana. You know how that is?"

"Sure, today is definitely one of those days, but it's not as bad for me as for the poor John Doe out in the drainage field."

"Right. We won't know cause of death until they do the autopsy and maybe not even then. We'll send the remains to Raleigh for a high tech analysis. In the meantime, I wonder why the guy got buried in this particular yard instead of a proper cemetery."

They paused while the Sailfish cruised in closer to shore. The fit young woman at the rudder was curious to find out why all the cops were swarming. She tacked back and forth, taking it all in.

"Sixty years ago Lake Norman didn't exist," Bearfoot continued. "If the John Doe's been here that long, he could've been a poor dirt farmer living on a hill above the Catawba River. Times were tough. Many folks couldn't afford fancy funerals so they'd bury their family members on the land—no big deal."

"I hope that's the explanation." She felt uncommonly sad.

Wayne said, "Before they dammed up the river and flooded the farms, Duke Power made every effort to move all the coffins from graveyards and relocate them. But it stands to reason they overlooked a few homegrown burials."

"Stands to reason," Diana echoed the sheriff but remained unconvinced. She hoped Liz and Danny would see this discovery in a positive light, like finally the poor man would get a proper burial, maybe even be identified. But while Diana didn't believe in ghosts, hauntings or bad omens, she knew that Liz did. Her red- headed girlfriend avoided black cats, walking under ladders and never left an umbrella open inside a house. Diana feared a body in the backyard would give Liz the heebie-jeebies.

"What worries me, Wayne, is what if the body got buried much later, like when the guy who built this house put in his septic system? Seems to me he would've come across those bones at that time." A cloud passed over the sun, sending a chill up her spine. "And why wasn't the body in a casket? Even a dirt poor farmer could manage some sort of box for a loved one."

Bearfoot frowned. "You're a trouble-maker, Diana Rittenhouse. Anybody ever tell you that?"

All the time, she thought. "Maybe I have seen too many TV crime shows."

She glanced at her watch. It was two o'clock, way past lunchtime. Liz was currently out of town visiting a sick aunt in Atlanta, but she was due home in Charlotte around suppertime.

22

Danny, on the other hand, always closed down his construction sites early on Friday afternoons so his crews could get a head start on the weekend. Soon she'd have to call him and tell him what had happened. It was not a conversation she looked forward to.

Just then the radio on Bearfoot's belt crackled and a tinny voice came through, "Hey, Sheriff, we got a guy in a pickup truck says his house is on this street."

"Blueberry Lane?"

"Yeah, that's what he says."

"Okay, pass him through."

They both watched the truck in question turn onto the street and pull boldly into the driveway of number 16. The driver opened his door and a huge greyhound leaped across his lap to freedom. The dog charged across the yard towards the dock.

"It's Amazing Grace!" Diana exclaimed.

Bearfoot thought she was crazy. "What the hell are you talking about?"

"The dog! Grace belongs to Liz and Danny. That's Danny who just arrived in the red Ford 150." So much for the dreaded conversation. The Powers-That-Be had taken it out of Diana's hands. "Danny knew we were having the sewer inspection today. He must've come by to check on the progress."

Suddenly Grace arrived, stuck her long nose into Diana's hands and slobbered kisses onto her fingers.

"Didn't this greyhound once belong to you?" Bearfoot asked as he scratched the animal's ears.

It was a long story. "She did, but then Danny fell in love with her. Let's just say Amazing Grace was an advance wedding present and leave it at that." She eyed Danny's shock of curly brown hair as he climbed from his Ford. His big dark eyes were

23

wide with confusion as he beheld the pandemonium unfolding in his future yard.

Before he could ask a single question of the cops milling everywhere, Amazing Grace broke away and clattered back down the pier and into the yard. With a burst of speed worthy of her pre-retirement years on the dog racing circuit, she charged the diggers and ignored their outraged protests, Grace jumped into the pit. Danny ran to restrain his pet while the workers screamed for help.

"What the hell?" Bearfoot stood up and chased after the animal. Diana followed. When they reached the excavation site everyone was frozen in a state of shock. "What the hell?" Bearfoot repeated.

Moby dropped to his knees at the edge of the pit. The earth shook under Diana's sandals as she and the sheriff arrived and peered down. Dappled shade from the willow grove danced across the freshly- turned earth below while Grace wagged her tail, proudly displaying a foot- long bone between her teeth.

The kid with the ponytail, knee-deep in mud beside Grace, wilted backwards against the loamy makeshift wall. Freckles stood out in sharp contrast to his dead pale face. "Don't look now, boss," he gasped. "But we got us two more bodies."

FOUR

A crying shame...

Once the shock wore off, Danny, who had no idea what was going on, shouted at Grace to drop the bone. Naturally the dog had a different agenda, so grinning ear to ear, she clamped down harder, sprang up from the pit and scampered into a hedge of blueberry bushes with Danny close behind.

Only Sheriff Bearfoot remained relatively calm and explained to Moby's men how to go carefully about freeing the two new skeletons from their muddy coats. "Go slow and easy, boys, and keep the gloves on."

The Iredell County coroner hovered like a bird of prey and called for two more ambulances. The crime scene cops snapped more pictures while Diana felt progressively sicker with each tentative dip of the shovel.

"Maybe it *is* an old graveyard," she ventured.

"I never seen a graveyard without coffins," Moby grumbled.

"Well, clearly this property will not get a septic permit anytime soon," Mr. Meeks said as he nervously beat a tattoo on his clipboard with a ballpoint pen. "All this is highly irregular."

"Ya think?" Diana mumbled sarcastically, then took a seat on the old tree trunk she'd used before. By the time Danny and Grace joined her—Grace now minus the bone, which had been appropriated by a grim coroner's assistant—Diana wondered if she'd somehow warped into some alternative reality. Maybe she'd wake up from this nightmare sometime soon.

"What the hell's happening, Diana?" Danny was clearly stunned.

"I wish I knew."

He stood behind her, one hand on her shoulder, the other on Grace's collar as the crew eventually stopped digging and crawled out of the shallow hole. The men stood at the edge, hands folded, heads bowed as they stared down. In the brief silence disturbed only by the soft lapping of waves and distant birdsong, Diana felt like she was in church.

"Hey, guys..." Bearfoot called to them. "You'd better come take a look."

Reluctantly, Danny and she moved in close enough to see the sad little tableau at the bottom of the pit. The two new skeletons were laid out side by side. One collection of bones was maybe five feet long, the other less than three. Again the clothing had rotted away, but she saw no shoes. Absurdly, her brain stalled on the notion that these two had been buried barefoot.

"Oh my God." Her quiet words were more a prayer than an exclamation.

"Mother and child?" Moby's voice was hoarse with emotion.

"Could be. And maybe the first corpse was the daddy," the coroner suggested. "No matter how it plays out, it's a crying shame. Do you see what I see, Sheriff?"

Wayne Bearfoot shifted uncomfortably.

The coroner wore crisp black trousers and spit-polished shoes. Nonetheless he grimaced, eased himself into the hole and removed a small silver penlight from his breast pocket. With gloved hands, he gingerly took up the woman's skull and tilted it sideways while the cops with cameras furiously took pictures. With the ball of his thumb, he gently dug mud from a small indentation in the skull's temple and illuminated the area with his flashlight.

"That's a bullet hole," he announced.

"You sure?" Bearfoot seemed incredulous.

"Absolutely." The coroner carefully stepped across the woman's bones and repeated the process with the smaller skull. "See here?" he crowed. "Same thing. Someone put a bullet in this child's head as well. They were both murdered—execution style."

FIVE

A sore spot…

By 3PM the gruesome party was grinding to its conclusion, so Wayne Bearfoot finally dismissed Danny and Diana. When he walked them to their cars, the signature bounce in his step was conspicuously missing as he mopped his dark forehead with a white handkerchief.

"I'm so sorry about all this, Danny. How do you think Liz will take the news?"

Danny shrugged his shoulders, which had wilted along with the brown curls plastered to his flushed face. "What should I tell her? That y'all found three corpses planted in the garden of her dream house?"

"She's not going to like it." Diana hung her head.

"You kidding? She'll freak!" Danny jammed his hands in his pockets and gazed at the sky. "I don't have one clue what to tell her when she steps off that plane tonight."

For once Diana couldn't come up with a single word of comfort or advice, so the three stood by in silence as first Ryman Meeks climbed stiffly into his car and drove away, followed by the ambulances.

"Who were those poor people?" Diana wondered as she looked back at the makeshift graves.

Wayne frowned. "Tell you the truth, we may never find out. Too much time has passed. The coroner in Raleigh will likely tell us their age, gender, maybe how long they've been in the ground, but precious little else."

Moby and his workers were seated along the chrome bumper of the silver tanker truck. They were sucking bottled waters, looking whipped and dejected as they watched two officers assemble a makeshift tents over the graves.

"How soon will the coroner know?" she asked.

"Maybe one week, if we light a fire." Wayne barked out a laugh. "But I don't see this as top priority. After four decades give or take, this case isn't just cold, it's dry ice."

She glanced at the downward slope of the sheriff's wide mouth. Wayne was usually so upbeat. This negative attitude was new and she didn't like it one little bit. "But you will follow through, right? You will identify these people, won't you?"

He sighed. "Maybe eventually. When we can free up an officer with nothing better to do, we'll take a look."

Diana calculated this mystery would remain on the back burner for a good long time, and the thought made her very sad. Sad for the forgotten three who had waited so long to be discovered only to have their fifteen minutes of fame fade to a postscript on the police blotter, and sad for Danny and Liz who might never find closure to the sudden loss of their honeymoon cottage. Surely they wouldn't proceed with the purchase under these circumstances.

"Hey, Diana, you're going to Liz and Danny's wedding, right?" Wayne abruptly changed the subject. "Are you also attending that big pre-wedding party for Bobby Porter tomorrow night?"

Diana shifted emotional gears. It had almost slipped her mind that Bobby and his longtime fiancée, Juanita Cruz, were the second couple in their small circle of friends to be stricken by

April foolishness. "Well, Matthew and I were invited so I guess we're going."

"Who's Bobby Porter?" Danny demanded.

How could Danny forget that incident several years ago, when Bobby's hermit father had been murdered for his land, Bobby had been charged, and then acquitted.

"C'mon, Danny, don't you remember when my old Peugeot got blown up, then you and Liz leased the Crown Victoria for me?"

"Oh right, *that* Bobby Porter. I remember the dude."

"I bet you and Liz were invited to his wedding," Diana continued.

"Maybe so…" Danny opened the passenger door of his Ford 150 and Amazing Grace hopped inside. "To be honest, I'm too worried about my own wedding to care about anyone else's."

"I understand, son." Bearfoot laughed as Danny climbed into the driver's seat. "Getting married is scary business. Hope you and Liz aren't rushing into it."

Diana punched Bearfoot in the ribs. "Stop that, Wayne. We all know Danny and Liz have been in love since they were little kids, so don't be giving Danny a hard time."

"It *is* scary though," Danny agreed as he turned on the truck's engine and coasted backwards out the driveway. "I don't know what Liz'll do when I tell her about the bodies. Maybe she'll want to cancel the wedding."

"Don't talk crazy, Danny," Diana pleaded as he drove away. "You'll get through this together." But the bridegroom-to-be did not respond. Instead, he cruised down the street and out of sight.

"Now look what you've done." She glared at Bearfoot. "Danny was already upset, and now he's questioning his wedding."

"Aw, you know how it is," Wayne teased. "Look at you and Matthew—perfect example—if any couple deserves an award for putting off the inevitable it's you two. When are you gonna tie the knot, Diana?"

"None of your damn business!" Wayne had hit a sore spot. She yanked opened Queen Vic's door and slid to safety behind the wheel. "If you paid half as much attention to your business instead of poking your nose into mine, maybe you'd identify those three lost souls and we'd all sleep better at night."

SIX

Commitment jitters…

She backed up and sped away to the sound of Wayne's laughter, which echoed all the way out to the intersection of Williamson Road. Then she turned north and retraced the path she'd followed that morning. As she crossed the bridge, the water was no longer bathed in sunlight. Instead, it had that choppy bruised look that promised a coming storm.

Perfect, she mused. Hadn't the day already offered enough turmoil? First the horror of the graves, then Wayne's teasing about Danny's wedding and Diana's lack of a wedding— would it never end? Since that morning, she'd come full circle and was again brooding about her beloved Matthew and his commitment jitters. So as the sky darkened, her chest began to ache with the doubts that had so recently, so unexpectedly, come to shadow their relationship.

In spite of all the emotional baggage Diana had carried from Philadelphia to North Carolina—a bitter divorce, estrangement from her two children and a certainty that she would never love again—Matthew had changed all that. Totally different as they were—Matthew an outgoing outdoorsy, traditional southern gentleman, she an introverted reserved Yankee more inclined to curl up with a good book than drown worms from a rowboat—they had connected at first sight, and that powerful bond had strengthened with each passing year.

They both seemed to have trouble believing that two opposite, fiercely independent humans actually deserved such a fine second chance, and yet that chance had been given. So now they needed to accept this gift, which to Diana, was more precious than the air she breathed.

So what had happened, what had gone wrong between her and Matthew? Violent rain suddenly sluiced across the windshield in gray sheets, blinding her, so she steered off the road to wait it out in a parking lot. She kept the engine running so that she could use the air conditioner and willed her racing pulse to slow down as she watched the brave, possibly suicidal drivers continue to flow out in the street.

Lately Matthew had seemed withdrawn. He was elsewhere, certainly not with her. They shared the same bed, still made surprisingly passionate love for a couple of middle-aged creatures, yet he was emotionally absent and the hurt was more than she could bear.

She switched on the radio and poor dead Whitney Houston's "I Will Always Love You" ignited the humid space. She and Matthew considered it their song, along with a zillion other sentimental Americans. Whitney had died of a drug overdose. Was it possible to OD on love? Had it happened to Matthew?

Diana turned the stupid radio off and concentrated on breathing in, then out. Was it her fault? Had she allowed the pressures of a sagging real estate market to consume her? Certainly she had completely forgotten about the Porter pre-wedding party coming up tomorrow night. Had Matthew also forgotten? Did he even want to attend? Fact was, they'd never even discussed it.

Maybe the problem was that Ginny Troutman, Matthew's unwed daughter and her seven-year-old child Lissa, had unexpectedly moved in with them the very day Matthew and Diana moved in together. Certainly their arrival had spoiled their dream of a test honeymoon before a real honeymoon, but Diana had grown to love Matthew's girls like her own daughter and granddaughter, so they weren't to blame.

She knew the recession also worried Matthew. *Trout's Place*, his gas station/repair shop/mini-mart on River Highway had suffered a fifty percent drop in revenue over the past three years, yet Matthew went faithfully to work each day and claimed their finances were okay. That very morning, Matthew had kissed her goodbye and left to do battle with a faulty carburetor, warning her that he might be home late for supper—not to worry. He'd said it was a rush job for a demanding Bank of America executive who wanted his car yesterday.

Matthew never complained, so why should she? Was she imaging things? Were their problems all in her head? That slim hope caused the brutal rain to cease and the sky to clear. All at once the edges of the charcoal clouds were edged with gold and the blacktop glistened as the traffic picked up speed.

While Diana wondered if there might be a rainbow, she realized that she hadn't planned anything for dinner that night, and she sure as hell didn't feel like cooking. So what could be better than Matthew's favorite—takeout barbeque, slaw and hushpuppies from Boss Hog? The restaurant was only slightly out of her way, so why not? On the other hand, she had better check with Matthew, because lately he hadn't had much of an appetite. Perhaps he'd prefer something less spicy?

She fished the cellphone out of her purse and speed-dialed Trout's Place. "Hi, Jody, may I speak with Matthew?" she asked when the boy who covered the night shift picked up.

"Hi, Mrs. Rittenhouse. I'm sorry, but Trout's not here."

That was good news. It meant Matthew had won his battle with the carburetor. "No problem, Jody. When did he leave the store?" She listened to an extra beat of silence.

"Thing is, ma'am, Trout never showed up for work today. Is everything all right?"

Not all right! Diana said goodbye and hung up.

There would be no rainbow.

SEVEN

Stigma…

Before pulling into traffic, Diana called the house and little Lissa answered on the first ring.

"Where the heck are you, Diana?" the child demanded. "Mommy and Grandpa are down at the dock, and I'm starving."

Okay, so maybe she wasn't getting her rainbow, but Lissa was certainly Diana's sunshine. Matthew's granddaughter, with her curling flame of red hair, dancing blue eyes and boundless energy, lifted her spirits when all else failed. Ginny, Lissa's mom, predicted that soon Lissa would be calling Diana "grandma," and the idea pleased her more than she cared to admit.

"When did Grandpa get home?" Diana asked.

"He was out fishing when I got off the school bus. Why does Grandpa throw all his fish back in the lake?"

Diana laughed. The answer was complicated, one of the many reasons she loved him. Long as she'd known Matthew, he'd revealed an almost Buddhist reluctance to kill any living thing. Unlike the archetypical southern male, he refused to hunt, practiced "catch and release," and more than once she'd seen him save a drowning moth from the sink drain and gently set it out in the bushes to dry.

"I don't know why, honey. Maybe Grandpa's playing a game with those fish? Maybe it's more fun to catch 'em again and again?"

"Well, I think it's silly." Lissa pouted. "I love fried fish and I'm starving!"

"Do you love barbeque and hushpuppies?"

Lissa's squeal of approval nearly shattered Diana's eardrum. "Are you going to Boss Hog?"

"Absolutely. I'll be home with supper in twenty minutes, so tell everyone to wash up and stay hungry."

"Awesome!" The child hung up.

By the time Diana turned into the long, unpaved road leading to Matthew's waterfront acreage, the storm had cleared and the sun hovered like an orange soccer ball above the dark ribbon of the far shore. The rain had washed the humidity away, leaving a fresh ozone smell clinging to the pine straw as she parked behind the Troutman's sprawling, unpretentious ranch home, one of the first structures on the lake. She made her way down the narrow path under the branches of the blooming dogwoods towards the warm light spilling from the kitchen onto the screened back porch.

She shifted the large aromatic white paper bags filled with barbeque, slaw, hushpuppies and extra of Matthew's favorite vinegar sauce into the crook of her elbow in order to fight with the floppy screen door, which always stuck after a rain. At that moment Ursie, the magnificent Doberman, charged out from the kitchen nearly toppling her along with dinner. As she found her balance, saved the food and also managed to pat Ursie's long nose, now peppered with gray, she saw the silhouettes of three heads turning away from the television at her arrival. Predictably, Lissa was the first human to greet her.

"Jeez, don't drop it, Diana!" The girl, already in her classic Babe pajamas printed with images of the little pink pig who thought he was a sheepdog, quickly snatched one of the white bags. Then she and Ursie, who really was a pig when it came to hushpuppies, headed for the kitchen table.

Ginny arrived next, but unlike her daughter, she was dressed for another night at Buffalo Guys. This was rustic music bar and restaurant she ran with Trev Dula, her childhood sweetheart, current lover, and the man who—it was recently disclosed—was also the father of Lissa.

"God, I'm starving!" Ginny rolled her dark eyes below her punk-cut black hair and grabbed the second bag. "Thanks so much for bringing this, Diana. I'm running late, no time to cook."

So what else was new? Diana thought wryly as she followed Ginny's tight jeans into the house. Matthew's daughter was Jill-of-all-trades at the club. She served as hostess, waitress, and sometimes the singing talent, but never the chef. This was fine with Diana, who loved feeding her new family. Even though Matthew was the better cook, she enjoyed the simple act of standing over the stove, trotting out her brief repertoire of specialties and watching them eat. Somehow it strengthened the cord binding her to them, or so it had seemed.

"When did your father get home?" she asked as Ginny dragged the red plastic picnic dishes from the cupboard.

"Beats me. He was down at the dock watching Lissa swim by the time I got back from my Goddess Club."

Ginny was no goddess, more like a reformed rebel looking for a cause. After her mom, Matthew's wife, died of cancer, she'd run away to Las Vegas, leaving her dad frantic with worry. Matthew had even hired a private detective to find his underage daughter, but Ginny had finally come home of her own accord. She'd returned with a child and a hard luck story that compelled everyone to forgive her. Diana figured that if Ginny and her old high school girlfriends aspired to be goddesses— more power to them.

She watched Matthew from the corner of her eye. He blew her a kiss, but didn't bother to get up for a more convincing welcome. Not long ago, he would have met her at the door, smothered her in a bear hug and testified as to how much he'd missed her before planting that kiss where it belonged.

"Must be something fascinating on television," she muttered unhappily.

"Nope, just the evening news," Ginny said. "Seems the local cops found three old bodies buried in someone's yard…" She paused to shiver and make a face. "Gives me the creeps."

Diana's heart contracted. She'd been so busy feeling sorry for herself, she'd put today's tragedy on the back burner. "Jesus, Ginny, I was there! That's the place Liz and Danny were planning to buy."

She rushed to the living room, leaving Ginny gulping like one of those fish Matthew liked to throw back. At the same time, Matthew rose from the couch.

"Lord, Diana, isn't that *you* on TV?" His tanned face was creased with worry as he held out his hand to her.

"And look, isn't that Danny with Amazing Grace?"

By the time Wayne Bearfoot's serious face filled the screen and described the macabre discoveries at Blueberry Lane, Diana was in Matthew's arms, her head on his chest as he rubbed the tension from her back and watched the news over her shoulder.

"What a mess," Matthew said. "I can't imagine how Liz and Danny must feel, and for the life of me, Diana, I'll never understand how you always manage to land smack dab in the middle of whatever trouble comes down the pike."

"It's not like I go looking for it." She peevishly rejected his comforting massage. "Unfortunately, Blueberry Lane is now what we Realtors call a *stigmatized* property."

He wrapped his large hand around her waist and guided her down beside him on the couch. "What exactly does that mean?"

"When something bad happens in a house—a murder, suicide, or sex offender lived there—our Code of Ethics prohibits us from revealing the unsavory facts to potential buyers. It's considered unfair to the sellers, who of course pay our commission."

"But what if people ask?" Matthew wondered.

"What if the house is haunted?" Lissa interrupted. "You'd tell 'em if there were ghosts, wouldn't you, Diana?"

"No, not in North Carolina. But I've hear that agents in New England are permitted to disclose a haunted house."

"They have more ghosts in New England?" Lissa collapsed into Diana's lap, dropping her curly head into the crook of her grandpa's arm. "Ghosts only come to North Carolina at Halloween, right?" she added uneasily.

Matthew propped Lissa upright. "Hey, I thought you were hungry, punkin? Why don't you go help your mama get dinner up?"

"I...am...not...a...punkin. If I was, you'd carve me up at Halloween."

When Lissa grinned, exposing the gap where a front baby tooth was missing, Diana decided she looked exactly like an adorable Jack O 'Lantern.

"Don't worry about it…" She smacked the child lightly on her rump to speed her on her way. "Halloween won't be here for seven whole months."

Once Lissa was out of earshot, they finished watching Bearfoot's report in grim silence. The part about the three skeletons, especially the bones of the little child being dug up, were the stuff nightmares were made of.

"Well, they won't send you to real estate jail for spilling the beans to Liz and Danny, because now everyone in the state knows to steer clear of Blueberry Lane." Matthew nuzzled the words against her neck, his breath warm and reassuring.

But Diana was still distracted. She sighed and set a trap. She couldn't help herself. "So, did you get that carburetor fixed today?"

He averted his eyes, and in the skip of a heartbeat, she feared he would lie. Instead, he matched her sigh and stretched out his long legs. "Nope, I decided not to go the work today."

"Really? What about that Bank of America guy who was so impatient to get his car fixed?"

Matthew yawned. "Jody said he could fix it."

She knew Matthew's assistant lacked the mechanical skill to change a tire. "So you went fishing instead?"

"Yep."

"All day?" She hated herself the minute the words left her mouth. Like a stigmatized house, she didn't want to be branded as a bitch incapable of trusting her loved one.

"No, honey, I only fished this afternoon. And before you ask, the rest of my day is not your concern."

Although he softened the rebuff with a crooked grin, Diana was stunned. When everyone gathered in the kitchen to stuff their mouths with pork, her stomach did flip flops, and for

41

the first time since she'd met her beloved Matthew, she felt afraid.

EIGHT

Full moon…

"I'm sure he didn't mean it the way it sounded." Liz tried to comfort Diana as the sun set over a grassy slope leading down to the remodeled Porter homestead. They had driven together to celebrate Bobby Porter and Juanita Cruz's pre-wedding party.

"Sure he meant it. Matthew basically told me to butt out."

Liz shook her curly red hair, which she wore long and loose for this occasion. Usually her unruly mane was confined in a ponytail, so she could disguise herself as a real estate agent. "Look, I've known Trout forever, and he's never evasive. Something else is going on, and he's not a convincing liar. Hey, maybe's he's been out shopping for a big ole diamond engagement ring and he wants to surprise you?"

Diana snorted. "Dream on."

Putting one sandal carefully before the other, so she wouldn't topple down the hill to where the other guests had wisely parked much closer to the house, it struck her how much this property had changed. Bobby Porter's daddy, old Jedidiah, had been murdered for this prime waterfront acreage, but in the end he had fooled the greedy developers by leaving the land to the state, to be dedicated as a public park. Jed had stipulated in his will that his house would go to Bobby, who would also receive a salary as the park's groundskeeper, thereby putting his talent as a gardener to good use. That arrangement had proven

43

ideal for the wayward son, who was now able to put down roots, marry Juanita and adopt Juan, his wife-to-be's nephew.

Diana squinted into the sun dying above Lake Norman, where the water lay still beyond the golf course and tennis courts, like a black reflective mirror. "I can't believe Matthew didn't come tonight. He and Bobby have always been so close."

"Yeah, those two have been best friends since grade school, right?" Liz latched onto Diana's arm as they made their way down the steepest part of the hill.

If Diana thought her sandals were treacherous on this terrain, Liz's killer high heels were suicidal. As usual, Diana was casual—slacks and a blousy print shirt—while Liz was all legs and cleavage in a stylish miniskirt, halter and designer scarf.

"Matthew claimed he didn't feel well," Diana said as they neared what used to be Jed's hermit shack, which Bobby had remodeled to a lovely craftsman-style bungalow, complete with a covered front porch.

"That's weird, because Trout's never sick." Liz said as she led the way up the stairs to a front door with a round porthole window, like on a boat.

"That's true. I've never heard Matthew complain of anything worse than a headache. My theory is all these weddings are making him nervous."

Liz gave her a strange, probing look. "You may be right. First Danny and I decided to get hitched, now Bobby and Juanita, and who knows who'll be next?" She paused. "Sorry, Diana, of course you and Trout will be next."

Diana returned Liz's vote of confidence with a smile she by no means felt.

On the ride to Bobby's they'd discussed nothing but the bodies found at Blueberry Lane. Liz had confided that when

Danny picked her up at the airport last evening and told her the news, she'd erupted like a true red-headed volcano and immediately wanted to back out of the deal. He readily agreed. But by the time they'd gotten home to Danny's place, Liz had changed her mind.

"You know, Diana, all couples have their moments of doubt," Liz whispered as she rang a doorbell set into the mouth of a brass fish head. "Take Danny and me. Last night he freaked when I told him I still wanted to buy 16 Blueberry Lane. He thinks I'm nuts."

Diana tended to agree. "Is that why he didn't come tonight?"

Liz shrugged dismissively. "Who knows? Maybe both our guys are feeling buyer's remorse?"

"God, I hope not." It was real estate truism that after months of looking and driving the agent mad with frustration, when the skittish buyer finally found his dream home and made an offer, the agent could almost count on that buyer waking up the next morning with severe reservations verging on hysteria. It was then the agent's job to soothe the panic, hold the hand and see the buyer through to the ownership he ultimately desired.

"Maybe it's the full moon?" Diana said. It floated like a Necco wafer behind a smoky veil of clouds in the darkening sky. "Maybe we're all a bit crazy." The unsettling thought sent a shiver up her spine, along with an odd premonition that something bad was about to happen.

And then the door swung open.

Instead of Bobby or Juanita, the tall Hispanic young man who greeted them was instantly familiar, and the recognition was mutual. His darkly handsome face under a shock of unruly black hair opened in a smile when he saw Diana, but just as quickly his

45

expression changed utterly. His deep brown eyes flickered with fear, like a buck surprised by a hunter's gun trained on his forehead.

"Don't I know you?" Diana tried to process it all.

Next the man's eyes went cold with an emotion akin to anger or hatred. "No, ma'am, I am sure we have never met." His heavily-accented voice quavered as he rapidly retreated into the crowded room.

Then Diana recognized something about the slope of his shoulders, saw a grove of willow oaks beside the lake and a figure disappearing like quicksilver before the cops arrived. "You're Lou, aren't you? You work for Moby the septic tank guy."

"No, ma'am, you are mistaken."

Suddenly he was gone, almost tripping over his feet in his hurry to disappear into the sea of laughing, dancing guests. For the second time in two days, she'd seen him bolt and disappear, and for the life of her, she didn't know why.

"Whoa, what was that all about?" Liz frowned as they moved into the room.

"Darned if I know. But I intend to find out."

NINE

Trouble…

Diana was determined to forget about Lou the mystery man as she and Liz began to mingle. After all, this was a party celebrating the pending marriage of two special friends, and clearly Bobby and Juanita had gone all out for the occasion. She noticed how Bobby had removed the walls between the living area, dining room and kitchen to create one big great room able to accommodate the several dozen guests. Juanita had set a long table against the rear wall. It was laden with goodies from both cultures—burritos, tacos, Mexican corn salad, along with southern fried chicken, hot biscuits and baked beans. A barrel of chilled beer and a rum and tequila bar beckoned, while the spicy aroma of the food made Diana's stomach rumble with need. She'd had little to eat all day.

"Yummy!" Liz nudged Diana's elbow.

"Are you hungry, too?"

"Not the *food*, Diana. Check out those two *guys*."

Liz's nodded at a pair of hunky executive types who were balancing plates and surveying the scene. They were precisely the kind of men Liz had pursued in her former life—guys on the rise and on the make.

"Easy, girl," Diana warned. "You're engaged to be married, remember?"

"Yeah, but Danny chose not to come, remember?" Liz winked. "A little harmless flirting never hurt anyone." And then she was gone, across the room to the male admirers who eagerly welcomed her.

Old habits die hard. For years Diana had watched Liz chasing the dream of a rich husband, only to be hurt time and again. Danny had changed all that by offering Liz the steady love she'd always craved. Although Diana's red-headed friend would likely never stop practicing her charms on the opposite sex, her heart belonged to Danny.

Diana wondered, though, what the two young execs were doing there, in a crowd consisting mostly of Bobby's country friends and women who patronized Juanita's beauty salon. They seemed out of place until she spotted John and Brenda Sorvino near the bar. Perhaps Liz's guys had come with the wealthy banker and his wife.

Before she could speculate further, young Johnny Sorvino burst from behind his daddy's back, closely followed by his look-alike, Juan Cruz. The two kids latched onto Diana's hands.

She bent over and gave each boy a big hug. "Wow, you guys have grown so much! How old are you now?"

"Ten," they answered in unison.

"Well, you still look like twins."

The boys giggled self-consciously, like being unrelated spitting images wasn't quite as cool as it had been four years ago, when Diana had first met them at age six. Back then, Diana had taken Juan along to an Open House she was hosting for the wealthy Sorvinos, so that Juan could play with the Sorvino's son. Juan had been kidnapped, mistaken for the wealthy Johnny.

Fortunately, both boys survived the ordeal and Diana suspected they would remain lifelong friends.

"Aunt Juanita's getting married!" Juan bragged.

"Yeah, to Mr. Porter," Johnny added, "and they're adopting Juan."

"I know, isn't that great?" She allowed the squirming boys to escape her embrace.

"Yep, I'd say it's great. In fact, it's doggone awesome," an adult voice interrupted. Diana nearly jumped out of her skin when the man sneaked up from behind and wound his arms around her waist.

"Bobby, you scared me to death!"

"Well, Miss Diana, terror becomes you."

"You should know…" She looked into his odd, pale blue eyes and recalled the dangerous times they had shared. Yet Bobby Porter now looked healthy and happy. Life with Juanita obviously agreed with him.

He folded his skinny arms and tugged at the bow tie bobbing under his Adam's apple. "Can you believe my bachelor days will be over in one short week? Nita and me are taking the kid along on our honey*moon* to Can*cun*. Neat how that rhymes."

"Very neat." She wasn't surprised that they were taking Juan on their romantic interlude. They absolutely adored that boy. "Isn't it hot in Mexico this time of year?"

"Some like it hot." Bobby grinned. "Besides, Nita figures it's time I met her family south of the border. Juan will see his cousins for the first time."

"Can I come to Mexico, too?" Johnny pleaded.

"Not this time, compadre," Bobby said.

After the kids ran off to the buffet, Bobby eyed her curiously. "Where's Trout? You'd think my best friend could get off his sorry ass and show his ugly face at my wedding party."

"Matthew's sick."

"Trout ain't never sick," Bobby scoffed. "I'd say the notion of me getting hitched makes him nervous as a chicken in a fox den. No offense, Diana."

"None taken." Yet she was getting mighty tired of everyone from Liz to Bobby questioning Matthew's intentions. She was the only one allowed to have doubts. "By the way, where's Juanita?"

He peered around the room, then shrugged. "She must've stepped out with her pal Luis."

"Who's Luis?" Diana glanced at the open door leading to the dark back yard.

"Calls himself *Lou* here in the States, but I call him *trouble.* Luis was a close friend of Nita's sister Maria, out in California. When Maria and her hubby got killed in a car wreck, it was Luis who sent Juan out here to live with us. So I guess I should be grateful."

"I guess." Diana continued to watch the door and wondered why Bobby judged Lou to be *trouble.* She sensed there was no love lost between the two men. "I met Lou yesterday afternoon," she confided.

Bobby was clearly taken aback. "Where would a nice lady like you meet a lowlife like him?"

She laughed. "Actually, we met in a septic drainage field. Lou came up from the hole with a man's shoe. He insisted we'd find money rolled up in that shoe, but instead we found the bones of a man's foot."

"What the hell?" Bobby took one step backwards.

"Hey, don't you watch the news?" She nodded in Liz's direction. "Liz will explain the whole thing. It happened at the house where she plans to live. Lou works for Moby the septic guy. He was just doing his job."

Suddenly Bobby grabbed Diana's elbow and guided her to a quiet corner. "We don't talk about Luis's employment status," he whispered. "He ain't even supposed to be workin' here. He's illegal."

Her eyebrows shot up. "So that explains it. I should have guessed. Your friend Lou took off in a hurry when the cops arrived yesterday."

"Sure he did," Bobby growled. "And he ain't no friend of mine."

Diana found this strange. In the past, Bobby habitually rubbed elbows with shady characters—cigarette smugglers to moonshine entrepreneurs—so why would he balk at a little detail like Lou's lack of a green card?

"Let's change the subject, Diana. Go grab you a beer." Bobby gave her a peck on the cheek, then rushed off to join the boys, who were tossing corn chips to Juan's half-breed dog named Wolf.

In spite of her growling stomach, Diana made a beeline through the back door. She was morbidly curious to confront Lou again and immediately got her wish. Following the sweet smell of marijuana drifting up from the porch swing, she caught Juanita and the so-called illegal sharing a joint.

"Hey, girl, I thought you gave that up!" Diana called at the pretty woman seated in the shadows. As usual, Juanita wore a low cut halter revealing a generous bosom, while the long legs extending from her short shorts were seductively crossed at the ankles.

Juanita laughed. "Now Diana, you realize I'm giving up men to marry Bobby, right? You don't expect me to give up everything, do you?" She graciously offered the joint to Diana.

"No, thank you!" Diana fanned at the air, pretending to be offended as she squinted into the bright moonlight for a better look at Juanita's companion.

"This is my friend, Luis," Juanita said. "Cute as he is, I won't need to give him up because I never had him. He belongs to my sister, Maria. At least he used to," she sadly amended.

"Lou and I have already met."

"I do not think so, ma'am," he countered, an angry glow in his eyes.

"Oh yes, we met yesterday at Blueberry Lane, when they found the bodies."

"What bodies?" Juanita coughed on her smoke.

"Your friend Lou ran away when the police arrived."

"No way, lady." He sprang to his feet, nervous as a cat as the headlights from an arriving car illuminated the parking lot below.

"Relax, I don't give a rat's ass about your immigration status," Diana said. "This is America. Far as I'm concerned, everyone's welcome." She had intended to put the man at ease, but instead he became more agitated when the car parked and a tall man got out.

"Shit, Juanita, why in God's name did you invite him?"

"Ave Maria, I'm sorry, Luis." Juanita stubbed out the joint and shoved it under the swing with her sandal. "But Sheriff Bearfoot is a good friend. I forgot Bobby asked him to come."

Diana recoiled when Lou suddenly jabbed her in the shoulder with a stiff finger. "Keep your mouth shut, lady. Comprende?"

She swatted his hand away, both furious and frightened by his implied threat, until Juanita quickly intervened.

"Go, Luis! But don't worry, Diana won't tell."

"She sure as hell better not." With that last warning, Lou quickly melted into the bushes.

It was the third she'd seen him pull a vanishing act. "What's his problem?" Diana sank into the chair, badly shaken.

Juanita sighed. "I'm sorry, Diana. It's a long story."

"So tell me the story. I'm a good listener."

TEN

Guilty as sin...

Instead of telling Lou's story, Juanita dragged Diana from the swing and pulled her inside to where the party had heated up. She led her to the bar.

"Relax, have a drink. Eat some food. Forget about Luis, okay?" With that, Juanita faded into the crowd, leaving Diana alone, frustrated and determined to know the truth before the night was out. If Juanita was driven by misguided loyalty to Lou, Bobby was not. Hadn't he called Lou *trouble* and said *he's no friend of mine*? She decided to wait for an opportunity, then finagle the facts from Bobby.

"What are you drinking, ma'am?"

The eager voice came from the smiling mouth of one of the two hunky executive types who had caught Liz's eye. Diana glanced at the dance floor, spotted Liz whirling in the arms of the dark haired one, then returned her attention to the blond.

"Rum and tonic, thanks."

"Comin' up." He began mixing her drink. "Your friend Liz is a great dancer. So's my buddy." He pointed at his friend. "Otherwise she'd have stuck with me."

"Did Liz tell your buddy she's engaged to be married?"

"Who the hell cares? Squirt of lime?"

"Yes, please." Diana accepted the drink and wandered away towards the food, all the while kicking herself for sounding like an old prude. Since when was she the morals police? She didn't give a flying fig if Liz cut loose and had some fun. It was another of those disgusting habits that die hard, but she was sick and tired of behaving like a middle-aged matron, a role she'd adopted after too many years as a divorced single. The truth was she was upset because Matthew wasn't dancing with her tonight, and she was desperately worried by the tension in their relationship lately.

"Hey, Diana, where's Trout?"

She groaned inwardly as Wayne Bearfoot sauntered up with a frosted beer clutched in his big hand.

"Matthew wasn't feeling well," she explained for what she hoped would be the last time. "Where's your wife?"

"Didn't I tell you? Marianne's pregnant again, due any day now. She wasn't up for a party."

"Congratulations." Over the years, Diana had lost count of all the Bearfoot children. At least Wayne and Marianne were a uniquely happy married couple.

"Thanks, Diana." He gestured at Liz, who was now slow dancing with the dark stranger. "Looks like she's having fun. I wonder how many kids Liz and Danny will have?"

"Can we change the subject?"

Wayne laughed good naturedly and lifted his beer in a toast. "Here's to Bobby and Juanita, Liz and Danny, Diana and Trout—may you all find marital bliss."

She grumbled and moved away, but Bearfoot stuck to her heels. "Listen, Wayne, have you learned anything about those bodies we uncovered yesterday?"

He did a double-take. "Good Lord, Diana, don't you ever quit? Seems like you can't leave a good mystery alone. You should have been a detective, not a real estate broker."

"Well?"

"Well, it's way too soon to know. We did send the remains to the coroner in Raleigh, but like I said, it'll be at least a week, maybe much longer until we get a result."

"Not your top priority, right?"

"Right." He studied her from the corner of his eye. "But hey, as a real estate broker you are well-connected. You wrote up Liz and Danny's Offer to Purchase, so who's the current owner? Maybe they know something about those surprise packages buried in their yard?"

Diana's mind raced as she recalled writing the offer. "The owners are Charles and Evelyn Miter. They occupied the cottage until they retired and moved to Florida."

"There you go. So how long did Chuck and Evelyn own the place? You think the Miters are murderers?"

He was making fun of her, but Diana's curiosity was piqued. She couldn't recall how long the Miters had owned 16 Blueberry Lane, but she made a mental note to check the Realist Tax Records first thing in the morning.

"Shouldn't you be looking into that, Wayne?"

"Oh, I reckon I'll get round to it. Now, if you'll excuse me, I require a taco or two."

As he moved away, Diana understood that following the Chain of Title was way down on the sheriff's "to do" list. She had also neglected to tell him about Lou, but just as well. She didn't want to cause trouble for the man, in spite of his disagreeable attitude. Besides, what did she know?

She waited until Wayne had walked off to chat with Juanita before helping herself to a plate of fried chicken tenders. Locating a chair in a quiet corner, she slowly nibbled the delicious morsels while keeping Bobby in her sights. By the time she finished, feeling much better with some food in her stomach, she finally saw her opportunity to catch him alone. She followed him out to the front porch, then trailed him to a hiding place behind an enormous magnolia tree, where he lit up a cigarette.

Hey, Bobby, I thought you gave those up?" she said for the second time that evening.

"Hey, Diana, I'm giving up my bachelor life, but ain't nobody gonna tell me to give up my smokes or my booze."

"Good for you." This place seemed to be the spot where Bobby kept his construction supplies. When she sat down beside him on a pile of stacked two-by-fours, she smelled alcohol on his breath and hoped the liquor would loosen his tongue. Bobby had long since discarded his bow tie and seemed quite relaxed.

"Are you havin' fun, Missy?" he asked.

"I'm having a wonderful time, thanks."

Much to Diana's surprise, Bobby suddenly scooted off the two-by-fours, stretched out on a sheet of plywood and stared up at the moon. His smoke drifted skyward into the leaves of the great tree and she feared he was about to fall asleep.

"Listen, Bobby…" she began carefully. "I wonder if you can help me. I'm a little worried."

When he partially opened his strange pale blue eyes she was reminded of Jedidiah Porter, Bobby's father, who had been murdered several years ago. The memory sent a chill down her breastbone in spite of the mild April weather.

"What are you worried about?" he said.

How to start? She noticed the cigarette had fallen from Bobby's mouth and was currently burning a small hole in the plywood. She flicked it away with her fingernail.

"It's about Juanita's friend, Lou. He frightens me. Something's not right about the man."

57

Bobby reared up on his elbows. His eyes were now fully open and burned with an odd intensity. "Did Luis say something ugly to you, Diana?"

"Well, not exactly. I guess he kind of threatened me. He warned me not to mention him to the sheriff."

Bobby began cursing under his breath, then swung his legs to the ground and sat upright. "You best steer clear of him, you hear?"

"Why, is he dangerous?"

Bobby spat on the ground, hitting the cigarette butt with bulls eye accuracy. "Nita won't be tellin' you this, but I think you should know the truth. Luis is a wanted man. The law out in California's been lookin' for him for more than a year, and he had the nerve to come here askin' Nita for help."

"What did he do?"

Bobby hesitated, but only one moment. "They say he killed a homeless man in Los Angeles. Something about a drug deal gone bad. I say Luis slit the man's throat with that little blade he carries everywhere, but Nita thinks he's innocent."

The moon drifted under a cloud.

"So what's the truth, Bobby?"

"I think he's guilty as sin."

ELEVEN

The chain…

Diana and Liz arrived at their office, Lakeside Realty, at precisely noon Sunday as planned. It was an ideal time to insure privacy, since most agents would be out to lunch or showing properties during the prime spring season. Also it allowed both women to sleep in and sleep off any ill effects of the Porter party the night before. Most importantly, it pretty much guaranteed that Liz, who was not currently licensed to practice real estate, would avoid bumping into their Broker-in-Charge, who seldom worked on the weekends.

It was hard working for a boss. Not long ago, Liz and she had owned a two-woman brokerage in Davidson, which they were forced to abandon during the recession. They had enjoyed being independent but ultimately realized that working for a large national company would relieve the financial pressures.

"I feel stupid sneaking in like this," Liz said after they'd both parked their cars in the back lot, which was invisible to street traffic.

"Well, next time don't forget to deposit your client's escrow check," Diana teased. "By the way, when is your hearing at the Real Estate Commission?"

"Next Wednesday. Maybe they'll reinstate me by the weekend."

"I'm sure they will." At least Diana hoped so. It was awkward having her teammate offline, not to mention hard work doing both jobs. Generally Liz handled the listings—measuring and marketing seller's homes—while Diana mostly represented buyers. It was usually a graceful duet and Diana felt downright clumsy without her partner. "Cheer up, Liz, I brought lunch." She held out a brown paper bag.

"Not too fattening, I hope. I need to drop a dress size to fit into my wedding gown."

"Tuna sandwiches, hope you approve." In fact, Diana had packed tuna sandwiches all around—for Matthew to take to the garage and for Ginny and Lissa to take, along with Ursie, to the dog park.

Diana unlocked the plate glass door to the rear office and without turning on the lights, they moved directly to Diana's cubicle, which was conveniently adjacent to the workspace—printers, scanners, and fax machines.

"Did I tell you about my wedding gown?" Liz persisted as she rolled an extra chair into Diana's small space.

Diana made a face. "I'd rather hear what you and Danny have decided about Blueberry Lane. Have you convinced him to proceed with the sale?" She despised the boring details of wedding planning. If the time ever came, she hoped Matthew would agree to elope and spare her the agony.

"You're no fun. Maybe I shouldn't even send you guys an invitation, if weddings are such a drag."

Diana sighed. "Please, Liz, can we just get down to business?" She booted up the company computer installed at her desk.

"Well, if you must know, I think Danny would be more willing to go along if we could get some closure about those bodies. He's superstitious and thinks their spirits will haunt us unless we identify them and send them home—whatever that means."

"That's why we're here." Diana typed in her ID and password, them logged onto the website for the Iredell County Registrar of Deeds. "We know you've offered to purchase the property from Charles and Evelyn Miter. Let's see when they bought the place…"

Diana plugged in the parcel ID for 16 Blueberry Lane along with the Miter's names and soon accessed their North Carolina Warranty Deed. "This is it and it's dated July 28, 1992."

Liz groaned. "Bummer. That means the Miters only owned it a little over ten years. If the bodies were buried forty-some years ago, like Sheriff Bearfoot said, then those folks know nothing about it."

"True. Would you rather they were the ones who put the bodies there?" Diana grinned.

"Very funny." Liz rolled her eyes. "What now?"

"I suppose you could call the Miters down in Florida and ask them what they know about the people who sold them the property."

"Yeah, right. What would I tell them? 'Hey guys, I'm the one buying your cottage, and guess what we dug up in your yard?"

"Good point. Possibly no one's told them what we discovered during Due Diligence. Maybe we should hold off on calling until we're sure the authorities have informed them."

"Or maybe if I call and spring it on them, they'll give Danny and me a discount."

Diana smiled. "I suppose that's a possibility, but as your Buyer's Agent, I advise you to wait until you're sure you're going forward with the purchase."

"I guess." Liz located Diana's brown paper bag and lifted out the sandwiches and a baggie filled with potato chips. "Will you run over to the kitchen and get us some coffee, Diana? I'm ready for lunch."

"Why don't you get it?"

"Someone might see me. Pretty please?"

Diana had learned long ago that it was useless to argue with Liz, so she wriggled out from behind her desk then cut through the workroom to the parallel hallway and company kitchen. "Don't touch my computer!" she called over her shoulder. Minus her license, Liz wasn't authorized to access anything in Lakeside Realty's database.

"Wouldn't dream of it," Liz answered.

The kitchen included a refrigerator, microwave oven, dishwasher and sink. She eyed the coffee machine, grateful that some kind agent had obeyed the office rule: "If you finish the joe, make some moe." And sure enough, a pot containing enough black sludge for several cups was steaming on the burner. Diana poured it into two mugs stenciled with the company logo, then gazed out a window to the back lot, where her Crown Victoria and Liz's Honda were being pelted by rain. Off in the distance a bolt of lightning crackled across the pewter sky above the barren fields. As she dutifully set a fresh pot of coffee to brewing, she noted how easily one lost track of the weather while hermetically sealed inside a corporate box.

She carried the liquid caffeine back through the workroom and surprised Liz, whose hands were hovering over the keyboard as her blood-red nails tapped the letters. "What the hell do you think you're doing?" She set the mugs down and slapped Liz's hands away. "You wanna get us in real trouble?"

"Oh, lighten up," Liz scoffed as she scooted over so Diana could take the captain's seat. "Check it out. The Miters bought 16 Blueberry from people named Larry and Candace Webber."

Sure enough, Diana scrolled through the deed and saw the Miters had purchased the property from the Webbers in 1992. "But when did the Webbers buy it? We'll need to do another search."

"Yeah, but not until after we eat."

They devoured the food in silence, allowing Diana's mind to wander back to the scene at breakfast, when Matthew had complained of dizziness and declined to eat his pancakes. He'd been as balanced as an acrobat the night before, when they'd made sweet, passionate love after Diana returned from the party. So she'd begun to hope that the disturbing sense of separation plaguing their relationship had finally dissipated, but then his abrupt departure from the table had ignited her worries all over again.

"Hey, did you ever find out anything about that rude Latino man at the party last night?" Liz interrupted as she licked her fingers, then wiped them on one of the paper napkins Diana had supplied.

"Not really." Diana had already decided to forget everything she'd heard about Lou the fugitive. She'd said nothing to Liz, nothing to Matthew, and had almost accepted the fact that Lou's problems were none of her business.

"Okay, then…" Liz eyed her skeptically. "Let's get back to work. I don't know about you, but I want to get home and cook Danny a proper Sunday dinner."

Diana wondered, was she also eager to get home? Putting it aside, she wiped her own fingers, woke up her monitor, then followed the Chain of Title from the Webbers as Grantors in 1992 to Grantees in 1985, when they had purchased 16 Blueberry Lane from a couple named Mike and Ruth Kimmel.

"At least we're getting closer," she said. "But in 1985 when Mike and Ruth sold the place, the buried bodies had been underground only twenty-seven years, still not long enough, and we've already been through three sets of owners."

"Don't give up. Find out when Mike and Ruth took ownership."

Diana laboriously traced the chain back to when the Kimmels bought Blueberry Lane from a woman named Margaret L. Koopman in 1973. She did the mental arithmetic, then turned to Liz. "Here we go, thirty-nine years. This is about the time the murders happened."

"So either the Kimmels killed those folks when they first bought the place, or else this Margaret L. Koopman did it!" Liz was thrilled. "But wouldn't these people be really old now?"

"That's a matter of perspective," Diana snapped. "They could be my age, or dead and buried. Only one way to find out."

"Track 'em down," Liz supplied.

Realistically Diana knew that locating these past owners might be easier said than done. And of course, there was another scenario neither had considered. "You know, Liz, what if it wasn't one of the previous owners who did the deed? It could have been anyone from whoever were the septic tank guys back then, to some murderous passerby who saw the dug holes and took advantage of the opportunity."

Liz's face fell. "Are you saying we'll never know?"

"It's a strong possibility."

"Then Danny will never buy the place."

During the dejected silence that followed, Diana heard the front door of the office open, and the agent on duty greet several of their fellow Realtors. "We'd better leave now." She gave Liz a pointed look and shut down her computer. Seconds later, they fled through the back door without being spotted.

"I feel like a thief in the night," Liz complained.

"You won't feel that way much longer," Diana reassured her. "I wish I had my umbrella!"

Heads down, trying to dodge the raindrops, they scampered through the puddles to their vehicles, but when Diana bent over to insert her key, she noticed something was wrong with her left front tire. "Damn it, Liz, I have a flat!"

The deluge intensified as Liz rushed to her side. "I hate to tell you, Diana, but you have *two* flats."

Sure enough, the left rear was completely down on its rim. When they checked all around, they saw that tires three and four were also deflated. 'What's going on here?" Diana shouted angrily above the roaring wind. "This can't be a coincidence."

"It's not a coincidence." Liz squatted down for a closer look. Your tires have been slashed. Someone did this deliberately."

Diana wiped the rain from her eyes and glanced over at Liz's Honda. "At least *your* tires are okay."

Yeah, but Mary Mother of God, look at that!" Liz pointed at Diana's windshield. "Who on earth would do that?"

When Diana crept around the car, her heart racing as she leaned on the hood for support, she saw what appeared to be the letters "MS" sprayed in red paint on the glass, dead center on the driver's side. And though she was too upset to respond, she furiously gulped the wet air and knew exactly who would do this to her.

TWELVE

Truth session…

"Are you sure it wasn't just a bunch of kids?" The earnest young trooper blinked as rain dribbled into his eyes. "A gang of teenagers have been hanging out in this lot lately, using that hill over there for skateboarding."

"No, Officer, it wasn't kids." Diana watched in misery as Liz drove away in her Honda, waving apologetically from behind the water streaming down the window. They had decided before the patrol unit arrived that Liz should go. She had no light to shed on the situation, so she might as well escape from the office before anyone realized she'd been there.

"Mind if I make a phone call?" she asked the trooper.

"No, ma'am, go right ahead."

She slipped into the shelter of her car and took out her cellphone. Only Matthew could help her now, and it was an added benefit that he'd gone to work at his garage today.

"May I speak to Matthew?" she asked when Jody answered on the first ring.

"He stepped out," the boy answered nervously.

Again? Seemed like every time she called him at work lately he was elsewhere. "Well, if you can locate him, please tell him I need him immediately, with the flatbed truck. I've had an accident and I'll be waiting in the lot behind my office."

"No way! Are you hurt, Diana?"

"I'm fine, but I have four flats,"

"Don't worry, I'll tell him."

By the panic in Jody's voice when he hung up, Diana was sure Matthew would get the message right away, wherever he was. She powered down her window and took pity on the soaked trooper hunched over in the storm. He was busily photographing the damage done to her car with his phone. "Listen, Officer, why don't we take this conversation inside?"

"Yes, ma'am, that would be fine." He readily agreed.

They both made a mad dash and ducked into Lakeside Realty, where Diana smelled her fresh coffee brewing and was grateful she'd made "moe joe."

"Want a cup?" she asked him.

"Yes, ma'am, that would be fine," the trooper repeated.

She rinsed and refilled the mug she'd used moments before, then filled a clean one for the young man who, according to his nametag, was Don Bower.

"So if wasn't the local skateboarders who vandalized your car, who do *you* think did it?"

Diana wrestled with the pros and cons of telling on Lou. She was ninety-nine percent certain he was responsible. She figured he'd done it to emphasize the warning he'd issued the night before. But if she revealed that Lou was not only illegal but also a fugitive wanted for murder in Los Angeles, then Lou's revenge could prove much more lethal than slashed tires and a red MS.

"Do you have any enemies? Pissed anyone off lately?" Don asked. "Pardon the language." He blushed.

"Not that I know of," she lied. Aside from Lou, Diana had angered a few disgruntled real estate customers over the years—sellers who believed they didn't get paid enough for their home, or buyers who really wanted that chandelier the sellers had refused to leave behind. But surely those unhappy clients weren't tire slashers.

"What about the other agents in this office? Has anyone else suffered damage to their property or noticed anyone suspicious hanging around?" the trooper said.

As she fought with her conscience, Diana heard two associates chatting in the front office. "I'm not sure, Officer Bower, but you could talk to the agents down there at the end of the hall."

"Good idea. Excuse me a minute…"

He took the bait and walked away. Diana knew she would have received a cautionary memo if indeed any of the other Realtors had had problems or suspicions, but there'd been no such memo. Yet Don Bower's absence bought her a few precious moments to collect her thoughts and decide what to do. Bobby Porter thought Lou was guilty, but Juanita did not, and certainly she didn't want to implicate an innocent man. She remembered, however, that Juanita had introduced Diana by her full name and possibly even told Lou where she worked. Bobby had said Lou slit a homeless man's throat with a little knife he carried everywhere—the same knife he used to slit her tires? The thought of such a man stalking her, damaging her car, was intolerable.

She leaned against the counter and stared miserably at the parking lot, where the wind was stripping white petals from a dogwood tree. The petals scattered to the flooded concrete and drowned in the puddles. At the same instant she saw the headlights of Matthew's flatbed truck slowly round the traffic circle leading into the lot. He pulled up right next to Diana's Queen Vic, then climbed out for a better look. Judging by his body language as he stomped around her car, then stalled at her windshield, she knew he was absorbing the whole ugly picture.

By the time he pushed through the plate glass door and spotted her in the kitchen, Matthew's anger had internalized into a seething calm, which always happened when he was truly furious. A half dozen steps and he gathered her into his arms and held her close. He pulled her head down on his shoulder and stroked her hair. He smelled warm and wet, like his cotton shirts when she lifted them from the washer into the dryer. Mostly he felt comforting, and some of her fear melted away.

"Are you all right?" he finally asked in a gruff whisper.

She merely nodded.

He tipped her chin upward and searched her eyes. "Why did this happen to you?"

In that moment, she knew she needed to confide in him, but maybe not everything, because Matthew had mixed allegiances to Bobby and Juanita. She didn't want his anger to blow back on them just because Lou was their friend. She listened, heard Officer Bower flirting with the girls up front, and decided she still had enough time to take Matthew aside for a truth session. She led him into the dim cocoon of her cubicle, pulled up the second chair Liz had used and they huddled.

She spoke softly, revealing more than she had intended as Matthew held her hand and stroked her palm with the rough ball of his thumb. When she got to the part about Lou being wanted for murder, Matthew stiffened and his face reddened, but he did not interrupt. Again she was grateful. At that point, he could have reacted as he had in the past—scolded her for getting involved and warned her against courting danger. But much to his credit, he waited until they heard Officer Bower's boots approaching down the hall. Only then did he clear his throat.

"You have to tell him, Diana."
And for once, she agreed.

THIRTEEN

Out on the town...

By Wednesday, Diana still couldn't put the incident behind her. She hadn't given Officer Bower much to go on but a string of unsubstantiated suspicions and a bizarre story about a supposed illegal named Luis, who may or may not have committed a murder in California. Granted, the bizarre tale had caused Bower's eyes to bug with incredulity as he took copious notes, but did he believe her?

She hadn't been able to resist calling him yesterday, and she'd discovered that the young trooper had indeed confronted poor Moby, the septic guy, who of course denied knowing anything about Lou's illegal status, because hiring him would then be a crime. Diana could almost picture big, congenial Moby puffing like a distressed whale, and she hoped she'd caused him no serious trouble. In the end, all Bower had learned was that Luis' last name was Colon, and that the fugitive hadn't returned to work since the bodies were found at Blueberry Lane.

Lou had completely disappeared.

When Diana climbed into her car and began the short drive home from a disastrous listing appointment, it struck her that since last Friday, her world had turned upside down. She'd been unable to concentrate on real estate, her family and certainly not her social life. At least Officer Bower had not yet approached Bobby and Juanita, which was a huge relief. She knew Juanita would be furious. Likely even Bobby, who had a long-standing aversion to law officers, would disapprove of her squealing. And since she had to face them both at their upcoming nuptials on Saturday, she prayed she would still be welcome.

Sighing deeply, she steered into the long private road to Matthew's house just as the sun was setting above the far shore. When she parked, little Lissa flew out the back door to greet her, closely followed by Ursie, barking excitedly at her heels.

"Welcome home, Diana!" The child threw her arms around Diana's knees and hugged hard, while Ursie paused to sniff Diana's four new tires.

"I'm really glad to be home, honey." She ruffled Lissa's Raggedy Ann head.

Next, Lissa broke loose and stood on her tiptoes to inspect Diana's windshield. "Cool, I see Grandpa got it all clean!"

"Yep, good as new." But it hadn't been that simple. Jody had scrubbed with a dozen varieties of obnoxious solvents before finding the right combination to remove red spray paint. Luckily, Lissa thought it was all a big game, harmless as hopscotch chalk on a sidewalk.

"Mommy has a surprise," Lissa announced as she scampered up to the screened porch, beckoning for Diana to follow.

Diana fervently hoped that Ginny's surprise would be dinner on the table, because Diana had made absolutely no plans to feed the family. She called to Ursie, who reluctantly abandoned the intriguing smell of new rubber, and they all went inside. A quick glance confirmed no food on the table, nothing cooking on the stove, and no promising odors wafting from the oven.

Then Ginny appeared, clapping her hands in an uncharacteristic explosion of glee. "Just in time, Diana!"

Matthew's daughter cried. "Get yourself dressed, we're going out on the town."

Diana was exceedingly weary. After dealing with the sellers from hell, who had insisted their home was worth more than the market dictated, complained that Lakeside Realty charged too high a commission, turned up their noses at Diana's subtle lilac perfume—citing a fragrance intolerance when their house stank of mold—Diana had kept her cool and remained professional. She'd lost the listing anyway.

"Not tonight, Ginny…" She tried to beg off.

Ginny pressed a long finger, topped by a black lacquer nail, against her lips. "Stop right there, I accept no excuses. Trev and I have been planning this for weeks, so you and Daddy have to come."

"But I'm really beat." Diana gazed pleadingly into Ginny's brown eyes, one shade darker than Matthews, then shifted her attention to the silver stud in her left nostril.

Next Ginny ran an impatient hand through her short brush of black retro punk hair and puffed out her full red lips in a pout. "No, you are coming, Diana. Trev's arranged a special table and planned an awesome meal. If you're really lucky, I'll get up on stage and sing for you."

So the plan was they were going to Buffalo Guys, Trevor Dula's rustic nightclub up north on the Catawba River.

"You won't sing," Diana objected. "Even *I* know Friday is Open Mic Night, and today is not Friday."

"Hey, there's no law. If you're the boss's girlfriend, you can sing whenever you damn well please."

Diana tried again. "Who will watch Lissa?"

"That's lame, Diana. I've arranged to drop her off at little Emily's, so the girls can have a sleep-over."

Diana had one more card up her sleeve. "What about your father? I can't believe he agreed to go out midweek."

"Sorry, wrong again. Daddy's in the shower as we speak. He's looking forward to it, so wear something sexy, will you?"

Diana gave up and sank onto a kitchen chair. She had lost the argument big time. If her beloved stick-in-the-mud Matthew had consented to go to the bar, the same Matthew who never touched alcohol, how could she say no?

"Okay, you win. When do we leave?"

"Half an hour." Ginny grinned mischievously.

"Then I'd better get a move on. It might take all night to find anything remotely sexy in my wardrobe."

"Maybe this will inspire you…" Ginny swept a bottle of white zinfandel off the counter, poured a glass of wine for Diana and one for herself.

"Thanks." Unlike Matthew, Diana was not a teetotaler, and lucky for Matthew, he had no problem with her drinking. She climbed wearily to her feet and checked her watch. "I better go see how Matthew's doing. You know how he loses track of time when he's singing in the shower."

"Right, and you know it hurts my eardrums when Daddy starts singing. Good thing I inherited my mother's vocal chords."

Diana laughed and headed down the narrow hallway to the master bedroom Matthew and she shared. The Doberman's long toenails clicked on the wooden floor as Ursie trailed behind her, so Diana made a mental note to enlist Matthew's help in trimming them tomorrow.

As she walked, she realized she was actually looking forward to an evening out. It had been a very long time since Matthew had agreed to such a thing, and it would do them good. Besides, she did love hearing Ginny sing. Her rich alto voice was smooth as warm honey, perfect for either a country ballad or classic rock. And although Diana had never heard Matthew's deceased wife Lynn sing, Matthew had mentioned that she'd had talent.

When they reached the closed bedroom door, Ursie pressed her cold nose into Diana's free hand, licked her fingers and whined plaintively. Poor thing wasn't allowed inside because their bedroom was the domain of Perry, Diana's foul-mouthed parrot, and dog and bird did not play well together. She patted Ursie's silken head, twisted the knob, slipped through the crack and closed the door behind her.

"Fuck you, Mama!" Perry squawked the moment Diana entered.

"Shut up, Perry!" Diana hollered back. Some days she bitterly regretted inheriting Perry from a grateful, but cantankerous, real estate client. The old man had left her the parrot in his will. The bird had picked up the curmudgeon's colorful language. He would likely outlive them all and was a source of endless embarrassment to his mistress.

She looked through the glass sliders leading to the deck and realized the sun had fully set, leaving behind pink fingers to stroke the water on the far horizon. She could now cover Perry's cage without feeling guilty. She would feed him, bring his water and put him down for the night, thank God.

When she set her wine glass aside and looked for the small plastic pitcher she used to fetch Perry's water, it seemed odd that Matthew wasn't singing. Unlike his daughter and granddaughter, Diana adored Matthew's off-key tenor, especially when he belted out old gospel tunes. She heard the water running in the shower, so she figured he must be in a more pensive, less vocal mood.

Locating the pitcher, Diana supplied her own music by whistling, then stepped into their steamy bathroom.

"Hi, honey, I'm home!" she called out.

When Matthew didn't answer, she guessed he was playing a game, planning to jump out at her from behind the curtain, like at the Bates Hotel. Turning the tables, Diana snatched the curtain and pulled it aside to jump in on him. But instead of finding him lurking in wait, she found Matthew slumped on the tile floor. He had fallen and hit his head on the faucet. Blood dribbled from a gash on the side of his forehead as he lay crumpled, naked, and unconscious.

Unaware she was screaming, Diana dropped to her knees and ran her hand into the soft hair on his chest, searching for a heartbeat. She was also unaware of the pulsing water soaking her as she got her hands under his shoulders and dragged his face and upper body out of the jet stream. With Matthew's head cradled in her lap, she rocked and wept until she heard Perry screeching and Ursie barking. Someone had let the dog into the room.

"What the hell happened?" Ginny stood over them, her eyes wide with shock and fear.

Diana pulled a towel over Matthew, as though guarding his privacy could somehow save him.

"Your father is alive!" she cried. "Call 911."

FOURTEEN

Alcohol and fear...

The emergency room at Lake Norman Regional Medical Center was eerily quiet compared to the many other times Diana had had the misfortune to visit. Indeed Matthew and she had been rushed here in an ambulance several years ago, just as they had tonight, on the very eve the hospital had opened. On that occasion, Matthew had been severely injured by an explosion intended for her. Another time she'd been the patient after being shot by her boss, her very first Broker-In-Charge after she moved to North Carolina. So it seemed, as she perched on the edge of the chair by Matthew's bed and clung to his hand, that somehow violent mishaps plagued her and those close to her. But tonight was different.

"Why didn't you tell me?" She squeezed his fingers harder, but he was still groggy from whatever they were dripping into his veins.

Tonight she was not the cause, so the usual guilt attached to those former hospital visits was not the issue. No, instead of being at the center of the tragic circle, tonight she was completely outside the loop, uninformed and excluded. Clearly Matthew was ill, and if he'd known this, why hadn't he confided in her?

"Is Dr. Rivers here yet?" Diana asked the nurse who had checked Matthew's vitals and grilled Diana about his medical history.

"No, ma'am, but I'm sure the doctor will come straight to this room when she arrives."

Diana felt numb, dumb and useless as the second hand on the oversize wall clock jerked slowly and painfully through the minutes following midnight.

"Has your husband fallen like this before?" the nurse asked pleasantly as she busied herself at the sink.

"No, never." The room smelled of alcohol and fear. The hyped-up air conditioning raised goose bumps on Diana's bare arms as she decided it wasn't worth correcting the nurse as to her marital status.

"Well, has he been dizzy lately? Hard of hearing?" the nurse continued while she sneaked peaks at the television mounted high on the far wall.

"Yes, Matthew complained of dizziness the other morning at breakfast." She recalled how he hadn't eaten his pancakes. Hard of hearing? Diana wasn't sure. Lately it seemed he often ignored her or failed to respond when she asked him a question. But since she'd been feeling insecure anyway, she'd attributed Matthew's unresponsiveness to boredom or indifference.

"That's a nasty cut on his forehead," the nurse cheerfully commented, "but it could've been much worse if that faucet had connected with his eye."

"That's very true." Diana gently fingered the gauze bandage the first responders had applied. Was it her imagination, or had Matthew noticed her touch? "Why did you ask about his hearing?"

The nurse dried her plump hands. "Oh, you know, your husband might have an inner ear infection. That would explain the dizziness and the fall."

Diana desperately wanted to believe her. Having raised two children, she was an ear infection expert. The symptoms were disturbing, but eventually they went away.

"I wish Matthew would see a doctor regularly, but he's allergic to the idea. He's never sick so he thinks check-ups are a waste of time. I tell you, a more stubborn man never lived."

"Hey, ladies, are you talking about me behind my back?" the deep voice rumbled up from Matthew's pillow.

Diana was so startled she nearly tripped over an IV tube in her rush to stand. She reached down and took his face into both hands. "Oh, thank God, Matthew! You scared me to death!"

"What happened?"

As Diana explained how he'd slipped in the shower while preparing for a night out with Ginny and Trevor, Matthew's brown eyes focused as he began to comprehend.

"You rode with me in the ambulance," he said.

"Yes, that's right. You fainted and cut your head."

"No wonder it hurts…" He tried to lift his right arm but found it taped to a needle, so he explored the bandage with his left fingers. "Will I have a big scar like a pirate?"

"At least you won't require an eye patch, Mr. Troutman, like Captain Hook," the nurse said.

He laughed and winked at Diana.

"It's not funny, Matthew. What's going on?" Now that she knew he wasn't going to die she was stricken by the irrational fury of relief. "Why didn't you tell me you were sick? If you were feeling dizzy, why didn't you see the doctor?"

"Listen, I think I'll leave you two alone to sort this out." With that, the jolly nurse left in a hurry.

"Well?" Diana demanded.

"Well, I hope my accident didn't scare Ginny and Lissa. Where are they, by the way?"

Diana tried to control her temper. "Ginny took Lissa to stay with Emily. The girls will get their sleep-over, after all. I suspect Ginny will be here any minute. But what about me? You scared the hell out of *me*."

"I really didn't mean to. Can we go home now?"

"Not yet, Trout." The soft female voice drifted in from the hallway in the body of Dr. Ellen Rivers. "Sorry I'm late. I got here as soon as I could."

"What took you so long, Doc? Were you delivering twins?" Matthew joked.

"Cut it out, Matthew!" Diana snapped, then spun to face the doctor. "I hope you didn't mind me giving them your name, Ellen. Since you've been treating me for years I didn't think you'd mind taking Matthew on as a patient. They demanded to know his primary physician before they'd admit him."

"That's standard procedure in all hospitals." Dr. Ellen, an intense, diminutive woman, eyed Matthew critically. "The EMS guys told me you had a fall."

"When do I go home?" he said.

"I'm sure he needs some tests, right, Ellen?" Diana asked.

Matthew took offense and pushed upright to a seated position. "*He* is right here. Please don't talk around me."

"Sorry, Trout." Ellen turned to Diana. "Fact is, Trout has already had a number of tests—blood tests, EKG, hearing—but they've all been inconclusive."

Ellen's words sucked the wind from Diana's sails. She sank back into her chair. "Wait, do you two know one another?"

"Trout has been my patient for almost a month now, ever since these episodes began." Ellen cast a dark look at Matthew. "Why didn't you tell Diana?"

He shrugged, unable to meet Diana's eyes. "Nothing to tell."

Diana felt like a small craft cut loose in raging rapids. "If I were sick, I'd tell you."

"Would you?" Matthew was suddenly serious.

When their eyes locked, Diana completely lost her bearings. "What's wrong with you? Of course, I'd tell you."

"We have an MRI scheduled for tomorrow," Ellen interrupted. "We made that appointment long before this happened."

"Why?" Diana could not breathe.

"I didn't want to worry you, honey. Not unless we had a reason." Matthew spoke barely above a whisper.

Ellen touched Diana's arm. "Brain tumor. We need to rule it out before we move forward."

FIFTEEN

Book of Ruth…

If anything else could go wrong, then it surely would. At least that was Diana's operational theory. She explained it all to Liz as she drove.

"They kept him in the hospital overnight for observation, and he'll get his MRI today. Matthew took those unexplained days off work whenever Dr. Ellen Rivers had him scheduled for tests."

"So now it all makes sense," Liz said. "Too bad he was carrying that burden all alone."

"I agree, but that's Matthew." Diana squinted at the GPS screen on her dash. "Maybe it's a southern guy thing that 'real men' must internalize and protect their 'little ladies' from all the bad stuff."

Diana's abusive ex, Robert Rittenhouse, a Yankee through and through, had been just the opposite. Robert whined like a schoolgirl until Diana handled all their problems.

Diana turned left off River Highway onto Greenfield Road and watched for signs to Westminster Village.

Matthew had behaved true to form that morning when he'd insisted that Diana shouldn't bother to visit the hospital until the MRI was done. His exact words: "You and Liz go out and have some fun. Forget about me for a while. We'll know soon enough what's happening." Because she'd realized it was useless to argue, she'd decided to take his advice.

"I'm not sure about your theory," Liz said. "My Danny's a southern guy, but he never internalizes. He lets it all hang out. He shares all his worries and wants me to make all the decisions that affect us both—except that decision about Blueberry Lane."

"He still wants to walk away from the deal?"

"Absolutely, unless we solve the mystery of those bodies real fast."

Liz and Danny had only two more weeks of Due Diligence, the time allotted to finish any inspections and decide whether or not to move forward with the purchase. So long as they canceled before the end of Due Diligence, they'd get all their Earnest Money back.

"You're right, time is running out, which makes today's adventure doubly important," Diana said with enthusiasm she by no means felt.

Liz and she were on their way to interview the elderly Ruth Kimmel, who along with her husband, Mike, now deceased, had purchased 16 Blueberry Lane in 1973.

Yet all Diana could think about was Matthew.

"Yeah, we're lucky Mrs. Kimmel still lives here in town," Liz said as they turned left onto Shadyside Boulevard, which led to the assisted living facility where the woman now resided.

Diana slowed to a crawl and watched for the correct entrance to the attractive complex. They had been lucky. After a long search in the county records they'd finally located Ruth by simply opening the local phone book.

"Are you sure she's expecting us?" Diana had left it to Liz to make the appointment, since Diana had been too distracted by Matthew's illness.

"Of course, she knows we're coming. At least she knew this morning."

As Diana turned into the "B" Section, where Mrs. Kimmel reportedly lived in Suite 34, she sensed Liz's uncertainty. "What do you mean by that?"

She parked close as possible to the covered circular entrance. The rambling, low slung Craftsman-style building had pale yellow clapboard walls and white trim.

"Let's just say Ruth seemed a wee bit forgetful," Liz said. "But I'm sure at some point she knew we were coming."

"Well that's just dandy," Diana groaned. Last thing she needed was to torture some poor old soul suffering from dementia with a story of bodies buried in the yard.

As they parked Queen Vic and headed up a walkway lined with spring flowers, the sun golden and the sky flawless blue, Diana tried valiantly to get with the program, but could not coax a smile.

"What's wrong with you?" Liz followed Diana through an automated door to a small, but gracious lobby. "You're behaving like an old grouch. Trout's gonna be okay. You said he'd be home by suppertime."

"Yes, that's right." She hadn't told Liz the whole truth, because even the remote possibility of a brain tumor was more than she could bear. Perhaps if she never mentioned it aloud, it would go away.

"Welcome to Westminster." A smiling, middle-aged woman with silver hair and sensible shoes extended her hand and asked how she could help.

Diana shook her hand. "We're here to see Ruth Kimmel."

"She's expecting us," Liz added.

"Are you sure?" Their hostess seemed skeptical. "Have you been here before?"

"No, ma'am," Liz answered.

"Then you'd better follow me, it's easy to get lost. Took me two full weeks before I learned my way around."

They readily accepted the woman's guidance through a virtual labyrinth of long, beautifully appointed hallways flanked by several formal dining rooms set with linen tablecloths topped by actual menus. Diana saw inviting lobbies where residents could entertain guests, game and television rooms, and even a gym. The place reminded Diana of Shady Oaks, the retirement community just north in Statesville where Vivian, her mother, currently lived. Only this place was newer and much larger.

Their guide paused near the gym where a young man sat slumped in a wheelchair, a large bandage wrapped around his head and a blank expression on his face. Diana's heart stopped, because surely this man was the victim of a brain tumor.

"Most folks don't realize we also have a rehab center on location," the woman bragged.

The handsome fellow in the wheelchair had also caught Liz's eye. "What's wrong with him?"

The hostess shook her head, and Diana held her breath.

"Motorcycle accident. We see way too many of those, but lucky for that guy, he'll get better."

Diana exhaled and her heart resumed beating. She fingered the cellphone anchored in her pocket like a lifeline. Any time now Matthew would call with his news.

They turned down yet another hallway and eventually stopped outside Suite 34. Their guide knocked smartly on the door. "This is Ruth Kimmel's place." All three waited, listening to the shuffle of slippers on carpet until the door cracked open and someone released the security chain. "Hello, Ruth, your visitors are here…"

Mrs. Kimmel's round face peered out. If she was surprised, she didn't show it. She reminded Diana of one of those dried apple-headed dolls sold by folk artists in the mountains. Her dark, wrinkled skin was the texture of a shriveled Macintosh and her beady little eyes resembled the dried currants those artists used for that purpose.

"Please come in. I've been expecting you." Diana had anticipated a high, elf-like voice from the pursed little mouth. Instead, Mrs. Kimmel's tone was as low and cultivated as a stage actress. "Please call me Ruth."

The Westminster guide quickly excused herself as Ruth ushered them into a small living room overlooking a tiny patio decorated by birdfeeders.

Ruth gestured dismissively at the multitude of Carolina wrens, titmice and chickadees fluttering beyond the glass door. "I attract the birds to amuse Mr. Reynolds." She pointed to an enormous white cat crouched with his nose to the door as he wildly lashed his tail. "Sometimes I let him outside to amuse myself."

The woman was not at all what Diana had expected. She glanced at Liz, who also seemed surprised by Mrs. Ruth Kimmel. After they quickly dispensed with the introductions, Ruth told them to sit on the couch and help themselves to the tea set out on an ornate silver service.

They did as they were told, because clearly Ruth was a take-charge woman. In a matter of minutes she had rattled off her life story, which she called "The Book of Ruth." Her biography included a long teaching career and world travels, especially to the Orient, as reflected in the cozy clutter of Japanese woodblock prints, carved ebony furniture and patterned carpets. The whirlwind resume made Diana's head spin and rendered Liz speechless.

"Are you sure you lived at 16 Blueberry Lane for twelve years?" Diana asked incredulously.

Ruth's melodic laughter was like a bass clarinet. "Oh, yes, but that was my husband Mike's idea." She touched her leathery face. "I ruined my skin at the lake by reading down on the sunny dock." She sat very straight on the edge of her chair. "Now would one of you people please tell me why you are here?"

"Well, I'm thinking about buying 16 Blueberry Lane," Liz offered meekly.

"So what?"

Diana took a deep breath. Where to begin? Obviously she'd get no help from her cowardly partner, so she decided to tell Ruth the story straight, hit her right between her little currant eyes with the bodies. By the time she was finished, Ruth had not moved a muscle, but Mr. Reynolds had left the birds to wrap himself around Diana's ankles.

"Really?" Ruth spoke at last, drawing the word out in long syllables, like grunts from a tenor sax.

"Yes, really." Diana persisted. "The police assume the bodies were a man, a woman and a child. Do you know who they were, Ruth?"

"No, do you?"

Diana didn't know what to make of the old lady. Was she offended, defensive, rude or just plain senile? "Was the septic system complete when you bought the house?"

"Don't know, you'll have to ask my husband."

Again Diana and Liz glanced at one another. They both knew Mike Kimmel had been dead for years.

"Perhaps Mike knew those people," Ruth added. "Or maybe you should talk to that old bat we bought the place from."

"Who was that?" Liz finally spoke up.

Ruth gazed at the ceiling, conjuring a memory. "Margaret L. Koopman was her name, and she was the most disagreeable individual I have ever had the displeasure to meet."

Diana knew from the Title Search that this was absolutely correct, so Ruth wasn't entirely crazy. "Where is Margaret Koopman now?"

"I don't know, do you?" Ruth said, "But she sold us the house cheap, I remember."

"Do you think Ms. Koopman still lives in Mooresville?"

"She doesn't *live* at all." Ruth cackled so shrilly she scared the cat, who took off into her bedroom. "Margie Koopman was as old as Methuselah when we met her, so she's six feet under by now, the devil take her."

The interview went downhill rapidly, so Diana and Liz thanked the woman and escaped as soon as possible. It seemed not much had changed when they left the building into the golden sun under the flawless blue sky.

"What do you think?" Liz asked. "Is Ruth a mass murderer?"

"I don't know, do you?"

SIXTEEN

Til death do us part...

A stormy Friday of violent rains washed all the remaining blossoms off the flowering trees. The lake flooded and overflowed, allowing large catfish to swim into the low lying portions of their front yard. But then Saturday dawned fresh and clear, a perfect April day. Inspired and grateful for the glorious weather, Diana and Matthew dressed in what Matthew called their *Sunday-go-to-meetin'* clothes and headed to Trinity Lutheran for Bobby and Juanita's wedding.

As they drove up Perth Road and turned left into the tiny town of Troutman, which had been founded by Matthew's ancestors, Diana felt like the two of them had been granted a heavenly reprieve. While she steered with her left hand and clung to Matthew's hand with her right, she hummed along to Nina Simone's rendition of "Here Comes the Sun" from one of her favorite CDs. And when they crossed the railroad tracks and approached the church, he smiled and gave her fingers a firm squeeze.

"Looks like this wedding's attracted a fair size crowd," he said.

Indeed the lot was full, so Diana wound through the residential neighborhood until she found a parking space half a block away, "Are you sure you feel like walking? I can drop you closer, if you like."

"Now listen to me, woman, I am not an invalid." To prove it he skipped around to the driver's side, did a little bow, opened her door and offered his arm. "So don't go treating me like one, you hear?"

"Loud and clear." She laughed.

Since they'd gotten the good news, he certainly hadn't behaved like an invalid. First they'd eaten a celebratory cake with candles when Matthew got home from the hospital Thursday evening. Next they'd shared an X-rated day of wild abandon while the storm raged, while Lissa was in school and Ginny off shopping. During their lovemaking, Diana had feared he was over exerting but soon became too involved to care. Neither had emerged any worse for the wear. They'd cuddled on the couch eating Matthew's homemade chili until the girls came home, and only Ginny had raised an eyebrow when she noticed the Cheshire cat grins on their faces.

"Doc Ellen says I shouldn't drive until I know how the medication affects me, but she didn't say no to anything else." Matthew winked as they approached the big red church door.

"Yes, and for that, I'm very grateful." Diana clutched his arm more tightly as they climbed the steps together. She was so grateful, in fact, that she wasn't even bothered by the memory of the last time she'd visited this church. That day had been the occasion of a funeral in the pouring rain. The deceased was Lori Fowler, a young woman who had been murdered, and the service had ended in the arrest of Trevor Dula, Ginny's boyfriend. Although justice had been served in the end, that day was better forgotten.

Unfortunately, Fate chose to remind her when she glanced back and saw Sheriff Wayne Bearfoot striding up the walkway. Though he had not been the arresting officer that day

91

at the funeral, he still represented the law and never failed to awaken Diana's darker memories.

"Well, if it isn't Trout and Diana." Wayne quickly caught up by taking the steps two at a time. "Big day, right?" He grinned suggestively. "Wonder who's gonna be next?"

Matthew ducked the question and shook Wayne's hand. "Diana told me Marianne's expecting again."

"Nope, not anymore," Wayne answered. "She delivered on Tuesday, a healthy baby boy."

"Well, that makes for a change," Matthew said. 'You already have five girls, don't you?"

"Good memory, pal. It won't hurt to have an extra little squirt of testosterone in my family."

Matthew gazed fondly at Diana. "Oh, I don't know. I enjoy living with all my girls."

As they all moved into the vestibule, the organ was playing and most folks were already seated. It never ceased to amaze Diana how Matthew, a quiet man by nature, always remembered everyone's name, number of children, all those social details one would not expect him to absorb. When they entered the church proper, Wayne peeled off to take an aisle seat near the very back, while a beaming young boy in a tuxedo appeared to lead them to their pew.

Diana did a literal double-take when the boy's spitting image came up from behind. "Okay, guys, which one is Juan, and which one is Johnny?"

"Juan has the red carnation." Johnny made a face, like wearing a flower wasn't much of an honor. "Since it's his folks getting married."

"Makes sense," Diana said as the boys led them to reserved seats up front. As they walked, she searched the many faces for a glimpse of Lou the fugitive. Would he dare show himself? Surely he'd anticipate that the sheriff would attend, since he'd been at the pre-wedding party, and Lou certainly wouldn't want to run into Diana if he'd slashed her tires—and she was sure he had.

"Sit right there." Juan gestured and departed.

"Wow, we must be honored guests," Matthew said as they settled into the third pew on the right. They had a clear view of Bobby standing in the wings, looking nervous, anxious and very much out of place in his tux.

"I never thought this day would come," Diana admitted. When she craned her neck and scanned those assembled, she saw neither a "bride's side" nor a "groom's side." Instead, Bobby and Juanita's motley crew of friends were scattered randomly, and everyone seemed eager, if not vaguely surprised, to see this knot tied. She'd seen some of these people at the party, but most were strangers until she spotted a familiar young blond man who looked uncomfortable in his tie and sports coat.

She tugged Matthew's sleeve. "Look, it's Don Bower, the state trooper who responded when my car was vandalized. I wonder why he's here?"

Matthew's frown made her wish she'd never pointed Bower out. Ever since the incident, even while he was hospitalized, Matthew had been upset by his inability to avenge her.

"Well, I suspect Officer Bower's here looking for Lou, or Luis—whatever he calls himself—but I can tell him right now, the bastard won't show."

"So let's forget it," Diana urged.

The subject changed abruptly when the organist struck up an unfamiliar tune that was clearly a processional march. The lilting meringue beat signaled Juanita's entrance. Just as the music was untraditional, so was the bride's short purple gown layered with red lace. Her outfit was more suited to a bullfighter's senorita than a sedate Carolina bride, and Diana positively loved it.

So, it seemed, did Matthew. "Lordy, hope she doesn't spill outta that bodice."

They all stood while Juanita flowed past to meet Bobby at the altar. By the time they sat down again, with the soft sleeve of Matthew's shirt caressing Diana's arm, she was fighting back tears—not just the usual tears of joy she always suffered at weddings—but the emotion of sheer relief.

As the minister began to speak, she recalled Matthew's exact words: "They call it *acoustic neuroma*, an auditory nerve tumor. It's non-cancerous and benign, and Doc Ellen says it starts out in the cells that wrap around the auditory nerve."

"So it's not cancer?" Diana's cellphone had delivered the good news Thursday afternoon, after she'd dropped Liz off from their visit with Ruth Kimmel.

"No, honey, it's not cancer. Looks like you'll have to put up with me a few more years."

"A *few* more years?" She'd still been in panic mode.

But then Dr. Ellen herself took over Matthew's phone. "Hate to break this to you, Diana, but Trout's expected to live a long life. Hope you can deal with that."

The minister began to read the vows, but Diana tuned out and gazed at the stained glass window depicting Christ on the cross. Ellen had also told Matthew that his symptoms of noise in his ear, the hearing loss and occasional imbalance, could all be controlled or corrected. She'd said that type of tumor grew slowly, if at all, so Matthew would require observation, periodic

MRI scans, and in the worst case scenario the tumor could be successfully removed by surgery performed through a microscope.

Diana closed her eyes and counted her blessings as Bobby and Juanita repeated their vows. She could smell the clean scent of Matthew's soap mingled with pungent fragrances from multiple floral arrangements. After almost losing him, she finally understood what was most important about keeping him. To begin with, she no longer required a ring or wedding because they were happy as they were. They needed no vows to keep them together, only love could do that. Finally, Dr. Ellen had promised that Matthew could lead a normal, active life—so what else mattered?

"You okay?" Matthew whispered against her ear. "Better open those eyes, because Bobby's fixing to kiss her."

Diana did as she was told, but while the audience was clapping and cheering for the main event, she took Matthew's face into her hands and planted a big kiss of her own, right on his lips.

SEVENTEEN

Splashy getaway…

Diana finished kissing Matthew while Bobby and Juanita exited arm in arm down the aisle amid wild clapping, cheering and wolf whistles from the rowdy well-wishers. When Matthew came up for air, a huge smile on his face, he swept Diana to her feet so they could join the recessional a few paces behind the newlyweds. They all flowed through the crowded vestibule and spilled out the church door into the sunlight, while the happy couple disappeared into the dark basement to shed their matrimonial finery in favor of more casual honeymoon clothes.

Are they still driving straight to Mexico?" Diana wondered.

"Oh, I 'spect they'll stop to fool around along the way." Matthew pointed to the outlandish van pulled up at the curb. "Check it out. Somebody did a real number on Bobby's ride."

Sure enough, the Porter's white landscaping van, already distinctive enough with its large, hand-painted flowers, now wore additional artwork including "Just Married" graffiti and a string of beer cans attached to the tailpipe.

"They'll make a real splashy getaway." Diana laughed as young Johnny Sorvino, still in his tux, handed them a baggie filled with rice.

"You're supposed to throw it when they come out," he confided in a whisper. "It's against the town ordinances, but we won't get in trouble if we sweep it up after."

"Don't count on that, young man." Wayne Bearfoot sneaked up from behind and clamped his hands on Johnny's shoulders, but the boy just grinned. In his civvies, Wayne didn't look the part of a fearsome sheriff.

"Who'll take care of Juan's dog while they're away?" Diana asked.

"That's *my* job," Johnny said. "My family is staying at the Porter place, kinda like a vacation, while they're on their honeymoon. So I'll look after Wolf."

"Sounds like fun." Matthew grinned. "You two look so much alike, Wolf won't know the difference."

"No way, Wolf *always* knows." Young Juan, who had exchanged his tux for shorts and a Bruce Lee T-shirt, burst from the church and began tussling with his double. "Wolf's sense of smell is much better than a plain old dog's. He'll get one whiff of Johnny and know he's an imposter."

Everyone laughed as the boys pretended to do battle as Ninja Warriors. All the while, Juan kept watch over his shoulder in anticipation of the newlywed's emergence from the basement. "Here they come!" he soon shouted. "Get ready with the rice!"

Again Diana's emotions bubbled up as hopeful tears as Bobby and Juanita ran the gauntlet of friends throwing rice and offering off-color suggestions for a successful honeymoon. Bobby blushed and dodged, but looked far more relaxed in old jeans and an improbable tropical shirt with colorful palm trees. Juanita flaunted one of her favorite shorts and halter ensembles to showcase her anatomy.

"Jimmy Buffet meets Dolly Parton," Wayne mumbled.

"Wish I was ten years old again," Matthew said as he pulled the boys apart, allowing Juan to escape to his soon-to-be-official parents.

Diana choked back her silly tears and waved at the couple, sincerely wishing them a long and happy life. It struck her that marriage, especially one involving a middle-aged couple bringing tons of baggage to the union, was much like the leap of faith required when one buys an old house. In spite of the insurance warranties and the sellers' disclosures, one never really knew what problems lurked inside those walls. So marriage was Caveat Emptor—Buyer Beware.

"I wish I could find me a young woman half as good looking as that bride," Don Bower said.

The words startled Diana, who hadn't noticed that the state trooper had joined them. The officer tugged off his tie and stuffed it in his pocket.

Wayne greeted the newcomer and shook his hand. "Hey there, Don, I didn't know you were friends with Bobby and Juanita."

"I'm not." Bower nodded at Diana. "I'm here on official business, thanks to Mrs. Rittenhouse."

"No kidding?" Wayne's eyebrows shot up as he gave Diana a quizzical glance. "Now why doesn't that surprise me? Good lord, Diana, what are you up to this time, with both the county and state law involved?"

As Matthew stiffened at her side, Diana wished she could disappear, melt right into the sidewalk outside the church door. It didn't surprise her that Bearfoot and Bower knew one another. In a small community like theirs, where the various branches of law enforcement were tripping all over each other, it stood to reason they'd compare notes and help one another with their separate investigations.

But did Wayne not know about the hunt for Lou and her tire-slashing incident? Was Don unaware of the three bodies she'd helped uncover at Blueberry Lane? Most likely both men were familiar with both crimes, but not the fact of her involvement smack in the middle of each.

She turned wearily to Wayne. "It's a long story. Let's not discuss it today." She looked out to the street where Bobby was cutting the string of beer cans off his tailpipe over Juan's objections. Juanita threw up her hands and climbed into the front seat of the van.

"But I'm curious," Wayne insisted. "I like long stories."

Much to her relief, Matthew interrupted. "Not here, Wayne." He took firm hold of the sheriff's arm and led him aside. Don Bower followed. Matthew installed the pair in the church garden, where they got lost in conversation under the stained glass window.

"Thanks," she said when Matthew returned and took her hand.

"No problem." He gave her fingers a little squeeze, then watched while Bobby won the battle of wills, cut off the beer cans, then tossed them like a bridal bouquet to the eager onlookers. Next both Bobby and Juan crowded into the front seat with Juanita. "That's funny," Matthew commented. "If I were Bobby, I'd stash that kid in the back with enough games and junk food to keep him busy all the way to Mexico."

"You old romantic!" Diana squeezed back, then they both laughed as Bobby's vehicle jerked away from the curb, belching black puffs of exhaust into a snowstorm of more rice.

"I'd also run my van through a carwash and get rid of all that *Just Married* nonsense before I cleared the town limits," Matthew grumbled.

"Not so romantic."

"Maybe not, but Bobby doesn't need to attract attention if he wants to savor his romantic moment."

"Bobby *does need* is a new muffler," Wayne interrupted, back too soon. "I'm surprised that old van passed state inspection. If I were you, Trout, I'd advise Bobby to bring that rattletrap into your shop for a new exhaust system the minute he gets home. I'd be shocked if some enterprising highway patrolman doesn't ticket him for polluting before he gets too far."

"Go away, Wayne." Diana sighed.

"Now is that any way to speak to a friend?" Wayne frowned. "Why didn't you tell me your car was vandalized, and about your suspect, Luis Colon? This is bad business, Diana. Officer Bower just confirmed that Colon really is wanted for murder in L.A., so they've put an All-Points Bulletin out on the man."

"Go away, Wayne," Matthew echoed.

"Only trying to help." The sheriff moved in close to whisper in Diana's ear. "And since you're in such an unsociable mood, I guess you don't want to know what the coroner had to say about those bones we dug up?"

Diana's ears pricked, but Matthew groaned.

"Please, Matthew. It'll just take a minute."

Matthew shrugged. "If it concerns you, it concerns me, so I reckon we should hear him out."

The sun rolled under a cloud, raising goose bumps on Diana's arms as people began drifting off towards their cars.

Wayne did not hesitate. "Well, just as we suspected, the bodies were an adult male, a woman, and a female child about four years old. As we calculated, those corpses have been buried at least forty years. But the coroner did make some additional discoveries…"

Both Diana and Matthew wanted to hear the final chapter, so Matthew signaled that Wayne should go ahead and finish.

"The male was fully dressed. They found brass buttons and good quality shoes. But the females were barefoot, and if they wore any clothing when they were buried, it was something flimsy that had long since disintegrated."

"What does that mean?" Diana's mind raced with the grim possibilities and she shuddered. The thought of violence done to a little girl that age was inconceivable. She hugged herself against the sudden chill.

"My theory is the females were naked when they were murdered, or else killed in their nightgowns, possibly while they were in bed. Unfortunately, it's way too late to get forensic evidence indicating rape."

Even Matthew was visibly shaken. "But what about this man? If he was the killer or rapist, then who murdered him? Obviously he didn't bury himself."

"Obviously." Wayne frowned down at his shoes. "It's a mystery. Truth is, we don't even know if the murders occurred on location, or elsewhere. Back then that yard was all dug up waiting for the septic system, so a lucky serial killer might have seen the site as graves waiting to be filled and took advantage of a perfect opportunity."

That possibility had also occurred to Diana. "But surely someone would have noticed a stranger planting bodies in the neighboring yard?"

"I'm afraid not, I've already checked," Wayne said. "At that time, 16 Blueberry was the only home on the peninsula, so theoretically the killer could have conducted a burial in broad daylight and nobody would be the wiser."

Suddenly Diana felt completely deflated on that joyous wedding day. If the crime was never solved, then Liz and Danny wouldn't buy their dream house. She watched in dejected silence as the minister exited the church and locked the red door behind him.

EIGHTEEN

Back in the saddle...

The new pancake house was Liz's choice, and considering what Liz had endured so far that day, Diana figured her partner had a perfect right to make the restaurant selection. Since the place was only a few blocks from their office, Diana caught up on some paperwork and waited for her cellphone to ring. When Liz called and explained she was traveling south on Interstate77, about to take the home exit ramp, Diana closed up shop and drove to the restaurant's parking lot to wait and worry. After all, Liz had given absolutely no indication of whether the North Carolina Real Estate Commission, at the morning hearing in Raleigh, had reinstated her, or taken her license away.

By the time Liz parked beside her and they walked together into the pancake house for a very late lunch, or perhaps an early supper, Diana was bursting with curiosity.

"Well?" she demanded as the hostess directed them to one of the more private booths in a back corner.

"I'll tell you after we order." Liz's face betrayed nothing.

So Diana fidgeted while her red-headed friend ordered the Wednesday special: Rooty Tooty Fresh N' Fruity, which included two eggs, two bacon strips, two sausage links and two pancakes with strawberries and whipped cream. Diana, who lacked Liz's fat-burning metabolism, opted for coffee.

"Just because you're buying, doesn't mean you shouldn't eat," Liz teased. "I didn't realize you were such a cheapskate."

"Hey, have you seen me getting rich on commissions lately?" Diana snorted. "Now tell me what happened before I ask for separate checks."

By that time Diana was convinced that Liz had good news, otherwise, even Liz would have lost her appetite. Sure enough, as the story of her hearing unfolded, Diana realized the Commission had simply warned Liz to never again delay the deposit of an earnest money check into an escrow account and then restored her license.

"Congratulations! You got off with a little slap on the wrist."

"Sure I did. What did you expect?"

"What I *do expect* is now that you're back, you'll work double-time to make up for lost time."

"Sorry, I didn't hear that." Liz feigned deafness as a gang of rambunctious teenagers cavorted at a nearby table. She concentrated on eating while Diana inhaled the warm, sugary smell of hot syrup and realized she was suddenly very hungry.

She avoided looking at Liz's food. "We missed you at the wedding Saturday. I thought you and Danny were coming?"

Between bites, Liz told the story of how Danny's mama, Liz's future mother-in-law-from-hell, had organized a birthday party for herself, which naturally took precedent over any other event. In turn, Diana described Bobby and Juanita's ceremony, including the unpleasant update Sheriff Bearfoot had provided.

Liz made a face and folded her napkin. "Bummer. Maybe I won't tell Danny the latest on the bodies until we get some fresh leads."

"*If* we get some fresh leads," Diana said, then quickly changed the subject. "Let's talk about the listing appointments I've been handling for you." Diana described the bad experience she'd had the day she visited the filthy foreclosure in old Mooresville where the vile, tattooed neighbors owned a vicious pit bull.

Liz made another ugly face. "Gross! But you went back and got the job done, right Diana?"

"Nope, I've been waiting for you. I have the bank's paperwork in the car, and since the property is only a few miles down the road, I figured we'd go together this afternoon. I brought my camera."

"Now?" Liz was appalled.

"Right now. Strength in numbers, wouldn't you agree?"

Liz was still moaning about the plan after Diana paid the bill and they stood in the parking lot. "You win, Diana, but let's take separate cars. Afterwards, I'm going directly home to Danny so we can celebrate me getting my license back."

"No problem, follow me…"

Diana drove deeper into the poor neighborhood. Back in the day, when cotton was king, the area had literally been designed to be on the wrong side of the tracks. She tried to picture what it was like back then as she turned left off Main Street and passed the abandoned mill, which rambled in glorious decay along an entire city block. She imagined the network of cramped mill houses painted in bright colors, with kids and laughter in the yards, when people still had jobs.

Glancing in her rearview mirror, she reassured herself that Liz was still following and was grateful for her company. Because frankly, she was downright scared to reenter that derelict foreclosure again without backup.

The sense of impending danger increased when she turned into the rutted driveway by the chain link fence, but the panic receded when she saw the fierce dog was not in the yard. She wondered if the animal was inside the house with his foul-mouthed owners, but if anything, the neighboring house seemed deserted. It was eerily quiet as Liz parked behind her and they exited their cars.

"Which house is it?" Liz asked.

"The one on the left." As they approached, Diana noticed that someone had installed a slide bolt on the door, so while the house vulnerable to intruders, at least it wouldn't blow open to the weather.

"Heck, it doesn't look that bad," Liz noted as they stepped inside and Diana turned on her flashlight. "But I wish the dumb banks would leave the damn power on. How do they expect us to sell these places?"

As Diana swept the beam around the kitchen, she was dumbfounded by the change—no more filthy broken dishes, no more graffiti on the walls and no more urinal smell. "This is bizarre. Somebody cleaned the place up—new paint, trash removed. It even smells halfway decent."

"But banks never remodel foreclosures, they just walk away." Liz was flabbergasted.

"Who cares? It's done." Diana handed her camera to Liz. "So let's take some good pictures and maybe we'll actually find a buyer."

Agents normally measured square footage from outside a house, but Diana wasn't inclined to crawl around in this particular yard, so she began inside while Liz snapped pictures for the Multiple Listing Service. She was running the tape along an inner wall when she noticed something shiny wedged in the crack between the linoleum flooring and the baseboard. Impulsively, she picked it up, then quickly dropped it.

"Oh shit!" she cried.

"What?" Liz scuttled across the room and stared down at the used hypodermic needle. "Holy shit! You didn't prick your finger, did you?"

"No, thank God."

"I hate to say it, Diana, but that's not just some innocent diabetic's insulin needle. Someone's been shooting up drugs."

"Heroin?" Diana gasped. "Is this a drug house?" Although she knew next to nothing about these things, she knew enough to be afraid. Taking a tissue from her purse, she carefully wrapped the needle and deposited it in a rubber waste can under the sink. "At least they're gone now."

"Who, the junkies? Jesus, I hope so. Are we done here?" Liz closed up the camera and beat a rapid retreat to the door.

Diana followed, locked the slide bolt and caught her breath. "Shouldn't we tell Bank of America about this?" She'd had very little experience with foreclosures. When she removed the listing file from her briefcase and turned it over to Liz, her partner merely shrugged.

"Hell, Bank of America doesn't care, and neither do I. With any luck, we'll never see this dump again. Let some other sucker show it and sell it."

It wasn't like Liz to sidestep a sale, even when the commission was small and especially since she'd been without income for several weeks. If Liz was spooked, then Diana was doubly reluctant.

"I'll complete the paperwork and enter it in the MLS tomorrow," Liz said. "Shall we call it a day?"

Diana glanced warily into the neighbors' yard, found it still to be blessedly free of either canine or human menace, and then gave Liz a big hug. "Glad to have you back in the saddle, partner," she quipped.

"Likewise, partner." Liz climbed into her Honda and waved as her headlights illuminated both Diana and the rusty fence. "Now go home to Matthew and stay out of trouble, will you?"

NINETEEN

Resisting arrest...

As Liz's tail lights retreated down the deserted street, glowing like a pair of closing red eyes, Diana auto-locked all her doors and backed out of the driveway. With Liz's admonition to "stay out of trouble" still ringing in her ears, she was determined to follow that advice and began looking forward to supper with the family. Ginny had promised to cook her famous spaghetti with meatballs as a special treat for her father, because like Diana, Ginny couldn't stop celebrating the fact that Matthew didn't have a brain tumor. They were both determined to spoil him rotten and loving every minute of it.

As she left the depressing neighborhood behind, passing the derelict cotton mill which now looked eerily like European cathedral ruins against the sunset sky, she fingered her purse. Inside was the special double CD set she'd bought for Matthew, "Lightning in a Bottle," a historic blues compilation, one of his favorites. She struggled with temptation as she considered slitting its plastic, shrink-wrapped skin with her fingernail and sampling the music during her drive home.

Diana pulled to the curb near the railroad tracks because it was hard to open a CD with only fingernails. The operation usually required teeth, truth be told. She lifted the package out to examine it under her dashboard light, and as she was looking down, she saw a flash of headlights in her rearview mirror. The dark-colored compact pulled up to Queen Vic's bumper, blinding Diana with its glare. As it idled, its siren burped a short, shrill warning—like the police do when they want you to stop.

She looked around in panic, wondering what guilty thing she had done, and where in God's name had this unmarked patrol car come from? Had it followed her from the neighborhood? Had she run a stop sign or made an illegal turn? Hard as she tried, she recalled no wrong-doing, but then, she had been distracted.

Her heart raced as she waited for the cop to make the next move. Her fingers trembled as she fumbled through her glove case looking for her license and registration. Dear God, what was she supposed to do? Turn off her engine? Leave the car? At the moment, all she could think of was the fact that the Real Estate Commission often confiscated agents' licenses following traffic violations. But what had she done? She waited.

And waited.

The siren burped again. Someone in the patrol car's dark interior placed a swirling strobe lights on the dash. Its flashing disoriented her. It reminded her of the portable LED lights Matthew ordered online for his tow trucks, and then she realized that anyone could buy the strobes, the sirens and all sorts of police paraphernalia on the Internet.

Diana gulped for air. Perhaps she was being paranoid, but everything about the situation felt wrong. Lately the Charlotte region had experienced a rash of robberies, even one rape, perpetrated by criminals posing as cops. She couldn't remember the details, but she was certain that these assaults had happened to single female drivers gullible enough to leave the safety of their cars. Even worse, what if the driver of the car behind her was Luis Colon? Officer Bower had claimed that the fugitive had likely left town, but maybe Lou was still around, lying in wait to even the score once and for all?

Making a quick decision, she waited for an opening in her lane, and then pulled out between a small sports car and an SUV. Her pursuer's siren wailed as he ducked into traffic one car behind her and followed her north on Main Street. Diana's heart skipped wildly as she fought through her panic and tried to get her bearings. When the SUV turned off to the right, leaving her alone with the cop right on her tail, her heart actually ricocheted inside her chest cavity until she feared it might explode.

The palms of her hands were slick on the steering wheel as she realized she was, in fact, only blocks from the Mooresville police station. If she could only make it there without wrecking her car, and if the joker behind her was really a cop, he could jolly well join her there and charge her with resisting arrest.

She encountered a red light at the intersection of Iredell Avenue, but when she stopped, the maniac hit his horn and rammed her rear bumper. The impact sent her face flying against the wheel. When she came upright, she tasted blood on her upper lip.

A sudden rush of adrenaline fueled her fury. Looking both ways and finding it clear, she ran the stop light and spun left onto West Iredell at twice the speed limit. If she was in trouble, let it be big trouble. Her tormentor blinked his headlights and kept pace all the way, but when she made a high speed, rubber-burning turn into the police lot, the crazy idiot accelerated and kept on going. She figured he'd soon intersect with Highway 150 and be gone for good.

Good riddance! Not until she parked beside an authentic police car, distinctly painted with black and white checkers to resemble a NASCAR racing flag, did she fully realize the enormity of her escape. She turned off her engine and sat absolutely still while her pulse rate returned to normal. The close call might have left her seriously injured, kidnapped, or worse. Finally, when her hands stopped shaking, she took a tissue from her purse and wiped away the blood on her lip.

As she stared at the warmly-lit station, which was characteristically quiet on that Wednesday night, she had to make a decision. She was already involved with the county and state police. Should she go for the Trifecta and tell the city boys the next installment of her bizarre, somewhat unbelievable story?

Or should she leave well enough alone?

TWENTY

Something monumental…

Diana and Matthew listened to his new CD as they drove through the soft night on their way to Buffalo Guys. Odetta's "Jim Crow Blues" was playing, then BB King and Buddy Guy. Matthew relaxed against the headrest, eyes half-closed as he hummed along to the familiar tunes, and Diana was gratified that her gift was such a great success. Oh, he complained that both she and Ginny were spoiling him, hovering too much, when he felt perfectly fine, which seemed to be perfectly true. His medication had cured his dizziness and his hearing was back to normal, except for those incidents of selective deafness when the women in his life nagged or refused to let him drive—like now.

"Turn left at the next road," he said.

"I know where I'm going, Matthew. How many times have I been there?" The doctor had never said he was unfit for backseat driving.

"Judging from your reckless driving in Mooresville Wednesday night, seems like *I* should be behind the wheel," Matthew teased.

She swatted his knee. "Luckily, I decided to speed up or the bad guy's would've got me."

Unlucky for her, Matthew and everyone else had found out about the incident because a model citizen, who just happened to be walking along the sidewalk during her high speed chase, had done his civic duty and reported the unlawful behavior to the cops. The Good Samaritan had strolled into the station at the same time Diana, sitting in the parking lot with a bloody lip, decided to come clean. By the time they'd both stood at the front desk blurting out their stories, the officer in charge agreed that since the two accounts matched perfectly, Diana was reckless, but innocent, and fortunate to be alive.

"Maybe you should apply for a job as a NASCAR driver?" Matthew continued to tease as they turned left onto Buffalo Crossing Road.

"Think so?" Diana stepped on the gas, sending Queen Vic speeding down the deserted road. In spite of Matthew's protests, she kept her pedal to the metal and didn't brake to a screeching stop until she reached Trev Dula's club. "How was my audition? Do I get the job?"

Obviously shaken, Matthew climbed from the car and pretended not to hear—more selective deafness. Diana giggled and took his arm. She figured a gal had to kick up her heels from time to time, and Buffalo Guys was the perfect place to do it.

Ginny's boyfriend had turned a disreputable old juke joint into a lively music bar several years ago. Tonight was Open Mic Friday so the place was jumping. As they walked up a path lit by Tiki torches to the clapboard building with a deck built out over the lake, Diana realized that the last time they'd planned to come here was the night Matthew collapsed in the shower and landed in the hospital. She clung more tightly to his arm.

"Ginny and Trev will be glad we finally made it." Matthew opened the door for her. "I wonder why they made us drive all the way up here? Seems like whatever's on their mind, they could have told us at home."

When they entered the dim club, a raspy-voiced local gal in a cowboy hat was belting out country karaoke up on the stage. Diana had a hunch what was up with Ginny and Trev, but she wasn't willing to speculate out loud.

As they moved along the sawdust -strewn floor, they were quickly accosted by a red-faced, muscular young blond man who gave them each a rib-cracking hug. "Welcome, y'all! We thought you'd never get here!"

Chip Henson, Trev's business partner, had attended high school with both Ginny and Trev, and they'd all remained great friends. In Diana's opinion, Chip was the most hyper-enthusiastic person she'd ever met, and she liked him immensely.

"The happy couple's waiting outside." Chip ushered them past the busy booths and dance floor, then out the back door to the deck, where Ginny and Trev were seated at a secluded spot near the railing. Their table faced the lake, where the moon and first stars struggled to shine behind the floating clouds. "So I'll leave you guys alone." Chip signaled a waitress, then quickly left.

Trev rose to shake Matthew's hand, which never would have happened when Ginny and Trev were high school lovers. Back then, Matthew had strongly objected to the young man's wild ways. If Matthew had known that Trev got Ginny pregnant when she was sixteen, a condition that caused the young girl to run away from home without telling either Matthew or Trev she was expecting, then Matthew might have murdered the boy. As it miraculously turned out, Ginny eventually returned with her enchanting little Lissa, and Trev had survived several tours of duty in Iraq. Experiencing war had left him with some deep emotional scars, but had also helped him become an impressive, responsible adult, who clearly worshiped both Ginny and Lissa.

"Glad to see you hail and hardy, Trout," Trev said.

"You can't keep an ornery old dog like me down too long," Matthew said as he pulled out Diana's chair.

"In my opinion," Diana said, "my old dog's too frisky for his own good. He's running in circles and chasing his tail to get back to work."

"Yep, I'm going back to work Monday morning," Matthew said with a firmness that defied contradiction.

"That's a relief," Ginny spoke up. "He's been underfoot around the house all day, until Lissa gets home from school, and then the two of them get so busy playing that she never does her homework."

As everyone laughed, Diana felt the tension of the past week drift away with the foggy breeze blowing across the lake. She gazed fondly at Trev and Ginny, who seemed to radiate light in spite of their dark, almost black hair and intense blue eyes. They could be mistaken twins, but for the electric sexual energy flowing between them.

Diana joined the kids by ordering cold draft beer served in ball jars, while Matthew asked for a pitcher of sweet sun tea. Everyone opted for Cajun battered catfish, Buffalo Guy's specialty, while Trev described how the catfish were caught fresh each day from below the very deck where they sat.

"You hire someone to sit here and drown worms every evening, do you, son?" Matthew winked.

Trev blushed in the candlelight. "Not exactly, sir, but I guarantee that the fish you're eating right now swam down river past here at one time or another."

"Sounds like a possibility," Matthew conceded as he popped a hushpuppy into his mouth.

They ate in companionable silence until the conversation inevitably shifted to Diana's most recent run-in with danger.

Naturally Ginny had kept Trev up to date, and like a good suspense novel, no one could leave it alone.

"Diana thinks it was that guy Lou who came after her, pretending to be a cop," Ginny began. "She thinks he wants to get even because she told the police he was wanted for murder in California."

Trev shook his head. "I don't think so. What would he gain by going after Diana? What's done is done. If this Lou character had a lick of sense, he'd be south of the border by now."

Diana noticed Matthew squirming in his chair, so she tried to change the subject. "Hey, aren't you going to sing for us, Ginny? You promised, remember?"

"Who slashed your tires, Diana?" Ginny ignored her. "Do you think it was Lou both times?"

"I think they were two unrelated events," Trev said. "Folks don't realize what an awful drug problem we have in Mooresville. My buddies on the Force swear that the cartels are taking over North Carolina. Didn't you say they spray painted a red 'MS' on your windshield, Diana?"

"Looked like 'MS' to me," Matthew grumbled.

"Well, there you go!" Trev crowed. "Haven't you heard about the notoriously violent MS-13 gang? They work as street-level dealers for the Mexican cartels, which send massive amounts of heroin into our state. The heroin is produced from opium grown in poppy fields throughout western Mexico, and Charlotte's the main distribution center for what they call 'black tar' heroin."

"You sound like a walking crime encyclopedia." Diana said. She knew that several of Trev's Iraq veteran friends had gone into law enforcement, but his knowledge of the drug criminals seemed unbelievable.

"I'm just interested, Diana. Mara Salvatrucha, or MS, was named for La Mara, a street gang in San Salvador."

Matthew pushed away his plate. "Sounds pretty far-fetched to me. More likely those letters painted on Diana's car were just some local punk's initials."

"Do you think Luis Colon belongs to a drug cartel?" Ginny's eyes were enormous.

Diana vigorously shook her head. "Of course not. Believe me, if Lou was getting rich dealing heroin he wouldn't be working for Moby, digging up nasty old septic tanks."

Diana hoped this theory was true. She also hoped Trev was right, that Lou's was long gone, not hanging around seeking revenge. Yet she couldn't shake the feeling that someone was stalking her with malicious intent. Nor could she accept that the tire slashing and the fake cop were unrelated.

Speaking of septic tanks, what's happening with those bodies you found?" Trev wondered. "Does Sheriff Bearfoot have any leads?"

Matthew frowned. "Please, Trevor, can't you let Diana eat in peace?"

"Yeah, how come they haven't brought in forensic experts and criminal archaeologists to comb that site?" Ginny demanded.

Diana pulled her sweater up around her shoulders to ward off a sudden chill rising off the lake. "You've been watching too much CSI TV, Ginny. This is Mooresville, not Miami, and our resources are vastly different."

"Still, a little girl and two adults were murdered, right?" Trev ordered another round of beers. "You'd think it would be top priority. They can do radiography on those bones, X-ray them for lesions or old breaks and determine if any of the victim's had

118

suffered injuries or abuse. Think about it, Diana, have they checked for missing persons back then? Have they searched the local headlines from forty years ago for news of a lost child, or lost family?"

"You should've been a detective, son, not a night club entrepreneur," Matthew said.

Diana stared through the railing to the dark water lapping gently around the pilings. She imagined big, sluggish catfish bumping noses just under the surface, attracted by the candlelight on the dinner tables. She wondered if she had just eaten one of their kin. Mostly she wondered if Bearfoot had bothered to scour the old newspapers, and if not, maybe she should investigate on her own.

When the waitress arrived to clear away their plates, everyone quit talking.

"Was the food okay, boss?" She winked at Trev.

"Great, Cindy. Now you can bring out our coffee and dessert."

"Sorry, I'm too full to eat any dessert." Matthew folded his napkin.

"I'm stuffed." Diana agreed.

"Well, that's just too bad, guys," Ginny said. "Because Chip made the cake special for you—for all of us, really."

Before they could protest further, a hush cushioned the night sounds, the crowd chatter from inside the restaurant became muted and distant, and Diana's emotions were sucked into a maelstrom of expectation. In that suspended moment, she sensed something monumental was about to happen, so when the disc jockey began broadcasting an electrified rendition of "The Wedding March," her premonition was confirmed.

Oh, my God!" she breathed when the waitress, followed by a beaming Chip, set down a three-tiered, multicolored cake ablaze with ten candles.

"One candle for each year we've known one another." Ginny took Trev's hand. "And from day one, we've never stopped loving each other."

"Amen." Trev nodded with tears in his eyes. "It took way too long to make it right, but now with your permission, Trout— yours, too, Diana—I'm asking Ginny to be my wife."

Matthew pretended to look to the sky for an answer, but clouds hid all his guiding stars. He cleared his throat. "Well, it's about time, young man." He smiled.

"Right answer, Daddy, because I wasn't about to give this up." Ginny dug into the pocket of her skirt and pulled out a glittering diamond engagement ring. Trev slipped it on her finger. "Do we have your blessing, Diana?"

By then a throng of curious onlookers had drifted from the restaurant onto the deck and they were holding their collective breath.

Diana blinked back the tears of joy blurring her eyes, but couldn't find her voice. Instead, she gave an emphatic "thumbs up," held it high, and the still lake suddenly echoed with the explosion of applause.

TWENTY-ONE

Family business…

Just before dawn, that dead time before light creeps into the sky and the first bird sings, Diana woke up in a cold sweat. She jerked upright and disturbed Matthew, who then rotated from his back to his side and draped his arm across her hips.

"Bad dream?" He yawned.

Was it a dream? She struggled to remember what had caused the panic, but the details were too fleeting to capture. She'd always been prone to these episodes in that twilight time between heavy slumber and consciousness, but at various stages of her life, the subject matter had shifted from unrequited love, to financial worries, to fear of dying, or losing someone she loved. Sometimes the angst was relatively unimportant in the great scheme of things, like choosing the right menu for an important dinner party or closing a difficult real estate deal. But never had she suffered an attack when she felt as safe as now, after making deep, satisfying love.

"Maybe the catfish didn't agree with you." Matthew was waking up.

"No, that's not it." She concentrated on breathing in and out, still searching for answers as Matthew slipped his knee between her legs.

He sighed. "I'm not surprised. Too much excitement for one week. First someone trashes your car, then you get chased through town by some jackass posing as a cop. I wish I could do something to erase it, Diana."

She felt his agitation escalate as his sense of helplessness took hold. She loved it that he was so protective, sometimes overbearingly so, but she hated what it did to him. Besides, she now realized her nightmare had nothing to do with evil guys from the outside world.

"Are you scared?" He coaxed her to lie down flat in bed again, so that they were lying side by side. "Forget all that. I won't let anything bad happen to you."

Matthew's eyes glistened in the available light as they locked with hers.

"Yes, I guess I'm scared, but it's not about the car, or the fake cop, or even the bodies..."

"What then, my love?" He touched her chin with the tip of his finger.

"Much worse. I've been dreaming about the mistakes I've made with my family." So finally she'd nailed it, the monster haunting her sleep. Matthew had always been troubled by the same demons, so he seemed to understand.

"I'm sorry, Diana. I suspect it's all this marriage talk stirring it up—first Liz and Danny, then Bobby and Juanita, and now my little Ginny..."

As Matthew's words trailed off, she knew he was spiraling downward into his own emotional miasma, which was as dismal as hers. He'd lost his wife to cancer, his daughter to the streets, and had always blamed his distraction, grief and lack of attentiveness for Ginny's running away. Diana had lost an abusive husband to a bitter divorce that cut a great divide between Diana and her children—Amanda and Robert, Jr. They'd accused Diana of alienating their father, and as the years went by, her children had become adults with lives of their own, and the divide had never mended.

"Have you heard from Mandy or Robby lately?" He read her mind and quietly took her hand.

"Nope, not one word." Reconciliation required willing partners, and somehow the years of guilt had prevented Diana from doing her part. "Maybe I'll write to them this week."

"Maybe you should call them instead."

He was right. Matthew knew she was the Queen of Avoidance, and although she was strong and independent in so many ways, she was helpless when it came to reaching out to her kids. Matthew and she had always been brutally honest when it came to admitting their failures as parents, but sometimes even the mighty love they felt for one another brought little comfort.

"Well, at least Ginny found her way home, and I know she and Lissa will be well-loved by Trev," she told him.

"Yeah, and they'll all be moving into Trevor's renovated farmhouse as soon as they're married," he added.

"So we'll be empty nesters." She completed his thought and realized that Matthew's father and daughter reunion had been exceedingly brief. Ginny and Lissa had arrived at Matthew's house only six months ago, the same day Diana moved in, and now they were leaving. "Are you okay with that?"

"What are you trying to say, Diana? Are you asking if I'll mind having the house for just the two of us?" He offered a lecherous chuckle. "That was the original idea, remember? This was to be our private honeymoon place, so I say bring it on! I can't wait to be alone with you." His hand strayed down between her thighs.

She believed him, so the panic she'd felt earlier retreated as the first light seeped through the slats of the Venetian blinds and Perry began chirping from under his cage cover. Diana did not point out that in order for Matthew's home to be their "honeymoon house," there'd first had to be a wedding. It simply didn't matter anymore.

"I've been thinking we need a vacation, Diana. When will you be free?"

His idea startled her. She couldn't remember the last time Matthew, the proverbial homebody, suggested a vacation. "Well, the Due Diligence period for the home Liz and Danny may, or may not buy, is only one week away. Once that's settled, I could go."

"Great! I've been thinking how pretty the mountains are in spring. We should visit Boone."

"Really, Matthew?" They'd first made love in Boone, in an old trailer on a mountaintop belonging to Matthew's uncle.

He began to move his fingers in a most provocative way. "I thought you'd be more excited."

Although Matthew's fingers were causing most of her excitement, she truly needed a getaway. If only she could shake the last remnants of her nightmare.

"What's wrong?" His hand stopped moving.

"Oh, it's this family business. Now I can't stop worrying about my mother. Mandy's in Florida, Robby's in Philly, so my kids have some excuse for not seeing me. But Mama lives thirty minutes away and I haven't visited her for two months. She's not getting any younger, you know."

"Who, Viv?" Matthew roared with laughter. "Hate to tell you, but Vivian will outlive us all. She's too stubborn to have it any other way."

Diana laughed too.

"And speaking of your mama, tomorrow's Sunday. Why don't we give the old gal a call and invite her out to lunch?"

Diana nodded and kissed him. Somehow Matthew always knew what she needed, and just to be sure, she found his fingers and urged them to go back to what they'd been doing so well.

TWENTY-TWO

Old girlfriends…

Mama chose to meet them at La Patisserie, a trendy brunch place on Brawley School Road. When Diana and Matthew entered the bustling restaurant they immediately spotted Vivian's white pageboy bobbing in a booth in the rear corner. She was not alone.

"Look Matthew, Mama's invited Linc."

"The more the merrier."

Matthew was in a great mood after taking over the driver's seat. After some gentle arm twisting, Dr. Ellen had lifted the ban on his operating motor vehicles and proclaimed him ready to return to work. Diana was relieved to see the spring back in his step and the old, ever-present grin returning with a vengeance.

"It seems she's spending an awful lot of time with Linc, considering they only met six months ago," Diana whispered as they approached.

Matthew waved agreeably at the older couple. "That's a good thing, Diana. Your mother deserves a little romance in her life, and besides, you said yourself, she's not calling and bothering you anymore."

Romance? Diana was incredulous at the very idea as they arrived at the booth. "Hi, Mama. Hi, Linc."

"Hello, Diana." Ever the gallant gentleman, Lincoln Davis climbed to his feet, nodded genially at Diana and shook Matthew's hand. "It's a pleasure to see you both again."

"Likewise." Matthew smiled as they slipped onto the bench seat across from the couple. "You both look well and happy. They must put something special into the water out at Shady Oaks."

"Sure, it's Ponce DeLeon's Fountain of Youth." Linc chuckled, and much to Diana's surprise, lifted her mother's hand and kissed it.

"Silly man!" Vivian giggled like a schoolgirl.

Diana didn't know what to make of it. Certainly she didn't begrudge Mama a life of her own and had always hoped that after her father's death many years ago, Viv would someday find someone else—but at age seventy-five? She picked up a menu and buried her face in it.

"So, how are you, Diana?" Mama pinned her with her famous, slightly disapproving, icy blue stare. "I can't even remember the last time you phoned me."

"Sorry, Mama." She could make an excuse and explain she'd been busy, but that would never fly with Vivian. Diana and Matthew had already agreed not to mention any of the recent unpleasantness—slashed tires, high-speed car chases, buried bodies, and especially Matthew's health. Instead, Matthew and she had decided to put all that away and enjoy the day to the fullest.

"I'm fine, everything's good." Diana prayed her smile did not look as fake as it felt, but she couldn't take her eyes off Linc's thumb rubbing her mother's knuckle. "How about you two?"

"Oh, good." Mama blushed.

"Yes, very good." Linc winked slyly at Vivian, two lovesick teenagers sharing a guilty secret.

Diana didn't want to be appalled. After all, she really liked Lincoln Davis. His parents were a Yankee and a southern woman, just like Diana's, thus the schizophrenic name. Linc always said he was born straddling the Mason-Dixon Line, and since Mama and he had become friends, Vivian's attitude had improved considerably.

The two were both residents at the Shady Oaks Retirement Community, both had been happily married and lost their spouses years ago. If not soulmates, Linc and Viv were intellectual equals and shared the same conservative values that Diana had always found extremely stifling.

"How's business, Matthew?" Linc asked.

While the men launched a discussion about everything from Matthew's garage and Mini Mart to Linc's reminiscences of his long career as a lawyer in Statesville, Diana squirmed under her mother's scrutiny. When they were together, Diana felt like a naughty adolescent. Mama thought she was too skinny, too busy, too liberal, and mostly too unattached to a permanent man in her life.

From the beginning, Mama had adored Matthew and pressured Diana to marry him. Oh, not in so many words, but with every gesture, comment, and once with a downright nasty remark: "men never pay for what they can get for free."

Or maybe it was all Diana's imagination?

She came out of hiding from behind her menu and managed a genuine smile. "What are you ordering, Mama?"

"Whatever Linc chooses. We always share."

Vivian was not big on Women's Lib, and Linc eagerly obliged her by ordering Ropa Vieja—white rice, black beans, sweet plantains, shredded beef and a side salad—two plates. Matthew asked for grilled chicken while Diana chose a baby spinach and cheese crepe.

While they were waiting for the food to arrive, Diana realized the men's conversation had switched from shop talk to former girlfriends. Diana's ears pricked with sudden interest.

"*Really*, Matthew?" Diana said. "I never knew you dated Mrs. Connor in high school." Today the woman, wide as she was tall, was little Lissa's jolly first grade teacher.

"Well, she wasn't Mrs. Connor then, she was Sherrie Weldon, and my heart nearly broke when she wouldn't marry me."

"I understand." Lincoln gravely shook his head of luxuriant white hair and stroked his dapper moustache. "I fell in love long before I met my wife. The girl was a local, much younger than me. She was a sweet and innocent farm child, while my folks lived in the city."

"*Really*, Lincoln? You never told me about her." Mama was as surprised as Diana by these heart-felt confessions.

"I wasn't proud of it." Linc stared at the table. "It was a terrible mistake."

"How was it a mistake?" Diana couldn't resist asking.

Linc hesitated a long time before answering. "She was married, you see. I should have known better."

Diana and Vivian glanced at one another, but neither woman wanted to pursue the matter, since the memory clearly caused Linc a great deal of pain.

"Well, these things happen," Matthew mumbled as their food arrived.

They ate in peace, each silently cataloguing his or her personal list of loves past and long gone. For Diana, it was not a pleasant exercise.

"Who wants dessert?" Matthew enthusiastically inquired when the sumptuous meal was finished. "I'm having one of those éclairs over in the bakery display."

"Vivian and I will share a caramel apple crepe," Linc announced.

Diana threw up her hands, her stomach stretched to capacity. "No way! Coffee will do me just fine."

"On a brighter note," Linc began over dessert, "Vivian and I have a surprise…"

Diana's stomach suddenly contracted in knots.

"We are taking a little vacation next month. Vivian has agreed to join me on a tour of France."

"Paris in the spring!" Mama chirped and actually clapped her hands.

"Oh, my God!" Diana gasped in shock.

"Sounds like fun," Matthew said neutrally as he licked a bit of chocolate from his finger.

This was really too much. What had happened to Diana's proper mother? Where was she hiding? Had Diana made such a pronouncement, Viv's first question would have been, "Who's your chaperone?"

Mama again grabbed Linc's hand. "Isn't it just thrilling? Aren't you happy for us, Diana?"

Diana managed to nod as she took a huge gulp of coffee.

"I'm glad you approve, Diana, because before we go, we want you to do us a big professional favor," Linc continued. "Will you start looking for a small house for us to buy? Nothing fancy—three bedrooms and a little land, a place where my grown children can stay when they visit and a garden for your mother to putter around in. I'll sign an Exclusive Buyers' Agency Agreement, of course, because we expect you to be paid for your trouble."

Diana almost choked on her coffee. When she finished sputtering, she found words. "Sure, I'll be happy to look for you." What else could she say? Had her mother gone mad? Maybe she'd missed it, but so far she'd heard nothing about marriage, and Vivian wasn't a woman to put the cart before the horse.

"Since we're leaving next month, you can start looking right away," Mama said.

"Yeah, sure."

It wasn't until the men argued over the bill, eventually splitting it, and after Matthew was back behind the wheel driving that Diana finally lost it. "How can Mama behave this way?" she whined. She ranted and cried until every objection or reservation she harbored against her mother's involvement with Lincoln Davis was aired like dirty laundry throughout the car.

"Are you finished?" Matthew calmly inquired. "Linc's a nice guy, and it sounds serious. What's the real problem, Diana?"

She thought about it long and hard while Matthew turned right instead of left off Brawley onto Williamson. "You turned the wrong way. Aren't we going home?"

"It's a pretty afternoon, so I thought we'd enjoy a drive. Isn't this the way to that house Liz and Danny want to buy? We're close, aren't we? I'd like to see it."

Would wonders never cease? "Okay, turn right at the next stop light and that will take us to Blueberry Lane."

They parked out front and Matthew cut the engine. "Cute little place with lots of potential," he said.

131

All Diana saw was a house never destined to become a home. As she stared at the structure and the lake beyond, an unseasonable chill hung in the air. She couldn't imagine Liz and Danny enjoying holidays—Easter, Christmas and Thanksgiving. There were too many ghosts.

And in light of the way she'd behaved with Mama and Linc at brunch, she asked herself a hard question: what skeletons were buried in her own closet, and when would they find peace?

TWENTY-THREE

Jellied doughnuts…

By Tuesday morning Diana was more than ready to get out of the house. With Matthew back at work, Lissa in school and Ginny floating dreamily room to room mumbling about wedding plans and flashing her diamond, Diana actually welcomed her required stint doing floor time at the office.

Her shift was eight-thirty to noon, theoretically a good time to answer phones and catch incoming leads, but this morning had been depressingly quiet so she'd hunched over the lobby computer and searched the MLS for properties for Mama and Linc. So far she'd located three likely choices: a restored 1920's bungalow in town with an English garden, a tract house overlooking a golf course, and new construction in a fifty-plus retirement community, where the yard and common areas were maintained by a homeowners' association. Diana guessed Mama would prefer the latter, because in spite of her telling Linc she wanted to "putter around in a garden," Vivian had avoided any kind of outdoor work for almost half a century.

Diana was printing out information about the properties when clapping and cheering erupted from the back room. She was dying to find out what all the fuss was about, but she was forbidden to leave her post and had to wait fifteen long minutes until a flushed and excited Liz emerged from the back room. She burst into the lobby with an armload of cards and small gifts.

"Can you believe it, Diana? They surprised me with a hero's welcome." She dumped her loot onto the high counter surrounding Diana's post.

"Why?"

"You know, to celebrate the reinstatement of my license. They said escaping the wrath of the Real Estate Commission was like surviving the Spanish Inquisition."

Diana gaped in disbelief as her partner strutted around the room. "How come nobody told me?"

"I guess they figured we're so close that you'd spill the beans."

"They were probably right." What a difference a week made. Liz had been a pariah, now she was golden. "Congratulations."

"Yeah, thanks." Liz slipped into Diana's enclosure and leaned over the monitor. Her long red hair tickled Diana's cheek. "What's this? Did you get a new buyer?"

Diana sighed. Liz's excess energy was exhausting, and the prospect of telling her about Mama and Linc, followed by Liz's predictable vote of approval, was daunting indeed. "Never mind, I'll explain later."

Liz shrugged dismissively. "Okay, but wait till you hear the story I've got for you!"

Diana quickly logged off her computer and rolled her chair back a few feet, escaping both Liz's hair and her heavy perfume. She took a deep breath and waited.

"Don't you want to hear?" Liz demanded.

"Do I have a choice?" She wished Liz would disappear.

"If you're going to be poopy, I won't tell you." Liz stomped from the lobby and disappeared behind the scenes, but all too soon she returned with a paper plate stacked with jellied doughnuts. "Left over from the business meeting. How many do you want, Diana?" Liz spread a napkin on the counter and pulled up one of the upholstered chairs reserved for clients.

"You know I'm not allowed to eat on duty." It was one of those stupid rules designed by corporate sadists. "But don't let that stop you."

"I won't." Liz took an enormous bite, finished slowly, then deliberately wiped an ooze of strawberry jelly from the corner of her red lips.

"So what's the story?" Diana was almost out of patience, but fortunately Liz picked up on the vibe.

"Well, believe it or not I went back to that awful house on Helms Street yesterday morning to place the 'For Sale' sign."

"Where?"

"You know, Diana, at the foreclosure, the drug house. Remember?"

"Right." She had hoped to forget.

"As soon as I took the sign from the trunk, this dude came out of the house next door with his badass dog snarling and snapping at the fence. The guy was half-naked, covered with tattoos. He looked me up and down, then guess what he said...?"

Did she really want to know? Diana lifted her eyebrows.

"The jerk asked me out on a date! He licked his lips, grabbed his crotch, then asked again! And all the while, the dumb dog was trying to break through the fence and eat me."

"Then what?" Either Liz was on a crazy sugar high, or else the encounter had actually turned her on.

"I told him why I was there—to sell the house and all— and he said 'hold on' and took the dog into his house."

To fortify herself, Diana broke the rule and took a doughnut.

"So I went ahead and put on the lockbox thinking I'd be long gone before he came back, but he was too fast for me. This time he left the dog inside, but he was carrying a big old briefcase. He called me over, propped it on the fence and popped it open. It was fuckin' full of cash! 'I'm buying the house,' he said. 'Here, take it'."

"Oh my God, what did you do?" Diana froze, doughnut in hand.

Liz paused to catch her breath. "It looked like a lot of money, maybe more than the asking price, but I knew I couldn't take it. I told him he had to come to the office and sign a contract. I hope I did the right thing."

Diana gave up and put the doughnut back down on the napkin. "Are you kidding? Of course you did the right thing. You know it's illegal to purchase real estate with large amounts of cash unless it's thoroughly sourced. Or do you want to get hauled before the Commission again? For all you know, that creep was offering drug money."

"Yeah, but…"

"No buts about it. Then what happened?"

"He wrote his name, Jose Nunez, on a piece of paper for when I changed my mind, and then he asked me to marry him!"

Diana rolled her eyes and buried her face in her hands. When she looked up, Liz was still unconvinced. Diana understood. They hadn't earned a decent commission check in ages, but this situation was impossible. "Look, give his name to Bank of America, but then forget it. Right now your big problem is Blueberry Lane, because you have less than a week left to make a decision."

Her red-headed sidekick was still conflicted, like maybe she'd let a good deal slip through her fingers, but Diana pressed on. "I told you that Ryman Meeks, the Iredell County Septic Inspector called. He gave the green light to add two more bedrooms at Blueberry Lane. So if you and Danny still…"

Liz interrupted. "Danny's got cold feet."

"What about you?" Had Liz been just another of Diana's buyer clients, her last remark would mean the deal was about to go south. But since Diana had no skin in the game, since she was representing Liz for free, all she cared about was her friend's happiness.

"Can we extend Due Diligence two more weeks?" Liz asked.

Another tricky maneuver. The sellers in Florida had already waited six weeks, so they might not be inclined to give that concession. "I'm not sure Charles and Evelyn Miter have been informed about the bodies, so it's hard to predict how they'll respond."

Liz snagged another doughnut and nibbled thoughtfully. "Yeah, they'll be shocked when someone tells them, but once they know, they should give us a discount. It's a stigmatized property, so they should jump at the chance to sell, even if they have to wait two more weeks."

"So I'll prepare an extension form, Liz. There's only one way to find out, so why don't you call the Miters right now?"

Liz smiled sweetly and batted her fiery eyelashes. "But *you* are my agent, Diana, so it's *your* place to call." She began walking towards the back room. "I'll be here another hour, so please let me know what you find out."

So much for the joys of mixing business with friendship.

Diana gazed mournfully at her fingernails, located the Miter's number and picked up the phone.

TWENTY-FOUR

Research junky...

"You should have brought Liz along, not me." Ginny complained as she and Diana entered the Iredell County Main Library in Statesville.

"Well, Liz doesn't have a library card, and it's not like I'm buying *Liz's* wedding dress after we're done with this chore."

"I should hope not!" Ginny blinked a couple of times, noted the blackmail attempt, and then strode up to the information desk to get directions to the newspaper archives. "That's what mothers do for daughters, not for their business partners."

Diana was truly touched by Ginny's remark, because she'd never before referred to Diana as anything like a mother figure. It almost made the odious task of helping Ginny choose her dress, and then paying for it, worth it. She was honored and happy to buy Ginny's.

"Still, research is Liz's thing, not mine." Ginny continued to bitch as they entered a lounge where the historic newspaper were stored on microfilm and DVDs.

"Unfortunately, Liz wasn't keen on helping," Diana said. "I even bribed her by offering to buy lunch, but it didn't work."

"So you bribed me with a dress instead?" Ginny's disarming grin was so like Matthew's—the silver stud in her nostril was not. Nor would her father approve of Ginny's butt-hugging miniskirt, an outfit that turned the heads of two middle-school boys hunched over homework.

"Let's sit over there…" Ginny indicated two side-by-side workstations. "You do the microfilm, I'll do the DVDs. Now, what are we looking for again?"

Diana had already explained the mission on the drive up. They would search local newspapers circa 1970's for the keywords "missing person," or anything to do with suspicious disappearances, but Ginny's head was in the clouds. So Diana repeated the criteria and handed her a list of the previous owners of 16 Blueberry Lane. It was the list she and Liz had compiled when they'd searched the chain of title.

"Remember, if you find any of these names, no matter what the context, please let me know. It could be important. I'm especially interested in the original owner, Margaret L. Koopman. According to Ruth Kimmel, the old lady Liz and I visited in the nursing home, Ms. Koopman was a disagreeable individual who's probably dead by now."

"And why do we care about her?" Ginny folded a stick of cinnamon gum into her mouth and offered one to Diana.

"No thanks." Diana waved the gum away. "We care because Ms. Koopman owned the property when somebody planted those bodies in the ground."

"Right, I get it." Ginny turned on her computer, accessed the files with her library card, and then passed the card to Diana. "This is all Trev's fault, isn't it?"

"I'm afraid so." Indeed, Trevor Dula had put the bee in Diana's bonnet that night at Buffalo Guys when he'd asked Ginny to marry him. He had suggested checking the newspapers from forty years ago for articles about a missing child or family, and Diana couldn't get it out of her head. Following Ginny's lead, she turned on the microfilm viewer and figured out how to use the thing.

"Why isn't Liz interested in all this?" Ginny asked. "She's the one buying the house, doesn't she care?"

Diana shrugged. Frankly, she wasn't sure Liz and Danny were still committed to the purchase, but Diana had spoken to the current owner in Florida and had managed to get a Due Diligence Extension of two weeks. As it turned out, the Miters had already been informed and questioned about the bodies, so Diana hadn't been responsible for breaking that ghastly news.

"Did the current owners give Liz a discount?" Ginny wondered.

"No, in fact, Mrs. Miter didn't seem at all concerned about the bodies and almost refused to extend. I don't get it."

"It is weird." Ginny agreed. "If that were my house, I'd pay someone to take it off my hands."

As they got down to work, Diana recalled that Evelyn Miter's only concerns had been the flowering trees just coming into bloom in Florida, because her allergies were killing her. Even weirder was the fact that Diana had remained intent upon pursuing the matter, but the hunt had become personal. Even if Liz didn't care, the mystery gripped Diana and she couldn't wait to get to the last page.

"Any luck?" Ginny asked wearily after an hour had passed.

"Not really." They were searching old issues of the Mooresville Tribune, Statesville Landmark and Record, and even a little publication called Barium Messenger. So far, Diana had found no people missing around that time. "Have you found anything, Ginny?"

"One small item, but maybe it's not important. I found the name *Henry Koopman,* but not *Margaret Koopman.* He was a Vietnam vet who got arrested twice for drunk driving, once for assault."

"No kidding? Koopman's a distinctive name. Maybe Henry and Margaret were related. Did you find his address?"

"No, sorry." Ginny stood, yawned and stretched. "But I'm beat, Diana. Can we quit now?"

Diana had also come to a dead end. Perhaps the old papers had no secrets to yield. "I agree, we're done with the library, but if you can bear with me a few more minutes, I'd like to go next door to the Registrar of Deeds."

Ginny groaned. "Please don't tell me you're doing real estate now. What about my dress?"

"No, I'm doing obituaries. I'm looking for Henry and Margaret Koopman's death notices."

Ginny followed Diana under protest. The county complex housed not only the library and Registrar of Deeds, but also the Hall of Justice and Board of Elections. It provided one-stop shopping for most official business, from political and judicial to the mundane.

"It won't take long," Diana reassured Ginny. "Why don't you wait outside here on that bench in the sun? Soak up a few rays. I'll be back in a few minutes."

Thirty minutes later, Diana returned empty handed. She'd found no record of any Koopman death whatsoever.

Ginny sensed her disappointment and patted a spot beside her on the bench. "I know you're a research junky, Diana, but you got nothing?"

"Nada." Diana plopped down, while Ginny returned her cellphone to her purse.

"Bummer," Ginny said, a sneaky grin on her face. "But maybe that's good news. It means Henry and Margaret are still alive, right? If you find them, you can question them."

"Wrong. It only means they didn't die in Iredell County. They could be dead in Peoria or Timbuktu for all we know. It's over."

"Not necessarily..." Ginny waggled her purple-tipped finger. "Contrary to what you may believe, I wasn't playing video games while you were gone, I was talking to Trev. I told him about Henry the Vietnam vet, and Trev knows how to find him."

Diana waited for enlightenment while the two middle-school boys from the library strolled past and wolf-whistled at Ginny. "Well, are you going to tell me?"

Ginny chuckled. "As you know, Trev's an Iraq vet, and he has connections. He says the odds are good that your Henry Koopman passed through the VA Hospital in Salisbury sometime upon returning from the war, and if you buy me a *really* nice wedding dress, he'll personally escort you to the hospital and help you find your mystery man."

Diana laughed. "Did Trev say what color dress and how much to spend?"

"He just specified low neckline, something sexy."

Diana glanced at her watch. If they hurried, they could visit the bridal shop and max out Diana's credit card before lunch. "What's Trev doing this afternoon?" she asked.

TWENTY-FIVE

The adult in the room…

As it turned out, Trevor Dula was unavailable, so after searching unsuccessfully for Ginny's dress, Diana dropped Ginny at the house and headed to the office, where she hoped to make some money. She had two potential clients who'd been sitting on the fence for almost a year. She'd shown them dozens of suitable properties, yet both were waiting until the economy improved, until prices and interest rates dropped even further—which wasn't going to happen—so likely neither would buy until Doomsday, and Diana would go broke.

As she charged through the front door of Lakeside Realty, plotting ways to goose her customers into action, her head still cluttered with the mystery of the bones, she plunged headlong into Dick, her Broker-In-Charge, as he stormed from the conference room. The collision caused her to drop her briefcase and the boss to splash coffee on his shoes, but she saw immediately that it wasn't the mishap that was upsetting him.

"Sorry," she gasped. "What's wrong?"

"Damn it, Diana! I don't know how you two manage to make so much trouble. You and Liz McCorkle—trouble magnets. Sometimes I don't know why I keep you on."

She'd never seen him angrier. He was apoplectic, with small veins bulging at his temples and tiny droplets of spittle foaming at the corners of his contorted mouth.

"Calm down, Dick. What's happening?"

He jabbed a stiff finger at the room. "Why don't you ask your partner in crime? She's in there right now with a manager from Bank of America and an agent from the SBI. Our company doesn't need this Diana. Really, I should fire you both!"

Diana felt her hackles rise. She never took a frontal attack lying down, especially when she was "not guilty" of anything more serious than eating on phone duty. She picked up her briefcase and glared at him. "So, am I fired, or not?"

He visibly wilted and backed off two steps. He wiped at his mouth with his sleeve, and stepping stork-like, one foot to the other, wiped coffee from the toes of his loafers on the backs of his trouser cuffs.

"Diana, you need to get in there right now and straighten this thing out, you hear? We'll discuss the rest later."

Dick was ridiculous, but Diana was shaken. Whatever the problem, she had no choice but to meet it with shoulders squared. So she entered the room, taking care not to slam the door behind her, and was most definitely not encouraged by the scene awaiting her.

"What?" She directed the question to Liz, who was scrunched up like a small, terrified red mouse in the chair at the head of the table. Two standing males, flaunting their power positions, flanked Liz on either side. One was a middle-aged balding blond, impeccably dressed in a custom suit, hundred-dollar tie, gold cufflinks—the bank exec. The other was a nerdy, non- descript fellow in a considerably cheaper suit with neither color nor character—the representative from the State Bureau of Investigation.

Diana put her briefcase down. "Well, is anybody going to fill me in?"

"You better take a seat, Mrs. Rittenhouse, I presume?" said the SBI guy, whose darting little eyes reminded her of a squirrel.

"No thanks, I'd prefer to stand." And why not? At five feet, ten inches, she was taller than these two even in her flats, and long ago her dear daddy back in Pennsylvania had taught her never to give up that advantage. "Who are you?"

They rapidly introduced themselves: Mr. Carlton the banker and Mr. Mendenhall the agent. The polished surface of the conference table was littered with photographs, file folders, and Liz's Client Book for Helms Street, so Diana suddenly understood all this fuss was about the drug house.

"I told Mr. Carlton about the cash offer, just like you said, Diana," Liz meekly began.

"And now all hell's broken loose." Diana completed the thought. By then the men had lost some bluster. "Why don't we *all* sit down and figure this out?" Diana waited until the men reluctantly took seats side by side at Liz's left, and then Diana sat at Liz's right hand, gave it a little squeeze of encouragement. 'Don't worry, Liz, you did the right thing, and we've done nothing wrong."

When Mendenhall cleared his throat, his Adam's apple jigged above his tight white collar. "Except that your fingerprints were found on a discarded dope needle, Mrs. Rittenhouse. May I call you 'Diana'?"

"No, you may call me 'Mrs. Rittenhouse'." As Diana's mind raced to process the situation, she realized that everyone was already focused on the Bank of America deal with the nasty neighbors, the foreclosure. "Yes, I remember now. I touched that needle while I was measuring at the baseboard, but I used a tissue to throw it away in the waste can under the sink."

Mendenhall frowned. "What else did you do to disturb the crime scene?"

"How did they know they were your fingerprints, Diana?" Liz wondered.

"Tell you later." Diana gave Liz a stern look and let go of her hand. Liz, of all people, should remember Diana's very first listing in North Carolina, when Diana's client was murdered and Diana fell under suspicion. Through no fault of her own, Diana's prints were in the system, and there was nothing she could do about it. She fixed on Mendenhall. "You should know this is absurd."

"Mrs. Rittenhouse, haven't you had a recent run-in with the MS-13 gang?"

Diana blinked in shock as she tried to recall what Trev had said about the drug cartels taking over the state, but at the time she had been so sure Luis Colon was to blame for her troubles, she hadn't paid strict attention.

"What's he talking about, Diana?" Liz's green eyes were enormous. "Is this about your tires?"

"I understand you were also involved in a high-speed chase in downtown Mooresville," Mendenhall continued. "Who was chasing you, and why were you running?"

"Agent Mendenhall, if you had a grain of sense, you'd ask yourself why, if I was transporting drugs, did I take shelter at a police station?" She'd decided it was time to change course and become the adult in the room. She turned to the banker, who thus far had said not one word. "Mr. Carlton, the house on Helms Street is your property, your responsibility, didn't you know it was a drug house?"

The man blushed to his blond roots. "No, we were unaware."

"Of course he was unaware, he never even saw the damn place," Liz spoke up. "The banks look at what they have on paper, turn off the utilities, then put on a padlock. In this case, there wasn't even a padlock."

Diana was glad to see Liz spark when confronted by her pet peeve. Since she handled all the foreclosures, she understood how careless some banks could be with their real estate assets. Once Liz had listed a million dollar waterfront home in foreclosure, but by the time Liz arrived, vandals had removed the priceless chandeliers, an upstairs pipe had frozen and burst, ruining the ornate plaster ceiling and hardwood floors below. And all that seemed tame when compared to the rotted food in the expensive refrigerator—exotic cheeses growing green beards.

"Has anyone from the bank even seen the property?" Diana demanded.

"Not until yesterday," Carlton admitted. "By then, even the neighbor Ms. McCorkle described was gone."

"The house next door, occupied by a Mr. Jose Nunez, as your partner accurately reported, had been stripped bare and abandoned, but Nunez and his partner could not eradicate the stink of the crystal meth they'd been cooking," Mendenhall explained.

"He had a partner?" Diana instantly pictured Luis Colon in that role. "What was his name?"

"I'm afraid we don't know. Although the place has been under surveillance this past week, our agents were unable to make an identification." The nervous little man shuffled the stack of photos through his fingers like a squirrel worrying a nut. "Perhaps you and Ms. McCorkle can help us with that?" He passed the photos across the table, and Diana and Liz began looking.

Diana had seen two neighbors in the beginning of April when she'd visited alone and found the bank- owned property trashed. When she and Liz had gone back together, it had been miraculously sanitized, but no one had been home next door. Finally, when Liz had returned by herself to place the sign, she'd seen only one neighbor, but had it been the same man Diana had encountered?

As they browsed through a combination of mug shots and candid pictures, the only things the disreputable subjects had in common were youth, amazing "body art," and Latin heritage. Eventually Liz and she were able to identify only one man—the same man—and Mendenhall confirmed he was Jose Nunez, so his partner remained a mystery.

"How much cash would you estimate Nunez offered you?" the squirrel asked Liz.

"Lord, how would I know? More than enough to buy that dump."

Carlton gravely shook his head. "It's a pity these criminals are such wealthy men."

"Since he's rich, maybe I should have accepted Jose's marriage proposal?" Liz giggled.

Mendenhall was not amused. His eyes flickered back and forth on Diana. "Describe the car chasing you that night."

"It was small, dark and fast. Sorry, that's all I know."

"Anyone besides the driver in the car?"

"I have no idea. Wish I could help more, but maybe you can answer one question for me? Who cleaned up the foreclosure?" She described the house before and after.

But Mendenhall was stumped, or pretended to be, and Carlton didn't have a clue.

"I don't get it," Diana said. "It almost seems like they'd cleaned it up because of me. When Jose saw me that first time, he didn't know why I was there, but my visit obviously upset him. Then voila, a week and a half later, the place was spic and span with a lock on the door."

"You were unexpected, Mrs. Rittenhouse, because you certainly don't look anything like the lowlife who normally frequent their drug house," Carlton said.

"Diana doesn't look like a NARC agent, either," Liz pointed out. "I think those guys were the ones who cleaned the place up, but not to impress Diana because she looked like a classy lady, and not because they thought she was coming back to arrest them...so why?"

Neither Mendenhall nor Carlton was inclined to take a guess.

"Maybe they thought I was the competition?" Diana joked. "They feared I was moving in on their turf."

This time Carlton laughed uproariously, but Mendenhall just twitched and fidgeted, because plainly the interview had yielded less than nothing. He quickly gathered up his files, said his terse goodbyes, and moments later he left.

Carlton, Liz and Diana exited the conference room directly afterwards, almost trampling their Broker-In-Charge, who was eavesdropping right outside the door.

"So how did it go?" Dick asked anxiously.

"Oh, these two gals are a great team," Carlton said. "I'll keep them in mind when I'm ready to buy or sell. You're lucky to have them."

Dick was speechless.

Liz turned to the banker. "What about the Helms house? Do I still have a listing?"

"Sorry, Ms. McCorkle, I'm afraid not. We've been instructed to take it off the market while the investigation's still pending." And then he left.

Dick left, too. Apparently their Broker-In-Charge was too embarrassed to apologize.

"Rats, now that the drug house is cleaned up, I actually could have sold it." Liz was downcast. "So, are we in trouble, or what?"

Diana sighed. "No, we're not in trouble, but we're back at square one."

TWENTY-SIX

Only the good...

Thunder rumbled through skidding black clouds, backlit by jagged white lightning, as Trev drove Diana onto the large campus of the W.G. Hefner VAMC. She'd been there once before, also in spring with azaleas blooming, but today the multitude of imposing brick buildings looked less like a lovely college campus, more like what they were—a facility dedicated to warriors damaged in ugly wars.

"Sorry about the rain." Trev drove his Jeep under a covered roundabout at the main entrance so Diana could stay dry. "I'll park, then meet you right inside."

She pushed through glass doors equipped with waist-high buttons so the handicapped in wheelchairs could enter without assistance, and when she stepped into the well-lit lobby, she was relieved to find the atmosphere more cheerful than she imagined.

"How can I help you, ma'am?" The pretty young receptionist was smiling and upbeat, much like any girl with her first job, eager to make a good impression.

"Thanks, but we better wait until my friend gets here," Diana said.

"Is it still raining hard?" The girl rose from behind her big desk, but reached for a walker to pull herself upright. When she navigated to the door to peer out, Diana saw she had only one leg and tried not to stare.

Afghanistan," the girl quickly explained. "IUD exploded under a laundry cart outside the mess hall, right near the cafeteria line. If you think it wrecked me, you should see what it did to our dinners."

Diana didn't know whether to laugh or cry. The offhand humor, like the girl herself, implied the injury was no big deal, but clearly this was not her first job. Instead, this brave receptionist had already seen more horror than most people experienced in a lifetime.

"I'm so sorry." Diana realized the apology was inadequate considering the sacrifice, but she couldn't think of anything else to say. She could offer a platitude about how much Diana appreciated the woman's service in keeping America safe, but in fact, she felt that a much wider apology was owed from the politicians who'd sent these young people into two wars not worth fighting. At least that was Diana's opinion.

"No, don't apologize. I'm good." The woman smiled. "Now that Iraq is almost over and Afghanistan's winding down, there'll be lots more like me coming home, and I'm glad I'm in a position to help them."

"Yes, I understand." Diana also smiled, but did she understand? The whole concept of these needless injuries made her furious. Trev, for example, had been wounded and his whole outlook on life had changed forever, yet she couldn't express her opposition to the wars without upsetting someone. So she hid her inner pacifist, and sometimes the effort made her physically ill.

"Have you come to visit a vet?" the girl inquired.

"No, we're hoping to find information about a soldier from forty years ago. It's a longshot, but we think he may have been treated here in the 1970s."

"Oh wow, Vietnam." The woman's smile drooped. "North Carolina lost hundreds of guys in that stupid war. We still have a few of those patients here even now."

Stupid? Had the woman really said that? Maybe Diana wasn't the only one with reservations about America's appetite for war. But before she could explore it, Trev burst through the door and stomped his feet on the welcome mat.

"Hey, Margo!" he greeted the receptionist by name.

"Hey, Trev, I'm surprised to see you again so soon."

Diana did a double-take. "You come here often, Trev?"

"Sure, he comes all the time," Margo answered for him. "At least once a month Lieutenant Trevor Dula brings cookies and books for the inmates." She winked at Diana. "Are you the lucky woman? I hear Trev's getting hitched."

"I wish." Trev grinned. "This is Diana Rittenhouse, my fiancée's future stepmom."

Even though Diana knew Margo was teasing, heat crept up her neck. Not so much at the thought of marrying a young stud half her age, but because Trev had used the "mom" word. It seemed like Diana was the only one doubting that Matthew would eventually pop the question.

"Nice to meet you, Diana. Now, Trev, tell me why you're here bothering me so late on a Friday afternoon." Margo wheeled her way back to the desk, and with some difficulty, shifted back into her chair.

In the meantime, Trev explained they were looking for the records of a man named Henry Koopman.

"You sure he served?" Margo asked.

"Yeah, but we don't know if he ever visited the VA Hospital. Can we find out?"

Margo frowned. "Is either of you related to Mr. Koopman? If not, I'm not permitted to release any information to you. Sorry."

Diana saw a mischievous flicker in Trevor's blue eyes as he considered lying, but then he thought better of it.

"Pretty please?" he said instead. "Can't you just take a peek and let me know if Koopman was ever here?"

"Did you say *Koopman*?" A tinny, amplified voice boomed from the shadows across the room, where a shriveled man was propped in the corner on a couch. "If you're talking about *Henry* Koopman, yeah he was here, and I knew him well. I still regret it."

"That's Mr. Johnson," Margo said. "Don't believe a word he says."

"Don't listen to that witch," Johnson squawked. "She can't walk too good, but she's plenty mean when she starts flying around on her broomstick. You folks wanna know about Henry? Come over here and sit a spell."

Margo nodded at the older man, who looked the right age for a Vietnam veteran. "It's not against regulations for Mr. Johnson to tell you what he knows. He maybe doesn't remember what he had for breakfast, but he hasn't forgotten one minute of his war experience."

"Damn straight." Johnson patted a spot beside him on the couch. "The lady can sit here by me."

As Diana and Trev approached, she noticed a round disc in Mr. Johnson's throat, a speaking device. It explained his odd, static-filled voice. When she took a seat beside him, while Trev sat nearby in an armchair, she also noticed that Johnson followed their progress by tilting his head, not with his eyes.

"I'm blind," he bluntly stated as he pointed a crooked finger at Trev. "But I recognize your voice, son. You've been here lots of times, so how come you don't give some of those cookies to me?"

"I usually visit the guys who served in Iraq, like me, but I'll put you on my list in the future."

"You better do that, boy, to thank me for the quality information I intend to provide. Who the hell are you, anyway?"

Diana and Trev introduced themselves, and without going into the gruesome details about the bodies at Blueberry Lane, explained they were researching a property that once belonged to a woman named Margaret L. Koopman. They wondered if she might have been Henry's wife.

The horrible wheezing hoot that followed alarmed Diana, until she realized that Mr. Johnson was laughing. When it was over, he wiped his vacant eyes and got himself under control.

"God Almighty, no! If old Koop heard you say that about Margie being his wife, he'd shit a brick." Johnson touched Diana's knee. "Excuse the language, ma'am, but it's the truth. Hear Koop tell it, Margie was the bitch from hell. Lord, how he hated that woman, even though she was his sister."

"His *sister*," Diana repeated, then glanced at Trev. "So I guess you knew the whole family?"

"Everyone knew the Koopmans, but no one had much time for that bunch. White trash farmers, don't you know? They were land-rich, but every last one of them had a mean streak wide as the stripe down a skunk's back. Especially Koop."

Diana and Trev continued to stare at one another as Mr. Johnson seemed to sink into a past that swallowed him whole. He grew silent as the rain beat a steady staccato on the roof, and then he reached out, like he was trying to grab hold of some memory.

Diana feared they were losing him. Trev cleared his throat and ran fingers through his wet black hair.

"Mr. Johnson..." he spoke loudly. "You knew Mr. Koopman through this hospital?

The old veteran's head snapped upright, as though some invisible puppet master was jerking his string. "When we were boys together, we all gave little Henry a bad time, called him 'chicken koop' on account of he was always so small for his age, but mostly because he was rotten inside. And that never changed. When he came back from Nam and ended up in here with the rest of us, he was worse than ever."

Diana inched as far away from the man as the small couch would allow. She had no sympathy for schoolyard bullies, but when she moved, Johnson's talon-like fingers clamped down on her knee.

"He thought he was a hero, you hear? But we all got hurt over there, him not as bad as some, so he deserved what he got."

"What did he get, sir?" Trev gently reached over and disengaged Johnson's hand from Diana's knee, then placed it on the old man's lap.

"Who, Koop? How should I know what happened to him? He got out and went home. End of story."

"Where was home?" Diana asked.

"Cross the river in Denver. We were both from Denver."

Diana's mind spun with the news. No wonder she and Ginny never found anything about the Koopman family. They didn't live in Iredell County at all, but rather in Lincoln County. "Is Henry Koopman dead?" She blurted it out.

Again the disturbing, wheezing hoot echoed around the room until Johnson was calm enough to talk. "I never heard he was dead, and why would he be? If losing his left arm didn't kill him, what would?"

"He lost his arm in combat?" Trev asked.

But Mr. Johnson had moved on to a different place. "Didn't you ever hear that song that got so popular a few years after Koop left? '*Only the Good Die Young.*' So by that measure, Henry's not dead. And if you need more proof—neither am I."

PART TWO

Matthew

TWENTY-SEVEN

Blueberry pancakes…

"It was Billy Joel's big hit from 1977," Diana said. "The album was called *Stranger.*"

Matthew looked up from his blueberry pancakes. "How do you know? Since when were you a popular music guru?"

Diana laughed, poured them both another cup of coffee. "Trev told me on the way home from the hospital. Also, you couldn't be alive in the late 70s and miss that song."

"I missed it, and we both missed our chance to die young, so does that make us bad?"

"It makes me very happy." She bent over and kissed his cheek, then sat down at the table to drink her coffee.

Matthew watched her lift the cup to her lips. The corners of her amazing blue eyes crinkled as she tried to smile and sip at the same time. The morning sun slanted through the kitchen window, making her short white hair shine like dry ice.

He adored her.

And he had caused her so much worry the past few weeks. In retrospect, hiding his health problem had been a terrible mistake. It had pulled them apart and made them both miserable. Sneaking around behind Diana's back felt all wrong, and had the circumstances been reversed, he would have been furious had she hidden an illness from him.

"What?" She caught him staring.

159

"Nothing. You look mighty pretty, that's all. Like a contented tabby cat sitting in that patch of sunlight."

"Why thank you, Matthew. You're downright lyrical this morning."

"Inspired, more like it." He toasted her with a forkful of pancake, then swallowed. Regrettably, he didn't consider himself lyrical, poetic or even adequate most times to express his love for Diana. But she knew how he felt by now, and someday soon he'd make it official.

"It's a beautiful day," she said. "Almost like summer. We should get out, Matthew. Take a ride, or something."

"Just two old fogies out for a Sunday drive?"

"Sure, why not?"

He rarely had her to himself on Sunday, the only day he was off. Too often she had floor time, or buyers to haul around, or an Open House, but that was the price of loving a real estate lady. This particular Sunday was peaceful indeed because Ginny and Lissa had left early that morning for an outing with Trev, leaving Matthew and Diana alone in the house.

"Where do you want to go?" he asked.

She began clearing dirty dishes off the table and fed Ursie the fatty ends of her bacon strips. The Doberman expected this treat on weekends and never left Diana's side until breakfast was over. Satisfied, Ursie licked her lips then charged out the back door in pursuit of a chipmunk. Diana filled the dishpan with water and detergent as she gazed out the back window.

"Would you enjoy a trip to Denver?" she asked innocently.

Matthew already knew where this was going. Ever since she'd returned from the VA Hospital, then found Margaret L. Koopman's address and phone number by simply looking in the white pages of the correct phone book, Diana had been on a mission. She'd pleaded with Trev, Ginny and Liz to accompany her on a visit to the woman, but they'd all turned her down flat.

"You want to talk to Ms. Koopman, don't you?"

"How'd you know?" Diana wrung out her dishrag.

"Honestly, Diana, you couldn't be alive in this house and miss that bit of information." It was all she'd talked about, and Matthew had overheard every conversation. He'd hidden his doctor appointments from her, and she'd tried to conceal her obsession from him. She knew it upset him—everything from the bodies, to the tires, to the car chase—all putting her squarely in harm's way. Yet he realized she couldn't leave a mystery unsolved. Courting danger was a way of life for the woman. She didn't go looking for trouble, but it always managed to find her.

He walked up behind her at the sink, resting his hands on her hip bones. "If this Koopman family is half as mean as that old veteran claimed, maybe you should take Ursie along for protection?"

"Yeah, right."

They both laughed at the family joke. Dear old Ursie looked like a junkyard attack dog and often terrorized folks by baring her teeth. But that was just her way of smiling, and the animal was more likely to turn tail and run from any conflict than stand her ground.

Matthew moved closer and wrapped his arms around Diana's waist. When he nuzzled the nape of her neck, she smelled like pancake batter and Ivory soap. "Maybe you should call her first. Could be Ms. Koopman is a church-going lady and won't be home until this afternoon."

"I'd rather surprise her."

This was typical of Diana. Bold as she was, she was shy about intrusion. She'd rather take her chances on the woman not being there than make a deliberate decision to pry. Then if Ms. Koopman just happened to be home, it somehow became a chance meeting that was meant to be.

"Hate to say it, but I don't know my way around Denver, Matthew."

She was fishing, but he was determined to keep her on the hook a little bit longer. "I can tell you how to get there..." He moved his hands higher and cradled her breasts.

"Stop it, Matthew!" She pretended to be shocked by his behavior. "My hands are wet, I can't defend myself."

"Just so happens I'm free this afternoon, if you wouldn't mind some company." He turned her gently around and pulled her into his arms. Even wet, her fingers felt good when she took his face into her hands and kissed him.

Once his mouth was free, he stipulated. "Of course, you'll have to let me drive."

"But what will we do with our morning, Matthew?"

He took her hand and led her to the bedroom.

TWENTY-EIGHT

The land time left behind...

Diana and Matthew could see the River Highway Bridge from their front deck. It was the main artery connecting the eastern and western shores of Lake Norman. The span also connected Iredell to Catawba County, and that afternoon as they crossed over, Matthew was surprised to see heavy boat traffic churning up waves beneath them.

"Lots of folks are out, considering it's early in the season," he commented.

"Must be global warming. It's the end of April, but it feels like June." To emphasize the point, Diana rolled her window all the way down, and Ursie, who'd come along after all, lumbered upright in the cramped back seat and shoved her long black nose out for a sniff of the fresh, watery air.

They were riding in Matthew's pickup truck because Diana refused to let Ursie travel in her "real estate car." Indeed Queen Vic, like an aging monarch, was kept clean and dog hair-free for the buying clients. Besides, Matthew had told Diana that if Ms. Koopman was really an old-school country woman, she'd likely feel more comfortable seeing his dusty truck invading her privacy.

They drove the next few miles in easy silence, appreciating the glorious day and basking in the afterglow of lovemaking. Different as they were, Matthew could never quite get over how natural he felt with Diana, how easy in his skin. He lifted yesterday's fast food container off the seat between them and took her hand.

"I wonder if her brother, Henry Koopman, lives with her?" he said.

"I hope not. He doesn't sound like a nice person, neither does Margaret, for that matter."

Diana proceeded to tell him a funny story about the afternoon she and Liz had spent with an eccentric old lady who lived at the Westminster Village Retirement Community. By the time she'd finished, Matthew was in stitches.

"Ruth Kimmel must've been an experience, but remember, Diana, just because she said Ms. Koopman was awful, doesn't make it gospel."

"So we should keep an open mind?"

"Absolutely."

They crossed two smaller bridges and soon arrived at the junction of Highway 16, which more or less ran parallel to the western shore, and Matthew took a left. As they drove past grocery stores, gas stations and various small businesses trying to make a go of it, he realized that this was the land time left behind. Unlike their side of the lake, with its close proximity to major highways, the western shore had no major roads pumping in life blood.

On their side, much to Matthew's distress, strangers from all over the nation had invaded to enjoy the lake, the mild climate and what had been a booming economy until the recession. Like many locals, whose North Carolina roots went deeper than memory, Matthew resented the outlandish mansions, the suburban sprawl, and the acres of concrete supplanting the family farms.

On the other hand, the great influx of humanity had allowed his business, *Trout's Place*, to thrive. More importantly, it had lured his beloved Diana who, like the others, had come seeking her fortune and a new life. In coming, she just might have saved his life.

"Do you know where to turn?" she asked him.

"Yes, ma'am, I sure do." In spite of the changes, the farmland unfolding just beyond the main drag seemed more intimately familiar to Matthew than most areas surrounding his own habitat. It felt more like the North Carolina of his youth, when there was no Lake Norman, only the sleepy Catawba River snaking down from the mountains, through the foothills, and finally into the Piedmont Plain.

When they left Catawba for Lincoln County, he kept his eyes peeled for Kidville Road. He cautioned Diana to watch closely for the Koopman name on a mailbox or sign post, because the phone book had offered no numbered address, only the name of the road. Out here in the country, farmers didn't require numbers to know where their neighbors lived. And as they passed through vast stretches of cornfields and cow pastures, occasionally punctuated by a house or a barn, Matthew felt truly transported to a bygone era.

"Are you sure we didn't miss it?" Diana fretted, and Ursie whined with boredom.

"I think we'll know it when we see it." But Matthew was worried, because many of the names on mailboxes were faded and unreadable.

"Wait, slow down!" Diana suddenly grabbed his arm. "I see it over there!"

Sure enough, unlike the others in these parts, the Koopman Chicken Farm sign was freshly painted and the complex itself looked prosperous. Diana hiccupped with laughter when Matthew turned into the long gravel driveway leading to a well-kept brick rancher, with four long metal buildings set back in the distance.

"What's so funny?" he asked.

"Are you kidding? The Koopmans own a chicken farm. As in 'chicken Koop.' It's hilarious, Matthew."

He chuckled obligingly, but didn't quite get the joke. In Matthew's experience, it wasn't uncommon for family names to reflect their profession. Smiths were once blacksmiths, Millers milled flour, Wainwrights made wheels. No big deal.

"But it's not at all what I expected," Diana admitted. "When you hear about an ancient woman living alone on her farm, you picture a ramshackle old frame house falling to ruin."

"Keep an open mind, remember?" he warned. "But just so you aren't completely disappointed, the old ruin you described is still here, but it's mostly hidden by those trees." He pointed.

"Yes, I see it." Diana held up her hand against the afternoon glare and squinted. "It must have been a pretty Victorian in its day. Was there a fire, Matthew?"

"Could be," he said, but it wasn't unusual for country generations to simply abandon the old homestead in favor of a smaller, more modern brick ranch. For the life of him, Matthew couldn't see it as an improvement, because the original buildings always had more character and grace.

As they approached the house, they saw a half dozen cats, all colors and sizes, milling around in the freshly cut grass. Ursie noticed, too, and began barking wildly.

"Oh, why did we bring her?" Diana groaned.

"She'll have to wait in the truck, that's for sure."

Five of the cats scattered, disappearing into the fields behind the house. The sixth, an enormous black creature with Halloween eyes, held steady, flicking his tail and growling softly at Ursie.

"I'll stay in the truck so she behaves herself, while you talk to Ms. Koopman," Diana said. "You're so much better with the natives, Matthew."

He gave her a stern, sideways glance. It was true Diana sometimes had trouble understanding the rural southern accents, and often her fast-talking Yankee ways put folks off, but this was her project. "We'll go together, Diana. I'll lock the doors and Ursie will be fine."

"If you say so…" She inched out of the passenger side, while Matthew slid from the driver's seat. "Maybe she's not home. I don't see any lights."

Matthew sensed Diana had cold feet, but they'd come this far and his curiosity was piqued. He locked the truck and moved towards the front door, Diana following. They walked up a sidewalk neatly bordered by daffodils, climbed three steps to an enameled green door, and Matthew rang the bell.

They waited and waited while the big cat rubbed against Diana's ankles.

"See, she's not home," Diana said hopefully. "I don't see a car anywhere."

"If Ms. Koopman owns a car, she likely parks it over yonder in that garage." Matthew guided Diana back down the steps and around the house to a driveway leading to a small apartment with a double garage underneath. "It's worth a looksee, don't you think?"

"I'm not sure this was a good idea. You were right, Matthew, we should have called first."

The cat came along, as though Diana had him on a leash, and if the escalated barking coming from the truck was any indication, Ursie did not approve of the situation one little bit.

Unlike the brick house, the garage apartment was old, same era as the abandoned wooden homestead, and it wasn't well-kept. Paint peeled from the walls and the steps up to the apartment were rickety, obviously unused. When Matthew peeked into the garage through a high window, he saw a new beige Cadillac sedan parked inside. The automobile was spotless.

"I think Ms. Koopman's here somewhere, and I'll tell you, I didn't need to bring my old truck to put her at ease."

But Diana had already turned around and was heading back to the truck when Matthew noticed a lone figure stomping through the field in their direction. She was coming from one of the big steel buildings where the chickens lived, and she looked none too happy.

"Hold your horses, Diana, Ms. Koopman's almost here." Matthew's "open mind" policy proved quite useful, because it appeared the woman was not elderly, eccentric or dangerous, as reported. She wore bright yellow rubber boots and designer jeans. She had professionally coiffed blond hair and obviously the best facelift money could buy.

"Are you Margaret Koopman?" Matthew smiled into her small dark eyes.

"Who else would I be?" the woman snapped.

Up close Matthew saw that she was much older than his original assessment. The hair was a wig, and the facelift gave her features a stiff quality, like they'd been stretched too tight.

"Koopman's my maiden name," the woman amended. "I took it back when my jackass husband left me. Question is, who the hell are you?"

Emboldened by Ms. Koopman's straight talk, Diana stepped forward, figuring she could speak that language. "I'm Diana Rittenhouse and this is Matthew Troutman. We hope you'll give us a few moments of your time and help solve a mystery."

Ignoring Diana, Ms. Koopman stared at the cat now wound around Diana's ankles. "Damn it, Snookums, how the devil did you get outta the house?"

At the same time, they all heard a tremendous crash. Suddenly Ursie came charging through the field, teeth bared, heading straight for the cat. Ms. Koopman screamed as Snookums yowled and ran for his life.

"Good lord, Diana, didn't you roll up your window?" Matthew shouted.

"I never dreamed she could squeeze through that little space!" Diana was devastated. She attempted to catch Ursie, but the dog wriggled free and got a taste of Snookum's tail before the cat climbed the nearest tree.

Diana and Matthew were so distraught they didn't notice when Margaret Koopman took a small revolver from her jacket pocket. Gripping it between both hands, she extended her arms and pointed it at Ursie.

"Call her off, or I'll shoot her dead," the woman said with no hint of emotion.

TWENTY-NINE

Rampage...

Matthew was almost fifteen feet from the woman, but without thinking, he put his head down and charged. The gun went off as he tackled her, and as they fell down, the bullet shattered a lower branch of the cat tree. Snookums screeched and shimmied up to the tippy top, while Ursie streaked across the meadow and cowered behind the pickup.

Diana was still screaming when Matthew rolled off Ms. Koopman and snatched her revolver. When Matthew tried to untangle, the old woman balled her fist and socked him in the eye.

"Damn, you broke my ribs!"

"I'd have broken more than your ribs if you'd shot my dog." Matthew disarmed the little weapon, tucked the magazine in his pocket, and then tossed it to the ground.

"Are you hurt, Matthew?" Diana rushed over and fingered the tender skin under his eye.

"Will you help me get her up?"

Together they hooked hands under Ms. Koopman's armpits and eased her to her feet. Matthew realized by the spring in her recovery that her ribs weren't broken, only her pride. She reached down, retrieved her gun, and tucked it back in her pocket.

She turned to Diana. "You best lock your animal in that truck, Missie, or I'll try again."

Of course, Ms. Koopman couldn't shoot unless Matthew chose to rearm her, and that wasn't going to happen. He nodded to Diana, who rushed to the truck where Ursie was whimpering. The dog was more than happy to jump inside.

"If you have a tall ladder, I'll fetch your cat," Matthew offered, hoping to salvage the situation. But Ms. Koopman dismissed the notion with an impatient wave of her hand.

"Don't bother. Snookums knows the way down on his own. He'll be waiting at the door come suppertime." She brushed off her expensive jeans and hobbled towards the ranch house.

Matthew trailed her. "My uncle, Stony Sheryl, kept chickens over in Troutman."

"I remember Stony, but he couldn't compete with us." She eyed Matthew more favorably. "I was past my child-bearing years when I married the boy next door. Lucky for us, he had six brothers in the business, so when we joined forces, wasn't no one could touch us."

"I can see that." He nodded at the impressive steel buildings where the roosters and nesters were housed. By now he had Ms. Koopman's number and knew flattery would get him everywhere. "I admire your enterprise, Ms. Koopman."

"How about you call me Margie, and I'll call you Matthew?"

"Yes, ma' am." He grinned. Now that they were on a first-name basis, she'd invite them in for tea in no time flat. When the invitation came, Matthew caught Diana's attention and waved her inside. "Mind if my friend, Diana, joins us?"

Ms. Koopman shrugged a begrudging assent. Clearly she preferred the company of gentleman callers. "Is this mystery you mentioned *hers,* or *yours*?"

Knowing Margie's preference, Matthew lied a little. "Well, I'd guess you'd say we both want some answers."

When Ursie was safely secured, with the truck windows rolled halfway up, Diana arrived just as Ms. Koopman was leading Matthew into what could only be described as a parlor. The small room off the entry hall was furnished with the ornate sofa and side chairs from the original house, complete with a round marble cocktail table at center of the arrangement. The room should have smelled like mothballs, but instead he detected the scent of fried sausage. And instead of tea, Ms. Koopman brought in bottled beer.

"Just water, please," Matthew told her as Diana entered the room.

"Speak for yourself, Matthew. I'll take one of those." Diana actually winked at Ms. Koopman and accepted the bottle. For once, she did not demand a glass.

Matthew was startled. Diana had the right idea, but it would take more than swilling from a bottle to win over Ms. Koopman, who distrusted Yankees, to be sure, but also females in general.

"How much should we tell her?" Matthew whispered when Ms. Koopman left to fetch his water. "About the bodies, I mean?"

Diana considered, then answered slowly. "You never know. She may already be perfectly aware of those bodies, because from the way she handled that gun, Ms. Koopman could have shot them and put them there."

Matthew shook his head. "Little lady like that? She'd have needed help to bury them. I don't think so."

"On the other hand…" Diana said. "If she had nothing to do with the murders, and the bones turn out to be people she knew—kin, for instance—it could come as quite a shock."

"So we best tread lightly?" Matthew asked.

"Just let her talk and see where it goes."

When Ms. Koopman returned, she carried not only Matthew's glass of water, but also an ice pack for his eye and a plastic bowl of corn chips.

She tossed him the ice pack. "I don't normally punch strangers. Sorry, Matthew."

"I'll live. How are your ribs, Margie?"

"Reckon I'll see the sunrise tomorrow." She took a noisy gulp from her bottle.

From the corner of his eye, he saw Diana react in surprise at the familiar repartee. She took a dainty sip and cleared her throat. "Thanks for seeing us, Ms. Koopman. I hope you can answer a few questions."

"So what do you want?" The older woman scowled at Diana.

Matthew noticed that she hadn't invited Diana to call her "Margie." He sampled his water. "Margie, did you ever own a property on Lake Norman, on a street called Blueberry Lane?"

She screwed up her face in concentration, spoiling the effect of the facelift. "Well, nowadays I could sure enough afford one of those fancy places, but I never much cared to live near the water."

"This was a long time ago, Ms. Koopman, back in the 1970s," Diana said.

Margie took another long drink to puzzle it out. As Matthew watched, a memory shifted across her eyes. "Well, yes, now I remember. It was over in Iredell County, but that piece of land belonged to my parents. They bought it for my stupid brother."

"Henry Koopman the war hero?" Diana asked.

Margie's whoop of laughter made her choke on her beer. "Henry sure enough called himself a hero, but just because he was dumb enough to lay down under a bomb don't make him a hero, now does it?"

Matthew shifted on the uncomfortable horsehair chair. "But he lost his arm in Vietnam, isn't that right?"

"Like I said, that don't make him a hero, it just puts him in the wrong place at the wrong time." Margie scoffed. "The war done nothing but make Henry meaner and more ignorant. When he decided to marry the local whore, my folks bought him that land thinking it would turn him around and help him and his slutty bride start fresh in life."

Matthew glanced at Diana, who was as shaken as he was by Ms. Koopman's nasty rant. "So did Henry and his wife live at Blueberry Lane?" he asked.

"It took them six long years to build that pathetic little house, and they never even finished it proper before Henry left."

Matthew pressed the icepack to his face. He couldn't be sure whether it was Margie's fist or her angry rampage causing his headache. Either way, the headache was a doozy, and Margie's long, bitter story flayed the skin off Henry who, according to his sister, had been a mean-spirited, abusive drunk who couldn't hold a job. Henry's wife had been too young for Henry and slept around. By the time Margie moved on to her own deceased husband, who was also good-for-nothing but providing money and man power for the chicken farm, Matthew had had enough.

He held up his hand in an appeal. "Thanks, Margie, I understand it's been hard for you, but can you tell us more about the property at Blueberry Lane?"

"What's to tell? I never even seen the damn place."

"But you're the one who sold it to Charles and Ruth Kimmel," Diana interrupted. "How did that happen?"

"That Jewish lady?" Ms. Koopman rolled her beady eyes. "Now that woman was a piece of work. Cold as ice, thought she was God's gift."

Matthew noticed red blotches climbing up Diana's neck, a sure sign that she was about to lose her temper. "I thought you said the property belonged to your parents?" He quickly intervened.

"They died," Margie explained dispassionately. "It almost killed them when Henry up and moved his family to Fayetteville, so maybe it was a blessing they got killed by that train."

"Your parents were killed by a *train*?" Diana seemed incredulous.

"Their old rattle trap stalled on the tracks is what the cops said, but I say they done it on purpose. When someone high up in the army was dumb enough to give my brother a job at Fort Bragg, and Henry moved without ever living in that sorry house at the lake, my parents couldn't bear losing the little girl—their only grandchild, don't you know?"

"Ms. Koopman, did you inherit the house?" Diana asked impatiently.

"Who else? Henry didn't want to know us once he had that fancy job. Didn't even bother to call when our folks died, so I figured the house was mine. I sold it. End of story." Ms.

Koopman finished her beer and slammed the empty down on the table. "Question is, why the hell do you care? What's this about?"

It was their moment of truth. Matthew looked at Diana for his cue, but Diana stole the line herself:

"Tell us about the bodies."

THIRTY

One true thing...

They left in a hurry. Although Matthew still had Ms. Koopman's bullets safely in his pocket, he couldn't guarantee the crazy woman didn't have more ammunition close at hand. For all he knew, she was deranged enough to reload and empty a few rounds at their backsides.

By the time they reached the truck, Snookums the cat was halfway down the tree and Ursie had given up. She was asleep, curled in the driver's seat. He quickly coaxed her into the back, hurried Diana into the passenger seat, auto locked the doors, and then backed out the long gravel drive fast as safety would allow.

One block down the road without incident, Matthew pulled off under a big oak tree and cut the ignition. He closed his eyes, took a deep breath, and leaned back into the headrest.

"Are you okay, Matthew?" Diana seemed frantic with worry as she touched his swollen eye.

"Are you?" he asked.

"Well sure, I'm fine. I refrained from strangling Ms. Koopman, didn't I?"

He knew she was still seething inside. "Ms. Koopman was an experience," he said.

"You think? Never a dull moment."

They recuperated in silence. As their pulse rates slowed, Diana stroked his face. Clearly she was concerned that the confrontation had tipped him off balance. Margie Koopman had not precisely chased them from her house, no swinging of rolling pins or throwing of broken crockery, but her verbal obscenities had certainly been effective propellants.

"Did she think we were cops?" Diana spoke up at last.

"She thought we were pains in the butt."

"Did you believe her story?" Diana asked.

"Which part?" As far as Matthew was concerned, most everything Ms. Koopman said was not merely suspect, more like a downright lie.

"The bodies. Did you believe her about the bodies, Matthew?"

He gently removed Diana's fingers from his face. She meant well, but she was actually making him dizzy. "Do I think the Jewish lady, Ruth Kimmel, was the killer like Margie said? I don't think so."

"She pretended not to know about the bodies, Matthew, but that seems impossible. When we uncovered them, it was all over the news. How could she not read about it or see it on TV?"

He sighed. "Margie strikes me as a soap opera watcher, so maybe she actually missed the news. Possibly her denial of any knowledge was the one true thing."

Sensing their distress, Ursie extended her head between them and licked Matthew's face. The sensation made him vaguely nauseous.

"The other true thing," he continued, "is that Margie hated her brother and his wife. She hated her husband and didn't seem too torn up by her parents' deaths. I wouldn't care to be a member of that family."

"Amen to that. But did she *kill* them?"

Originally Matthew had not suspected Margie, but now he wasn't so sure. "Question is, whose bones were in those graves?"

So far it had gone unspoken, but he supposed Diana was thinking the same thing—a man, a woman and a little girl—what if the bodies were Henry Koopman and his family?

They stared at one another.

"Maybe it's a good thing we didn't mention they were a man, a woman, and a little girl," Diana finally said it aloud. "If Ms. Koopman is innocent, then it would have been cruel to put that thought in her head without proof."

"Besides, she said Koopman and his family moved to Fort Bragg," Matthew pointed out.

"She also said they'd never heard from Henry again. Isn't that convenient? With her brother and his family gone, Margaret inherited the house at the lake."

"And with her parents dead, she got the chicken farm. Do you think she drugged them and left them on the railroad tracks, Diana?"

She laughed, so he laughed too, but the effort made his head spin. He gripped the armrest for support.

"Listen, Matthew, it won't be hard to find proof. I'll call Fort Bragg to verify that Henry really worked there, and you can ask Wayne Bearfoot if one of the skeletons we found had only one arm."

Her ideas seemed to make sense, but Matthew couldn't concentrate. "Sounds like a good plan, Diana, but can it wait until tomorrow?"

"Of course, it has to wait. Today is Sunday, remember?"

Matthew sensed the moment when Diana caught onto his infirmity, because she stiffened beside him and stroked his arm. Next it seemed like she was yelling into his ear.

"Are you sick, Matthew? How can I help?"

He swam up from somewhere deep under water to ask her.

"Can you drive us home?"

THIRTY-ONE

Wax wings…

Matthew soon felt fine, but Diana insisted that he had to see Dr. Ellen. The next day, after a quiet evening and a good night's sleep, although his symptoms had receded, he made the appointment anyway. It was easier than arguing, and in truth, he was a little worried himself. After all, he wanted to be around to enjoy their future together, for Diana's sake as well as his own.

He waited until she'd left for the office, then sneaked into her jewelry box and quickly found what he was looking for. He slipped it into his wallet along with the second part of the surprise, and then went to see the doctor. If everything went well, he'd finish with Dr. Ellen in time for the lunch meeting he'd arranged with Wayne.

"So, what did the doc say?" Wayne asked as they slid into a booth at the local chicken joint.

"She said I'm okay, not to worry. My balance, my hearing, everything's good now. So she figured the punch in the eye caused a temporary setback."

Wayne whistled softly as he beheld Matthew's black and blue shiner. Matthew knew from the bathroom mirror that he looked like half of Rocky Raccoon, or maybe Rocky Balboa—either way, he was not a pretty sight.

"I'd hate to see the other guy," Wayne said as he shook salt onto his sausage and egg biscuits.

"Gal." Matthew corrected him. "An old lady punched me."

Wayne laughed. "Not much of a *lady*, if you ask me. Did you deserve it, Trout?"

Matthew hadn't yet decided how much to tell the sheriff. Diana wanted proof before they implicated Margaret Koopman or assumed that the unidentified bodies were her family. But he was inclined to come clean about all they had discovered and describe the various scenarios they had envisioned.

"That cholesterol will kill you," Matthew said as he stalled.

"You should talk, buddy..." Bearfoot pointed at Matthew's fried chicken, mashed potatoes and gravy. "And I know you didn't pull me away from my other duties to discuss our questionable dietary habits."

Matthew hesitated only briefly, deciding that leveling with Wayne was best for Diana. She shouldn't take it upon herself to solve his case, confronting potentially dangerous players on her own.

"It's about those bodies, Wayne. I think Diana's stumbled onto something." He began at the beginning, explaining how Diana and Liz had followed the chain of title for Blueberry Lane back to the original owners, how Diana and Ginny had located a veteran named Henry Koopman by running across his old DUI convictions in an archived newspaper at the Statesville Library, how Diana and Trev had discovered Henry's old address by interviewing a cantankerous patient at the VA Hospital in Salisbury... and finally, he admitted that Diana and he had visited Margaret L. Koopman in Denver only yesterday.

"So Ms. Koopman socked you." Wayne eyed Matthew with curiosity. "Before you tell me her story, can you explain how you got dragged into this, Trout? It goes without saying that Diana couldn't leave it alone, but you don't usually stick your nose in other people's business."

"Actually, all this should be *your* business." Matthew hadn't intended to be so blunt. To Wayne's credit, he'd listened for thirty minutes and drained a full pitcher of iced tea, without interruption. Yet he resented Wayne's criticism of Diana, when she was actually onto something. If the sheriff pursued her theories, then she wouldn't have to.

Bearfoot pinned him with his dark, Cherokee eyes. "My Indian forefathers were great trackers, Trout, and I'd like to think it's in my blood. So as a matter of fact, I have been on that same trail. I bypassed the tax records, the library, the hospital, and I certainly never spoke with Ms. Koopman. But I have arrived at the same starting point—the Koopman family. So will you please tell me what Ms. Koopman said?

Matthew poured himself more tea and described yesterday's adventure. When he was finished, Wayne stopped laughing long enough to surprise Matthew.

"Yes, I knew all about the train accident and how Margaret inherited the house, but what's her brother got to do with it?"

While Matthew was impressed by all the effort his friend had put into a cold case, the great red tracker had lost the scent at a crucial juncture. "Wayne, did you know Henry Koopman had a young wife and a four year old daughter?"

The sheriff stopped eating, his third sausage biscuit poised midair.

"And another interesting fact..." Matthew persisted. "Henry Koopman was missing his left arm."

Wayne put his sandwich down and pushed his plate away. By then most of the lunch crowd had left the restaurant, so in the relatively quiet dining room, the clatter of cookware and the voices of workers joking in the kitchen seemed exaggerated.

"Well, that changes everything." Wayne slowly shook his head. "The medical examiner wondered about that missing arm, but until now, we couldn't put a face to it."

Matthew was confused. "That day at Bobby Porter's wedding, you knew about the arm, so why didn't you tell Diana and me?"

Bearfoot frowned. "Believe it, or not, Trout, it sometimes benefits law enforcement to withhold facts from the general public, even the two of you. It's a balancing act. We want to make the identification, but we don't want to tip our hand. You'd be surprised how often a guilty party will reference a bit of knowledge he's not supposed to know, making our job a little bit easier."

Matthew slid part way out of the booth. "I understand, Wayne, but what next? If those bones belonged to the Henry Koopman family, who'd want to murder them?"

"Most murders are committed for love or money. I don't know about love, but your Margie Koopman had a money motive. I guess I'll have to visit her now."

"You better wear a Kevlar vest and practice your judo moves." Matthew laughed. They had paid in advance, so Matthew was now eager to leave and get to the jeweler, but Bearfoot grabbed hold of his arm.

"Keep this to yourself, Trout. That's not a request, it's an order."

Matthew glanced across the street to Lakeside Realty, the office was a stone's throw away. "I'll have to tell Diana."

"Much as I'd like to keep it from that woman, I know you'll include her and I can't stop you. But promise me that you'll make her back off from here on out. Can you do that, Trout?"

"I truly appreciate what you're saying, Wayne, but that's one promise I can't keep. You know Diana, she follows her own lights."

"Right. Just like the mythical Icarus donned his wax wings and followed his lights too close to the sun. And we all know what happened to him."

THIRTY-TWO

May Day…

Icarus' wax wings melted and he plunged to his death. Crash and burn. The mythic doomed man fused with an image of Diana and invaded Matthew's early morning dreams. This disturbing vision wasn't related to the obvious criminal intrusions from the outside world, but rather it was a spiraling kaleidoscope of Matthew's inner turmoil. He saw downward swirling children—Diana's Robby and Amanda, whom he had never met, Ginny and Lissa—all imperiled by his inadequacies in the strobe-lighted maelstrom of falling.

Eventually Matthew jerked to consciousness, thankful to be safe in his own bedroom, the covers undisturbed. He blinked in confusion, unsure whether it had been Perry's obscene chattering or Diana slamming drawers that saved him.

Either way, he was grateful. "What day is it?"

"Have you seen my phone?" she said.

Suddenly he was fully awake. "Today is May Day, my love. Do you know what that means?"

"It means Liz and Danny have one week to make a decision about the house," she grumbled. "But they still haven't had an inspection or ordered a survey, and no one cares but me."

"No, it means we find some ribbons and dance around the maypole, Diana. Then I will crown you my Queen of May."

"Please, Matthew, have you seen my phone? I meant to charge it last night, but now I can't find it anywhere."

"Diana, did you ever call Robby and Amanda last week?" Feeling suddenly grateful to be alive on such a fine spring morning, he swung his legs off the side of the bed and wiggled his toes in the carpet.

Dressed only in her bra and panties, Diana spun to face him, her hands angrily balled on her hips. She was absolutely beautiful.

"Get serious, Matthew. Everything I need is in that damn phone, and I'm already late for work."

"Everything?" he asked suggestively.

But Diana had already disappeared into their walk-in closet. By the time he pulled on his shorts and jeans, she emerged fully dressed. "I'd love to stay and chat, Matthew, but I have to go. If you find it, will you please plug it in? I'll run home at lunch and pick it up."

"Okay."

But Diana was already gone.

By the time Matthew washed up, fed Perry and arrived in the kitchen, Ginny and Lissa were also gone. His daughter had left a note on the fridge saying she was taking Lissa to school, then going to the grocery: "Nothing left for your breakfast but cold cereal, sorry," Ginny wrote.

Matthew wouldn't eat cold cereal even to prevent starvation, but his enthusiasm remained undaunted. When he opened the back door, Ursie charged through a patch of jonquils and greeted him smelling like grass and lake. He fed her extra wet food with her dry, and everyone was happy.

He even found Diana's phone when he flopped down to read the morning paper. It had fallen between the couch cushions while they were talking deep into the night—about the bones, of course. He told her how Wayne had confirmed that the male skeleton had only one arm. So it was no longer necessary for her to contact Fort Bragg to verify Henry Koopman's employment, because it was a moot point. Even Wayne now believed they had identified the victims, so it was time for Diana to bow out. She had agreed.

Or had she?

He pondered the question as he drove to work. Even after he'd greeted Jody, who religiously opened *Trout's Place* each morning at 5AM, Matthew wasn't exactly sure Diana had said "case closed." He slid a slice of pizza into the microwave and helped himself to a cup of freshly brewed coffee.

"Didn't Diana fix your breakfast, boss?"

"Ran out of groceries." Matthew eyed the sweet rolls, pop tarts and other perfectly good breakfast foods on the shelves. They sold these items for twice what they cost at Food Lion, which was precisely why both Diana and Ginny had forbidden him to bring them home.

"Trout, if you'll mind the store for a couple of hours before my shift ends, I'll do the two oil changes back in the shop."

"Can you handle those on your own, son?" Matthew shoveled the pizza onto a napkin and took a bite. Jody was great with the customers, but lacked the aptitude for working on cars.

"No problem, Trout."

While Matthew savored the hot blend of cheese and pepperoni, Jody rolled up his sleeves and pulled on a greasy coverall. As he watched the kid, it occurred to Matthew that Diana had said something about the need for DNA testing. She swore it could be done, even on old bones. She also said knowing *who* the victims were wasn't the same as knowing *why* and *who* killed them. So maybe she hadn't given up, after all?

As fresh doubt gnawed at Matthew's gut, along with the spicy pizza, he heard the nearby howl of sirens coming from the direction of the Interstate. Moments later, a fire engine screamed past, and then another. They were sounding their horns and scattering traffic off River Highway. Many of the cars sought safety in Matthew's parking lot.

At the same time, Jody appeared, flushed and excited with his CB radio. "Sounds like a bad one, Trout. Near as I can tell, a car exploded in the southbound lanes, with traffic backed up halfway to Statesville. Fatalities. I expect they'll need a tow truck, boss. What do you think?"

Matthew listened to the static crackling from Jody's box and couldn't make hide nor hair of the lingo. But the boy was a born ambulance chaser and got an adrenaline rush each time there was an accident.

"Can I check it out?" Jody shucked off his coverall.

Matthew cracked open a bottle of anti-acid and swallowed three colorful tablets. Last time he'd sent Jody out on reconnaissance, the kid had disappeared for two hours and they hadn't even got the repair job.

"Thanks, anyway, Jody, but I'll do it." Matthew retrieved his keys from the counter.

"Aren't you even taking the tow truck?" The boy's face fell. "You're missing the chance to bring in business."

"Not yet. You don't want to crash the party without an invitation."

He left Jody pouting and headed back into the glorious day. Clearly the crash had occurred a few blocks away at Exit 36, so Matthew, like everyone else, crawled forward at a snail's pace.

But he didn't mind. He rolled his windows all the way down, oblivious to the exhaust fumes, and sang along with "Lightning in a Bottle," the CD Diana had given him.

As expected, a cop redirected everyone onto Williamson Road before they neared the exit, which was blockaded by flashing lights and emergency vehicles. While the others scrambled to figure out detours to their important destinations, Matthew turned into a residential neighborhood and drove to a street that dead-ended at a lot overlooking Exit 36.

He pulled into the empty lot, waited until Buddy Guy finished a guitar riff, and then climbed from the truck. When he first peered over the rise to the blacktop, all he saw was billowing smoke interrupted by four streams of high pressure water jetting into the conflagration. But then a breeze lifted the filmy black curtain and Matthew saw the car. It had once been white, judging from the mangled hood and front bumpers, while the rear of the vehicle was all but pulverized. It was a Ford Crown Victoria.

It was Queen Vic.

THIRTY-THREE

Hallucination…

Matthew dropped to his knees on the rough ground. He leaned forward for support, both hands in the weeds as he fought dizziness and nausea. When he looked again, a heavenly stage hand had lowered the black curtain, concealing the accident. He vomited the pizza, and once the convulsions ended, looked again. If anything, the smoke was denser than before.

Losing track of time and unable to get a second look, he climbed unsteadily to his feet and leaned against his truck bumper. This couldn't be true. It had to be a hallucination, an extension of the Icarus dream. His hands still shaking, he opened the door and fell into the driver's seat.

Dr. Ellen had warned him these things could happen— sudden disorientation bearing no resemblance to reality—yet as tears streamed down his face, Matthew could still see the mangled wreck of Queen Vic in vivid detail.

When his vision cleared and his hands stopped shaking, he took his cellphone from the glove compartment and speed-dialed Diana's office.

An unfamiliar male voice picked up.

"No, she's not here," the man said. "I've been on duty since eight- thirty, and Diana hasn't come in."

Matthew couldn't remember how he'd formed the words to say goodbye, but he reasoned that maybe Diana hadn't gone to the office. Maybe she had a buyer, or a listing appointment? He tried her mobile, but his call went directly to voicemail. Diana's recorded voice asking him to leave a message brought on a fresh wave of tears.

He tried again, but then pictured her cellphone charging on their bedside table, he'd plugged it in himself. He glanced again at the chaos down on the highway, but was still unable to get a clear view. So far, he hadn't heard an ambulance rushing an injured passenger to the hospital.

Jody had said there were fatalities.

Since he couldn't think what more to do, and since it couldn't be true, Matthew twisted the key and backed out of the empty lot. Although he had no memory of driving, he eventually found himself back on River Highway. He arrived at his home on autopilot, and Ursie greeted him with pure exuberance, proving again that nothing was wrong.

He entered the house, no one home, and lay down on the family room carpet near the hardline phone, with his cell cradled on his chest. Someone would call, he reasoned, so he closed his eyes while his head spun. Ursie licked his cheeks, then curled up beside him, her head on his lap, while Matthew tried to cast it all as part of his nightmare. He heard waves on the beach, birds in the yard and the steady ticking of the grandfather clock in the hall.

When it struck noon, Matthew counted twelve gongs. Sometime later, Ursie jumped up when the back door opened. He recognized her footsteps before he heard her voice, before she knelt beside him.

"Oh my God, Matthew, are you sick?" Diana said. "Why are you crying?"

THIRTY-FOUR

About the car…

For a long time they just held one another, lying on the floor with Ursie, while Matthew explained.

She kissed his face and wiped his tears away. "But you can see I'm fine, Matthew. I'm right here and Queen Vic's parked in the driveway."

"I don't understand. It looked exactly like your car, Diana."

"I am so sorry."

She followed him into their bathroom, held him round the waist and laid her head between his shoulder blades as he splashed his face and brushed his teeth. She canceled her afternoon appointments. "Are you feeling okay? Do you need to lie down, Matthew?"

He took a cold drink of water. The dizziness and nausea were gone, replaced by a sweet relief that turned his bones to jelly. "I'm not sick, but I'd love to lie down, if you'll lie with me."

She was almost convinced, unbuttoning her blouse, when the doorbell rang. Ginny wouldn't bother to ring, neither would most of their friends or neighbors.

"Probably some misguided Bible Beater looking for converts," Matthew grumbled.

"Well, we have to answer it."

Disappointed, he followed her to the door. Since Ursie had been barred from the bedroom, the dog saw an opportunity to get even by loudly barking at the stranger on the other side of the screen.

Diana seemed to know the squirrely little man fidgeting on the doorstep. "Oh, Agent Mendenhall, what are you doing here?" she exclaimed.

"I'm waiting until you lock that animal up, and then we will talk."

Even before Diana introduced him, Matthew had placed their visitor as the State Bureau of Investigation agent who had interviewed Diana and Liz at the real estate office. While Diana had been stingy about revealing the content of their conversation, so as not to worry Matthew, she had described Mendenhall in humorous detail, and she'd been dead on.

Matthew dragged Ursie out the sliders to the fenced front yard, coaxed her out onto the deck, then pulled the drapes closed. "All clear." He signaled Mendenhall into the family room and urged him to take a seat, while Diana went for iced tea.

The man had the audacity to choose Matthew's personal recliner. "Mr. Troutman, I can't tell you how relieved I was to see Mrs. Rittenhouse's car out there in the drive."

Diana arrived and handed everyone a full glass of tea. Mendenhall blinked at her with his dark, beady eyes. "I thought you were dead."

"So did I," Matthew mumbled.

"So did Officer Don Bower," Mendenhall added. "He was on patrol and reported the accident as suspicious, and since he recognized the car and figured it involved you, Mrs. Rittenhouse, it got back to me quite quickly."

As Matthew tried to piece it together, he pictured Bower, the young, rosy-faced state trooper who'd responded when Diana's car had been vandalized. They'd seen him again at Bobby Porter's wedding.

"I called your office, then your cellphone," Mendenhall complained. "But I couldn't locate you, so I expected the worst."

Matthew noticed that Diana had suddenly gotten pale as she wilted down onto the couch beside him. She had managed to comfort him without thought to her own situation, but now that Mendenhall was here, the intimations of her own mortality had begun to sink in.

Like Matthew, she'd been backed up in traffic, but she'd never seen the accident. "Why did you call it 'suspicious'?" she asked.

Mendenhall took time to gulp his tea, his Adam's apple bobbing. When he finished, he put the empty glass on the table and played with his fingers. "To begin with, the wreck was no accident. By all accounts, the Crown Victoria exploded, scattering debris everywhere. It appears someone put a bomb in the car, timed to go off when the speed reached sixty-five."

"So it was deliberate," Diana said in a weak voice.

Matthew took her hand. "Why would anyone want to hurt Diana?"

The SBI agent ignored him and turned to face Diana. "It now seems that everything that happened to you was about the car, and it likely started that first day you visited the house on Helms Street."

"That was April Fool's Day, even before we found the bodies at Blueberry Lane."

"Those bodies are a whole separate issue, ma'am." Mendenhall blew it away, it wasn't his case. "The point is, the

195

Helms Street neighbor, Jose Nunez, saw you that first day and soon after that, someone cut your tires and painted the letters MS on your windshield."

"Yes, that's right."

"You had just left Helms Street the night you were chased through Mooresville, so it's likely someone spotted your car leaving the neighborhood and attempted an intervention."

"Intervention in what?" Matthew demanded.

As the sun rolled around to the west side of the house, a shaft of light sliced through the crack between the drapes and illuminated Mendenhall's face. The little man was blushing.

"The gang wanted to send a strong message to the competition, and they likely believed Mrs. Rittenhouse was a key player."

"Diana a *drug dealer*?" Matthew roared with laughter, embarrassing the agent even more.

"We now know MS-13 has local competition. The rival dealer and his wife own a Crown Victoria exactly like Mrs. Rittenhouse's. We believe that first day on Helms Street, La Mara thought their competition had located their drug house, so they cleaned up that operation and tried to warn you off."

"Warn *me* off?" Diana snorted. "Does this competitor's wife look anything like me?"

"As a matter of fact, yes she does, ma'am." Mendenhall cast his eyes at the floor. "The couple is highly respected in our community. They own a big expensive house on Lake Norman. The man, a mild-mannered pharmacist, even belongs to the Chamber of Commerce. At least he did—until today."

"He died in the car?" Diana gasped.

"We believe so, but what's left of the body is unrecognizable. We do know there was only one person in the car when it exploded."

Matthew felt unreasonably angry. "Why did it take you so long to put all this together? And when do you expect to arrest those responsible?"

"I understand your anger, sir." The agent got jerkily to his feet in preparation for a fast retreat. "To be honest, we never would have suspected this pharmacist if Mrs. Rittenhouse hadn't gone to Helms Street in a Ford Crown Victoria." He smiled balefully at Diana. "I'm sorry for your trouble, ma'am."

He rushed to the door, but turned back one last time. "And another thing, Mrs. Rittenhouse, that pharmacist's wife isn't half as pretty as you."

PART THREE

Diana and Matthew

THIRTY-FIVE

Complications...

"So it was never about you?" Liz snorted in disgust as she followed Diana through a gracefully arched trellis covered with pink tea roses.

"Apparently, not." Diana was also frustrated, because while she was glad to be done with tattooed hoodlums out to kill her, the media had been annoyingly close-mouthed about the details, and she was curious.

"You say the pharmacist is dead, and they've definitely tied him and his wife to a homegrown drug operation?" Liz paused to sniff a rose.

"Right on both counts, Liz. I gather the guy graduated top of his class at Duke and was a devoted family man. Unfortunately, his big house was about to go into foreclosure and he couldn't make the payments on his expensive German car."

"Well, at least the bad guys blew up the pharmacist's old Crown Victoria instead of the Mercedes." Liz reached down to pick a handful of violets hidden in the ivy at the base of the 1920s bungalow.

"He was cooking the books at his drugstore and pilfering pain killers for a network of kids to distribute on the street. Because of his squeaky clean white bread image, not to mention his own innocent children in Little League, the media has cut him a break."

"C'mon, Diana, the man is dead and his widow is looking at jail time. What more do you want?"

Diana sat on a stone bench under a huge magnolia tree to wait for her mother and Lincoln Davis to arrive. "I guess I want them to catch Jose Nunez and his partner, whoever that might be, and then see them punished."

Liz sat beside her. "I totally get it, but then the cops will call us in to testify, is that what you want? I'd just as soon put it behind me."

Diana stared into the mossy green depths of a lovely old stone koi pool, where the big orange fish were hibernating sluggishly near the bottom. She hoped the warm weather would soon bring them back to life. "I still believe Juanita's friend, Luis Colon, was involved somehow."

"Let it go, Diana. Your mom and her boyfriend will be here soon, so let's get into real estate mode and sell them this house."

The bungalow was the first of three Diana had selected to show them, but she already knew Viv wouldn't like it. "Mama says she wants to get out and dig in some dirt, but I don't think she means it."

"Well, it sounds like fun to me. Do you really know the names of all these plants, Diana?"

Before Diana had a chance to show off her Botany 101, she saw Linc's flashy Chrysler glide to the curb. Seconds later, he helped Vivian from the car and they headed under the trellis in their direction.

Liz elbowed Diana's ribs. "Not bad. Your mama found herself a handsome old dude. Love the hair and the suit," she whispered.

Knowing Liz's obsession with matchmaking, Diana had revealed as little as possible about her mother's new romance. Even the tiniest hint of a trip to the altar had Liz salivating to meet Linc. While she claimed to be along simply to scope out the property, Diana knew Liz was angling for juicy details.

Yet Liz was right. Linc looked as dapper as always in a crisp tan suit and a green silk tie that perfectly matched his amazing eyes. Even Mama had gone to unusual pains to look spiffy and youthful in a patterned sundress. When the older couple approached, Diana introduced Liz to Linc, and everybody hugged.

Already Mama was eyeing the garden with alarm. "What do you call this style of landscaping? It looks like a lot of work."

"Naturalization, Mama. It appears wild and untamed, but it still requires a fair amount of weeding, seeding, fertilizing and the rest."

"I knew that." Vivian gave Linc a worried look. "Maybe it's more appealing inside."

Wisely, Linc kept his mouth shut and gallantly opened the door once Diana had retrieved the key from the lock box. When they stepped into the entry hall, Liz pointed out a small stained glass window casting colored dapples on the heart-of-pine floors.

"Yes, it's nice, but who would choose these awful colors?" Mama moved briskly room to room, from the hunter's green hall to the maroon dining room and goldenrod living room. The kitchen retained its original patterned ceramic tile floor and metal sink. "Guess these folks didn't believe in upgrading. Isn't it true, Diana, that sellers should neutralize the house before putting it on the market? So the buyer can picture her own stuff in a place?"

"That's one theory, Mama." Indeed most Realtors advised their clients to do just that. But in the case of this stunning original craftsman-style cottage, "neutral" equaled "neuter." Sanitizing would sap all its character.

"I think it's charming!" Liz exclaimed. "I wouldn't change a thing."

"Isn't there a master on the main?" Mama scowled.

"Mother, I told you before, all the bedrooms are upstairs. You could convert the downstairs study."

Unlike many properties, this vacant bungalow had not been "staged" with fake furnishings. Instead, it just seemed empty and smelled vaguely like aged burnt wood.

Mama wrinkled her nose at the fireplace. "I suppose we could change to gas logs."

Diana sighed and glanced at Liz, who seemed truly enamored of the place as she drifted along touching the window seats and peeking into cedar-lined closets.

Liz mounted the staircase. "Don't y'all want to see upstairs?"

"Don't bother." Mama glanced at Linc. "I don't think it suits us, honey."

"Whatever you think, darling." These were the first words Linc had uttered since they entered.

"No, listen, you guys, it's awesome!" Liz thrilled. "I can see myself living here."

Until that moment, Diana had assumed that Liz was "puffing," which was real estate lingo for exaggerating the good qualities of a property. But now she realized that in spite of Liz's usual preference for all things modern, she really did admire the place.

"Curb your enthusiasm, Liz. Remember, you're already under contract for another property," Diana said, but Liz had already scaled the stairs and was out of earshot.

Linc peered wistfully into the paneled study, where he possibly visualized his law books displayed on the floor to ceiling shelves. Yet even if he felt a tug of attraction, he'd never express an opinion contrary to Viv's preference.

"Liz seems like a lovely young woman," he said. "And Vivian tells me she's getting married."

"So it would seem," Diana said.

"Well I never thought I'd see Liz settle down before you, Diana. How is Matthew these days?" Mama asked pointedly.

Viv was on her usual fishing expedition, but Diana refused to bite. She turned back to Linc. "Liz and her fiancé were planning to buy a fixer-upper on the lake, but we've encountered a few complications."

"*Complications?*" Liz was back down. "I'd call dead bodies buried in the yard very serious complications."

Linc's bushy white eyebrows dipped down in a frown. "What's she talking about, Vivian?"

"Let's not discuss unpleasant things on such a beautiful day," Mama said.

"Oh man, where have you been?" Liz tapped Linc's arm. "It was all over the news the first weeks of April. How could you miss it?"

Diana noticed that Linc seemed agitated. Obviously he didn't enjoy being odd man out.

"I was away, you see, visiting my daughter in New England," he defensively replied. "Why didn't you tell me about this, Vivian?"

"It's nothing to do with us, and besides, who wants to dwell on such a gruesome topic?"

But Linc couldn't let it go, surprising Diana with the intensity of his interest. Perhaps it harked back to his days as a court prosecutor.

"Liz, do you think your property was built on the site of an old cemetery?" he persisted.

Liz guffawed. "Not hardly, unless it was a graveyard for murder victims."

"Were these victims of gang violence?" he asked.

"Please, can we change the subject?" Mama took hold of Linc's arm and steered him towards the door.

"I don't think Mooresville had a big gang problem in the 1970s," Liz wryly responded.

"So it's a cold case." Linc pulled an old fashioned hankie from his vest pocket and mopped his face.

"Are you feeling all right, honey?" Mama urged him to rest on one of the window seats. He obliged by sitting and loosening his tie.

Diana was stunned. She'd never seen Linc anything but cool, calm and supremely collected. By contrast, this panicky man was a stranger.

"He has a slight heart condition," Mama explained as she fluttered around at a loss.

"I am perfectly fine." Linc insisted. "But tell me, Liz, where is this property of yours?"

"16 Blueberry Lane."

THIRTY-SIX

Ushering in summer…

"Honestly, Matthew, I was afraid he was having a heart attack," Diana said as they carried an Adirondack chair from the shed to the yard. "But he wouldn't see a doctor."

"Can't say I blame the man. Sometimes it's better not to know you're sick, then maybe it'll all go away." He lowered his end of the chair to the ground.

"That's called denial, pal, and I won't tell Dr. Ellen you said that." She lowered her end, so the chair faced the lake.

Matthew straightened and stretched. He smiled at Diana, who looked wonderful in her shorts and a sleeveless blouse, the first summer clothes of the season. Every year at this time, she was embarrassed by her long white legs exposed in shorts. She complained that her fair complexion looked like someone had dusted her with flour. Soon the freckles would emerge, after the sunburn, and Matthew loved watching every phase.

They walked back to the shed for the second chair. He was determined to get at least part way through Diana's "honey-do" list. "Maybe I should replace those shingles?"

Diana stopped and squinted at the roof. "I don't like the idea of you up on a ladder. Why don't you get a free roof from the insurance company, like everybody else?"

Matthew considered. It was true that after a damaging ice storm earlier in the season, most of their neighbors were cashing

205

in. But he still had reservations about whether getting a whole new roof was ethical when a few shingles would do the trick.

"Mama even canceled their other two appointments, Matthew, and I think they would have loved the last house on my list. It was weird, because once he caught his breath, Linc didn't seem all that sick."

He realized she was back on the subject of Viv and Linc. Matthew also recognized that if Diana's mom was half as protective as her daughter, Linc was in for a lot of fretting and fussing. "I wouldn't worry about it. They can see the other two places another day."

"That's not the point, Matthew. What if Linc really has a serious heart condition? What if they leave Shady Oaks, move into their own home and then he becomes disabled? I'd hate to see Mama saddled with an invalid the rest of her life..."

Diana stopped abruptly mid- sentence as she realized the impact of those words. Matthew also stopped as her statement hit too close to home. The scenario was exactly what he'd feared for Diana, that someday his acoustic neuroma would disable him and he'd become a liability.

"Oh, it wouldn't matter at all if Mama and Linc really love one another," Diana quickly amended and took his hand. "They should proceed full steam ahead and not worry. I'm sure it'll be fine."

"I'm sure it will be." But once spoken, the thought cast a pallor on the afternoon. He looked down at the beach, where Ginny and Lissa were playing tag in the sand. It was Friday, but his granddaughter had the day off from school thanks to a teachers' conference, so the whole family was home together.

They went into the shed for the other Adirondack chair. Next they'd set up the picnic table. It was all part of the traditional ushering-in-summer ceremony. As they worked, Matthew recalled that only last Tuesday he'd thought that Diana had died in a car crash, but that hadn't been true. Bottom line? No one knew what life had in store, so maybe it was better to anticipate the best, not the worst, and get on with it.

"Linc seemed to get sick when he heard about the bodies at Blueberry Lane," Diana continued as they began lugging the heavy chair. "Come to think of it, he grew up around here, just like Mama. He was a young man forty years ago. I wonder if he knew the Koopmans?"

"I lived here, too, and I didn't know them," Matthew said.

"Yes, but you were just a little boy then."

"Did your mama know them?"

"Oh, Matthew, I didn't ask. I never even mentioned the name, because by that time the whole day I'd planned was falling apart."

"Right." They placed the second chair beside the other, like the stupid *his* and *hers* bathtubs in those more-sex-for-old-guys commercials. After that dumb thought, Matthew focused on two good things: they had purchased light-weight resin chairs for the rest of the family, and it was time for a break. He wandered over to where Ginny and Lissa were collapsed in the grass.

"Hey, you two, who wants ice cream?"

THIRTY-SEVEN

Trouble in Paradise...

Diana picked Vivian up at Shady Oaks and drove her to property number two. Although the Saturday morning was unseasonably hot, the atmosphere inside Queen Vic was definitely frosty.

"What's wrong, Mama?" They parked in the short driveway leading to a front-loading double garage. The brand new builder's model wasn't a house to inspire rapture, but it did have a small, straight-forward yard and overlooked a pond and the seventh hole of a nice golf course. "Don't you want to see this house?"

Still sulking, Vivian climbed from the car and stomped to the front door. Diana followed with her Suprakey in hand.

"You may have noticed, Diana, that I am alone. I wanted *us* to see this house together, but Lincoln is gone again."

This much was obvious, but so far Mama had offered no explanation. Diana fetched the house key and they entered a standard layout with a vaulted family room straight ahead, study and master off to the left, kitchen and dining to the right. Everything smelled of fresh paint and sawdust. "Listen, Mama, if you like this place, we'll come again when Linc gets home."

But Viv walked straight out French doors to the back deck, where she sat on a bench the workmen had left behind and stared out at the pond.

Diana sat beside her. "Do you want to talk about it?"

"This is all your fault, Diana," Mama moaned.

Taking a deep breath, Diana decided to wait her out. Naturally Viv blamed her for the problem, but this time Diana didn't have a clue what it was.

Finally, Mama took a tissue from her purse and daubed her nose. "Why did you have to start talking about those damn bodies you dug up? Ever since then, Lincoln hasn't been himself."

To put a fine point on it, Liz was the one who had mentioned the bodies, but Mama wouldn't see it that way. "Is Linc feeling better? Did he ever see a doctor?"

"No, Diana, that's the problem, isn't it? Ever since we looked at that bungalow last Wednesday, I've been begging him to get a complete checkup, but he refuses. Finally, he got so mad at me he went off to visit his son in Raleigh. And I'm not sure when he's coming back."

Diana was beginning to get the picture. This wasn't about anything she'd done, it was about Mama's hen-pecking, which Diana knew, being her only child, could be a powerful motivation for running away. "Don't worry, it'll all blow over."

Yet Mama would not be consoled. She glared at a sole golfer putting in the distance. "Do you remember when we all had lunch at La Patisserie? Lincoln and Matthew got to talking about old girlfriends...?"

Diana did not recall the details, so she kept silent.

"Well, Lincoln mentioned his first love, an affair with a young married woman," Viv continued. "He said it was a terrible mistake, but I believe he still loves her."

When Diana looked again, she saw Mama's eyes were red from crying. Apparently one was never too old to be infected by jealousy. "That's just plain silly, Mama. Since he knew that girl, Linc's had a happy marriage with children, and now he loves you."

"No, he does not love me."

This was Mama's way of verbally putting her foot down, and Diana knew better than to argue. They both watched the golfer, who eventually got frustrated trying to make the putt. He furtively looked around, toed the ball into the cup, then marked his scorecard.

"He cheated," Mama said.

Was Mama talking about the golfer, or Linc?

"Have you talked to Linc about this?"

"Yes, of course!" Mama tossed the tissue on the deck. It skittered across the lawn. "He denies it, claims he only cares for me and wants us to spend the rest of our lives together."

"So why don't you believe him? I do."

Wrong response. Mama rose from the deck and rushed back into the house. Diana wasn't anxious to follow, because in this mood, Mama couldn't take "yes" for an answer. Yet she expected Diana to convince her that she was the most desirable woman on earth, and it was Diana's duty to try. By the time she caught up, Mama was standing in the kitchen, arms stubbornly folded across her chest. She was complaining about the lack of cupboard space.

"You say you believe Lincoln loves me, Diana, but who are you to judge? Why haven't you married Matthew yet? I tell you he loves you. Don't you believe me?"

"Don't go there, Mother," Diana warned. "This isn't about me. We are here to preview this house. If you don't want to do that, we're leaving."

Viv clammed up and began opening silverware drawers, then slamming them shut. In the meantime, Diana wondered whether Mama's trouble in Paradise stemmed from Linc's health issues, commitment jitters, or perhaps it actually had something to do with the bodies at Blueberry Lane.

"Mama, when you were a child here in North Carolina, did you happen to know a family named Koopman?"

Surprised, Viv stopped abusing the drawers. "Koopman? No, for heaven's sake, and what does that have to do with the price of beans?"

"Nothing, just wondered." Clearly Mama wouldn't know if Linc had known the Koopmans, so it was best to let the subject drop. "Shall we take a look at the garage?"

But Vivian was at the front door, ready to leave. "Forget it, Diana. Maybe you're right. Maybe Lincoln does love me, but he won't love this house."

Diana rushed after her. "Why not?"

"Because it doesn't have enough space for a woodworking shop." Mama rolled her eyes. "And now Lincoln's got it into his head that he wants to build things. He used to be a carpenter, don't you know?"

THIRTY-EIGHT

Heart-to-heart...

Matthew was at a loss.

After a fight with her mama, Diana had decided to make peace by taking Vivian to dinner at some restaurant. He wasn't invited. Lissa was at a sleepover at one of her little girlfriend's, so Matthew was deprived of the pleasure of babysitting. Ginny was working this Saturday night at Buffalo Guys.

Matthew was bored and troubled.

On Tuesday, Liz and Danny would be forced to make up their minds, one way or another, about Blueberry Lane. Once that was settled, Diana would be free—or so she promised. Then, if everything went according to plan, he'd take Diana away for a special vacation.

But before any of that happened, he had to speak privately with Ginny

The last thing he wanted was to spend the evening in a noisy tavern surrounded by a crowd of young folks drinking, dancing and whooping it up, but he didn't have much choice. It might be his last chance to catch Ginny alone, so when he arrived at Buffalo Guys, he asked Trev to position him somewhere where he could have a little quiet time with his daughter.

Trev sent him out to the deck overlooking the lake, and Matthew chose a table near the railing, where he could gaze down into the dark water. While he waited, he remembered what this establishment had been like when he was a little boy. Back then, it was the Catawba River flowing beneath this deck, before Duke Power dammed it up to create Lake Norman.

In those days, Buffalo Guys had been an old juke joint. Matthew's daddy brought him only once—Daddy drank a beer, Matthew had a root beer. A rough crowd used to patronize the place, not a suitable environment for children.

"Daddy, what are you doing here?" When Ginny arrived, her big, dark eyes were wide with surprise and panic. "Is something wrong?"

"No, I just wanted to see my best girl."

"Has something happened to Lissa?"

He patted the chair beside him and nodded for her to take a seat. "Relax, everybody's fine. I know I don't visit here often enough, and that needs to change. Right now, I want some quality time with my only daughter."

Still suspicious, Ginny sat down. "That's really nice, Daddy, but this our busiest night and I'm waiting tables. Maybe we could put off quality time until we're back at the house?"

He laughed. "I know, honey, but this is the only time I can get you alone, and we need to talk."

"Oh no, bad news! Is it your health, Daddy? Something you're afraid to tell Diana?"

By the look on her face, Matthew realized he wasn't much good at these heart-to-hearts. He never had been, and maybe that had been one reason Ginny had run off all those years ago. He reached out and took her hand, hoping to reassure her. "I promise it's all good, Ginny, if you'll hear me out..."

"I get it! You want to talk about my wedding. Don't worry, Daddy, Trev and I don't want anything big—just family and a few friends. We don't even expect you to pay for it."

213

"Please, Ginny, can I get a word in edgewise?" Matthew let go of her hand so he could reach into his pocket and show her what he picked up at the jeweler's. "I don't want to talk about *your* wedding, I want to talk about *mine*."

THIRTY-NINE

The creeps...

By three o'clock Monday afternoon Diana was beside herself. She checked her watch. They should both be here by now, Liz and the home inspector, but of course they were late. It seemed she was the only one who took "time is of the essence" seriously, because this was the last day of Due Diligence and if the inspector found anything major wrong, Liz was flat out of time to do anything about it. She had been pressuring Liz to get with the program, Matthew had been pressuring Diana to commit to a vacation the coming weekend, so she felt like a human pressure cooker ready to blow.

Even feeling out of sorts, Diana experienced a powerful tug of déjà vu as she pulled into the driveway at 16 Blueberry Lane. Almost afraid to look, she glanced at the big side yard and saw, much to her relief, the landscaping company had done a tolerable job of eradicating the old gravesites. After the forensic team had finished, the septic people updated the system, the lawn guys filled in the holes, leveled the soil and reseeded. So today, one month and four days later, it appeared nothing had ever happened.

But it had.

It did.

As she made her way up the dirt path, still littered with pecan shells, she no longer visualized what a gem this property could become with the coaxing of Danny's skilled hands, nor did she try to conjure the spirits of those who'd originally lived there, because now she had a pretty good idea who those people were and what had become of them. The very idea sent a bone-deep chill vibrating through her skeleton as she sat on the top step to wait.

She watched the whitecaps ruffling the water on the Main Channel across the road, then looked backwards to the cove at this property's dock, which was as still and placid as death. She wondered what had taken place forty years ago when the murders occurred. Had it happened in broad daylight, or on a moonless night? Were they killed here, or elsewhere? Margaret Koopman had claimed the family had never actually lived in this house. They had all moved to Fort Bragg instead of taking up residence.

By the time Liz finally arrived, exceeding the speed limit in her Honda, Diana's imagination was running wild with depressingly morbid thoughts, so she was grateful for the interruption. When she stood to greet Liz, her hands were clammy cold in spite of the heat.

"What took you so long?"

"I'm running on McCorkle time, not Rittenhouse time," Liz shouted as she skipped down the path. "Would you believe I've only seen this place once, Diana? I hardly remember what it looks like."

"Well, you'll soon find out..." Diana fetched the antique skeleton key that had so charmed her before. She braced herself, and when the door creaked open, they both went inside.

The room still smelled faintly of must, aged wood and old ashes from the large brick fireplace. Diana also noticed a new smell, like decayed meat.

"Yuck!" Liz wrinkled her nose. "Place needs some airing out."

"I agree." The odor put her off. It sent Diana reeling back into that bad space she'd been just before Liz arrived. The lack of family photos and empty wicker rockers on the front porch now seemed more sinister than before. The pine paneled walls were suddenly too close, and when she stood in front of the fireplace, she noticed for the first time, a large dark oval pattern on the floorboards where a rug had once lain.

"Does this place feel spooky to you?" Liz's eyebrows shot up.

"Don't be silly." But in her present state of mind, it was worse than spooky, it gave her the creeps. "C'mon, let's finish the walk-through."

The tour didn't take long since the house was so tiny. They found the source of the smell in the master bedroom, where a dead squirrel lay in a small pool of dried blood. He lay stiffly on his back, his thin legs stretched outward and his beady eyes staring at the ceiling.

"Ooh, gross!" Liz squealed.

"Jesus, how did that happen?" Diana wondered.

"It's so sad."

But to Diana, it was absolutely tragic. "I've seen this before. He must have dropped down the chimney, then couldn't crawl out."

"But what made him bleed?" Liz demanded.

Diana saw at once. Sometime, likely during the big windstorm last week, a large branch had fallen from the oak tree out front and cracked a small hole in the bedroom window. The jagged edge of glass was tinted with blood. "He cut himself trying to get out."

217

"But when he realized he didn't fit, why did he go so far?"

"Wouldn't you?" Diana wearily asked. "Don't worry, when the home inspector gets here we'll ask him to clean up the floor and dispose of the squirrel, then I'll call the listing agent and tell him about the broken glass."

But Liz walked quickly from the room and stared across the road, where the sun was already sinking in the sky. "The inspector's not coming, Diana," she said at last.

"Why the hell not?"

"Because I cancelled him."

The announcement left Diana speechless,

"You see, I've decided I don't want this place," Liz said. "Danny's okay with it now, but I've changed my mind."

"If you knew that, why didn't you call and head me off?"

"I didn't make the final decision until I was on my way. I called the inspector on my cell, but I knew you'd already be here, Diana. I figured I owed it to you to show up and break the news in person."

"But why the sudden change of heart?"

Liz smiled bashfully. "I fell in love with that 1920s bungalow we saw with your mother and Linc. That's the house I want, and I intend to buy it."

FORTY

Bad karma...

Matthew was worried about Diana. She'd been edgy and withdrawn ever since returning from Blueberry Lane last night. He hoped this romp in the woods would cheer her up and distract her. So with Ursie restless in the back seat of the truck, they pulled into the parking lot at Lake Norman State Park. When he parked, he paused to study Diana.

"Listen, honey, I'm really sorry the deal fell through. I know how hard you worked to make it happen for Liz and Danny."

She sighed and dropped back against the headrest. "It's not that, Matthew, and you know it."

He did know it. The whole depressing adventure had taken its toll. "So, did you tell those owners in Florida the sale was off?"

"Yes, and that was a weird thing. Instead of being upset, Charles and Evelyn Miter were thrilled. It seems they were hoping it wouldn't work out so they could keep the place. Evelyn suffers from allergies during Florida's hot season, so they intend to remodel Blueberry Lane and live in North Carolina spring through summer."

"That's a good thing, right?"

She gave him a curious look. "Yes, I guess it is. In some bizarre way I like the idea. I hope they utterly change that house, erase the bad karma and give it new life. Just so I never have to see it again."

"Amen to that."

Ursie licked Diana's ear and she actually laughed. "We better let this beast loose before she explodes."

When they opened the truck, their dog trampled them in her rush to escape. She shot into the woods like a sleek black arrow. After recovering from the onslaught, Matthew and Diana left the truck and followed her up the path.

"Is she okay off leash?" Diana wondered.

"Well, this being a weekday, I don't think we'll meet any other hikers on this route, so she'll be fine."

"Thanks for this day, Matthew."

"No problem." It was uncommon for him to leave *Trout's Place* during the week, but he'd been making special arrangements. Matthew had already hired two part-timers—a mechanic to help Jody in the garage and a girl to watch the store—so that Matthew could take Diana to the mountains that weekend.

The footpath they'd chosen today was one of several nature trails cut through the park. It snaked up a steep hillside through dense pine, river birch and scrub brush forest to a ridge overlooking the lake. Once up they reached the summit, folks could hike for a couple of miles above a sparkling blue inlet, where the water washed against the vivid red clay shore. And although Ursie had only been there once before, she took the lead and they followed.

Part way up, the overgrown path disappeared. They grasped onto some available saplings to orient themselves and catch their breath. In the meantime, Ursie barked excitedly in the distance.

"She must've flushed out a squirrel," Matthew said.

"I hope to God she doesn't catch it." Diana groaned.

Instantly sorry, Matthew wanted to bite his tongue and take it back. She'd told him about the dead squirrel they'd found at the house, and the incident haunted her. He waited, hoping the moment would pass.

"After Liz left, *I* buried him, Matthew," she said at last. "Oh, not out in the septic area…" she quickly explained. "I took him to the vacant lot across the road. I picked him up with some paper towels I keep in the trunk, but since I didn't have a shovel, all I could do was put him under some leaves."

"That was good enough. It was the right thing to do." He gently touched her sleeve, not knowing how else to comfort her. During the night, she'd awakened and told him how dead spirits seemed to infuse the Blueberry Lane house with evil. She'd had a nightmare about murders in the bedroom and in front of the old fireplace, and Matthew had done his best to make her feel better. "You need to put this behind you, Diana."

"Yes, I know. But it's not over."

FORTY-ONE

A honeymoon high…

Once they'd finished the hike and climbed down from the forest, even Ursie was beat. Diana's legs trembled with that good rubbery feeling that proved she'd done virtuous exercise, and as they boosted Ursie into the truck, she realized that for the first time in days, she felt clear-headed and happy.

"Whew!" Matthew exhaled as he melted into the driver's seat. "I'd say that got the old blood pumping."

"I'd say." Diana agreed. She peeked at Matthew, looking for any signs of ill effects, but saw none. He'd never once complained of dizziness or lost his balance. Instead, he seemed invigorated and supremely healthy. It was all right.

"I'm really hungry," he said. "What about you?"

"Guess so… not sure. I'll let you know once my body calms down."

Once they were underway, with Ursie snoring in back, Diana had a bright idea. "Since we're here, why don't we swing by the Porter's? We can check up on the place to make sure everything's okay while they're on their honeymoon."

"And then we'll eat?" Matthew winked, then made the turn. "Aren't the Sorvinos living at the house while they're gone?"

"Please, Matthew, I'm just curious." Mostly Diana just wanted to prolong the moment, to breathe more fresh air and absorb the healing of clear sky and open land before returning to reality.

The last time she'd visited the Porters was the night of Bobby and Juanita's pre-wedding party. She and Liz had viewed Bobby's renovations to the old homestead in the dark, so she was eager to see everything in daylight. When they drove up the rise and rounded the bend, she looked down at the house and saw a familiar white van, its smooth paneled sides were hand-painted with large, colorful flowers.

"Oh my God, Matthew, Bobby and Juanita are home!"

"They just rolled in, by the look of it."

Sure enough, Bobby was lugging suitcases, Juanita's arms were loaded with grocery bags, while young Juan was flying around the yard in a joyous reunion with his half-breed dog, Wolf. With canine precision, Ursie ceased snoring and started barking at Wolf.

Diana panicked. "What should we do? We don't want to intrude when they're just settling in."

"Too late, they've spotted us," Matthew said as Juan began waving wildly. "Now we'll have to go down and at least say hello."

As expected, they were welcomed with pure exuberance. On a honeymoon high, Bobby and Juanita dropped the luggage and groceries, and then literally dragged Matthew and Diana from Matthew's truck. While everyone was talking at once, Ursie miraculously revived from her hike. She leaped out and began cavorting with Wolf. Moments later, after helping Bobby and Juanita carry in their stuff, Matthew and Diana were also inside.

"Where are the Sorvinos?" Diana asked.

"They left just before you got here," Juan said, then turned to Matthew. "But I want you to know, Mr. Troutman, that

223

Wolf was never fooled by Johnny. He may look exactly like me, but Wolf's sense of smell is much better than a plain old dog's, so he always knew Johnny was an imposter."

Everyone laughed, just as they had that day at the wedding when Juan had made exactly the same prediction. When Diana reached out to hug the boy, with whom she shared a special bond, it was hard to believe that the wedding had taken place more than a month ago. So very much had happened since.

"Did you miss Wolf?" she asked.

"Oh yeah, but not as much as he missed me." Juan turned to his aunt Juanita, who now was also his stepmom. "Can I be excused?"

Without waiting for permission, Juan ran back outside where he, Wolf and Ursie were soon engaged in a pretend fight game—all jumping, lunging, and growling at once.

"So, your honeymoon was good?" Matthew asked.

"You bet." Bobby moved in from behind, gathered Juanita into his arms and nuzzled the back of her neck. His wife's expression said it all—that for her, it was also very good.

Inevitably, the couple invited them to stay for lunch. The grocery bags proved to contain the makings for what Diana called old fashioned Philly hoagies—crusty Italian rolls, mixed cold cuts and cheeses, peppers and onions, and if desired, a dusting of oregano and a splash of oil and vinegar dressing. Diana was still reluctant to intrude, but Matthew was starving, so his need prevailed.

Diana zoned out as the animated conversation swirled around her. Instead of listening to the details of all the exotic sights they had seen and spicy foods they had eaten, Diana watched the family. Juan and Juanita were many shades tanner, like Mexican natives, while Bobby's sunburn was still peeling.

The longtime couple behaved like newlyweds, renewing Diana's hope that sometimes second chances really could work out.

Afterwards, when the men surprisingly offered to wash the dishes, Juanita took Diana aside.

"Can we talk in private, Diana?" She led her out the back door to the same spot, under a giant magnolia tree, that Bobby had taken her the night of the party. It was the site where Bobby kept his construction supplies. Like Bobby, Juanita lit a cigarette and perched on a pile of two-by-fours. The setting made Diana feel like her life was in rewind, only now it was bright sunlight rather than pale moonlight.

"There's something I need to tell you…" Juanita began.

Diana fervently hoped Juanita wasn't about to give her a blow-by-blow account of the couple's post nuptial sex life. She was nervous, so she made a stupid joke. "Well, if you're going to tell me you're pregnant, then you better stop smoking."

Juanita coughed on her laughter. "No, I'm not pregnant. But I'd like to be…" she shyly added. "Bobby and me have talked about it, and we want a baby of our own."

That was surprising. For Diana and Matthew, second chances didn't include child-bearing. She'd forgotten that Juanita was still young enough to consider the option, but she was flabbergasted all the same.

"But that's not what I wanted to tell you. Sit down, Diana."

When she joined Juanita on the two-by-fours, Diana was apprehensive. The two had never discussed anything remotely personal, but Juanita came right to the point.

"Now I know how you feel about my friend, Lou Colon, but you need to hear me out…"

A shiver lifted the hairs on Diana's arms and suddenly she longed to escape.

"Are you listening, Diana?" Juanita's dark eyes were riveting. "I know it was you who tipped the cops to him, and Lou knows, too. I didn't say anything at the time, but I was real mad, Diana. They came round to our house and hassled Bobby and me. They asked if we knew where Lou was. Bobby wanted to turn him in, but I stopped him."

Diana didn't know where all this was going, and part of her didn't want to know. "So what happened?"

Juanita squared her shoulders. 'Well, we snuck him out, Juan and me. That day we got married? Lou was hiding in the back of the van when we left the church."

"No way! Didn't Bobby know he was there?"

"Nope. Juan and me had made up a game, like Lou was supposed to be his uncle. Once we got into Tennessee, Juan actually climbed in back with Lou and they played together all the way to Vegas. They had plenty of food, and Lou had a sleeping bag. I always got our suitcases when we stopped at motels, so Bobby never caught on…"

"Until we reached the Mexican border," an angry voice interrupted.

When Diana spun around, Bobby and Matthew were standing there. Matthew's eyes were wide with disbelief.

"Juanita knew they'd search the van," Bobby continued. "So she had to make a plan. She wanted everyone to pretend that Luis was her brother, Juan's uncle. One of Luis' outlaw pals had even made him a fake passport."

"And you went along with this?" Matthew asked Bobby.

Bobby shrugged unhappily. "What else could I do? If the border patrol got wise, we'd all have been in deep shit."

"So Lou got away?" Diana was stunned. At the same time, she now realized that Lou was likely not part of the drug ring. He hadn't chased her through town in a fake police car, because he was already gone. She'd been wrong all along.

"Si, he got away!" Juanita said triumphantly.

"But was he guilty of murder?" Diana asked.

Bobby spread his hands in defeat. "We'll never know."

FORTY-TWO

Out of sync...

The next morning Diana felt vaguely ashamed and definitely foolish as she dressed for the day. She had a history of wading knee deep into trouble, but lately it seemed she was in over her head. She'd been wrong about Lou, wrong about MS-13 being out to get her when they only had a problem with her car, and finally, when Sheriff Bearfoot called just as she was heading out the door, she discovered she was wrong about the bodies, too.

"Based on your theory, Diana, I asked the chief medical examiner to run some difficult and costly DNA tests on those bones. Days later and a few thousand dollars poorer, he conceded the male was likely Henry Koopman, but only because the skeleton was missing an arm. Unfortunately, it was impossible to link him to the two females."

"What do you mean?"

"Well, the woman was the mother of the little girl, but Henry Koopman was not the father. So they could've been anyone, not necessarily a family."

"But those bones were so old. Is the DNA test really definitive?"

"They claim human bones contain nucleated cells called osteocytes, which are inside the collagen fiber and can retain viable DNA much longer than forty years. I'm sorry, Diana."

She explained it all to Matthew, who trailed her to the car, trying to console her. "The way I see it, Diana, it's better this way. For Juanita's sake, I'm glad Lou wasn't guilty of those crimes against you, and I'm glad the drug cartel knows they made a terrible mistake and no longer have you in their crosshairs. And as for those bodies, would you like to be the one telling Margie Koopman that her whole family had been murdered?"

"She'll find out about Henry anyway. Bearfoot will have to tell her," Diana pointed out as she slid into Queen Vic.

"Sure he will, but from what we witnessed, I doubt if Ms. Koopman will shed any tears for her brother. For that matter, I doubt she'd cry even if that poor little girl had proven to be her niece."

Diana wasn't sure how Margaret Koopman would feel, and although Matthew disagreed, she still suspected the woman had something to do with the killings. Certainly she'd had a financial motive and an almost pathological hatred of Henry and his wife.

"What's on your agenda today?" Matthew called as she was leaving the driveway, lost in her speculations.

"Oh, I'm showing Mama and Linc the last house on my list."

"So Linc's home now?"

"Guess so, he was the one who called to set it up."

"Well, good luck with that." He waved as she left.

Diana knew she'd need all the luck she could get to find the right place for Mama and Linc. She'd expressed her frustration to Matthew, who typically, told her not to worry about it. As she neared the upscale retirement village, where a cluster home was for sale that perfectly fit the older couple's needs, Diana realized her real worry was loss of perspective. Her radar was out of sync. She was losing her touch. How could she be so wrong about so many things?

When she stated her business to the gateman, then drove slowly into the Silver Bay complex, she was forced to admit that Matthew was right—it was time to bow out. Let law enforcement deal with Margie Koopman, if indeed there was any crime to deal with. Diana needed to get on with her own life, the one she wanted with Matthew.

She found the "For Sale" sign at the end of a cul-de-sac. The semi-detached duplex was tastefully constructed of brick and composite shingles. Each unit maintained privacy from its Siamese twin by sharing only a partial common wall between garages and by facing in different directions. The bi-level she liked for Mama and Linc angled towards a valley with a view combining forest and city lights on the far hillside.

Diana saw she was the first to arrive. She pulled into the driveway and was automatically backing out to park at the curb, when she realized this maneuver was not necessary. The first safety precaution Realtors were taught was "never let the client block you in. Always position your car on the street pointing out, in case you need to make a quick getaway." This was especially true at Open Houses, where crowds of strangers visited with potentially evil intent, even more important when one was a solo female agent.

Diana laughed and pulled all the way up the single driveway to the garage. No problem when it was Mama and Linc blocking her in. So deliberately putting all worries aside, she switched the radio to NPR and listened to the opposing presidential candidates locked in a verbal slug fest in advance of the upcoming election.

The heated rhetoric was so entertaining, she hardly noticed when Linc's Chrysler pulled in on her tail. And she didn't realize until Linc was tapping on her glass that Mama wasn't with him. She powered down her window.

"Hello, Diana, your mother has the flu," he explained before she could ask.

"Oh?" Until that moment, she hadn't even known that Mama was sick.

"Vivian hoped to come right up until the last minute, but in the end, I put my foot down. She wasn't well enough."

"I'm sorry." Diana's first reaction was *here I go again.* Last time she'd shown a house to Mama alone, it had not worked out well. Now the situation was reversed, and she had a sinking feeling the result would be no better.

"I hope you don't mind, Diana." As always, Linc looked exquisitely put together in dark slacks, a herringbone sports coat, dark gray shirt and white silk tie, which matched his snowy, perfectly cut hair.

"You still want to see it, right?" She couldn't leave him standing there looking like a highly-paid anchor newsman. "I'll get my briefcase…"

"Great."

Like many gents of his generation, Matthew included, Linc liked to open doors for women, and he always let the lady go first. This led to an awkward moment when Diana fiddled with the lock box to retrieve the key, and then had to hand the key to Linc, so he could open the door. Finally, he stepped aside so she could precede him into the house—which was another real estate no-no: "never let the client get behind you." Of course Linc wasn't going to bash her over the head, rob or rape her. But he did, in fact, pull the door firmly shut behind them, then twisted the lock.

Startled, she held out her hand. "Give me the key, Linc, so I don't forget to replace it in the lock box."

But he had already slipped it into his trousers pocket. "Don't worry, I'll remember."

Slightly annoyed, she decided to let it go. As a modern feminist, sometimes even Matthew's chivalry was a bit too much, but Linc really was of the previous generation, so he had a legitimate excuse. "Where would you like to start, up or down?" she asked him.

But Linc had already moved ahead on his own, which struck Diana as odd. When she caught up, he was in the kitchen, leaning with his elbows on the central work island. He was tossing his car keys hand to hand, and when he looked up at her, Diana hardly recognized him.

Linc's habitually ruddy complexion was much redder than usual and she noticed a strange twitching in his left cheek. Most disturbing, though, were his eyes. Usually as placid as still green pools, today they darted back and forth, almost without focus. Alarming as that was, she couldn't tell if the emotion moving those eyes was anger, fear, indecision—or all three.

"What is it, Linc? What's wrong?"

As he tried to compose himself, she saw he had a small army knife on his keychain. She hoped he wouldn't open that knife, because while she didn't feel precisely threatened, she was uneasy. It seemed whatever demons tormented him, they needed to come out.

"Does Mama know you're here with me?" In a flash of clarity, Diana remembered that it was Linc who had made the appointment. She'd never even spoken with Mama.

"No, I came without telling her," he confessed in a deep, trembling voice. "This needs to stay between you and me, Diana."

Last time they'd been together, Mama had confided that she and Linc had been fighting over his old girlfriend. Today Diana desperately wanted this to be about Mama and Linc's relationship. She hoped he was here for advice, but she feared that wasn't the case.

"I don't understand..." she said.

"I know you don't." He gazed up at the ceiling, looking for what? A hovering spirit to tell him where to begin? "Why did you ask Vivian about a family named Koopman?" he demanded.

Diana's heart jumped into her throat, where it beat so hard she could hardly speak. She had no idea why this mattered to Linc, but it seemed this was about the bodies and always had been.

"When Vivian told me you asked her, I went back and checked the local newspapers from early April, the ones I missed when I was visiting my daughter in New England. I read all about your discovery at Blueberry Lane, and I'm sick about it, Diana."

As he moved from behind the counter and approached, Diana suddenly understood that she was alone with him, trapped in this house. She checked to see if he had opened his pocket knife, but he had not, and although in the past she'd never felt anything but safe and relaxed in Linc's presence, now she was afraid.

"You see, I knew the Koopman family very well, Diana—both Henry and his sweet wife, Kessie. And as God is my witness, I had hoped to never hear those names again."

While he was speaking, Diana maneuvered around so she could run out the door, but Linc was too fast for her. He spread his big arms and blocked her exit.

"I'm in trouble here, Diana. I am so sorry, but I cannot let you go."

FORTY-THREE

Busy signals...

Matthew had decided to take another morning off, because everything at the store was set up for their vacation. The two part-timers were working out well, operations proceeding smoothly. And since Diana was away for her appointment with Vivian and Linc, it was a perfect time for him to make his secret calls to Boone. He'd been debating with himself about whether to keep his reservations at a fancy mountain resort, or ask his uncle if Diana and he could stay in his camper trailer on the ridge top.

When he and Ginny had discussed it the other night at Buffalo Guys, she'd said he should definitely choose the resort, but Matthew was conflicted. The first time they went to the highlands together, Diana and he had borrowed the camper. It was the first place they made love, so the romantic memory was indelibly etched in his mind, hopefully in hers as well. In the end, Matthew had decided it was best to let Diana decide before they left for Boone.

So first he called the Watauga County Registrar's Office, to be sure he understood the process of getting their license. Next he was about to dial three different Wedding Officiants, when the phone rang in his hand. Glancing at the caller ID, he saw it was Diana's mom.

"Hey, Viv, what's up?" he answered at once.

"May I speak to Diana?" Like Diana, Vivian wasn't one for telephone small talk, she always got right to the point.

"She's not here. I thought she was with you."

"Of course she's not with me? Why would I be calling?"

Matthew recalled Diana's parting words. "Well, when she left this morning she said she was on her way to show you and Linc a property."

The silence at Viv's end was palpable. For a moment, Matthew thought he'd lost the connection. Finally, Viv cleared her throat.

"That's ridiculous, Matthew, there must be some mistake. To begin with, Lincoln is in Raleigh visiting his son. Besides, after last time, we agreed we'd only look at properties when we were together."

Then Matthew was silent. Either he'd misunderstood Diana, or she had some secrets of her own. "No, Viv, I'm sure of it. Diana told me Linc called to make the appointment."

"What property?" Her voice betrayed her skepticism.

"Some retirement village. Silver Bay, does that sound right?"

"Jesus H. Christ!" Vivian shouted. "What's wrong with that man? Yes, Silver Bay was on our list, but damn it, Lincoln wouldn't go without me. Something's wrong."

Matthew vigorously agreed. Also like Diana, Viv never, or rarely, cursed or blasphemed, and she'd just done both. Plus, Matthew had observed Viv and Linc together, and Linc would never dare to cross her. If anything, the man was solicitous to the point of being obnoxious, so Viv was right. Something was very wrong.

"Maybe Linc was on his way home from Raleigh when he called Diana," Matthew suggested, hoping to placate her. "Maybe he wanted to surprise you?"

"Not on your life!" Vivian fumed. "I'm worried about Lincoln. He hasn't been himself lately. Sometimes I feel like I don't know him at all."

By then, Matthew was also concerned. "Listen, Viv, why don't you hang up, and then I'll call Diana on her cellphone. I'll let you know what I find out."

"You do that, Matthew." With that, Vivian disconnected.

Matthew speed-dialed Diana, but his call went to her voicemail—a long message explaining why the caller should choose Diana as his Realtor. The advertisement always annoyed him. He waited a few minutes, and then got a busy signal. Had she picked up his call too late, and then forgotten to end it?

Matthew wasn't inclined to panic, but while he gave Diana a chance to call him back, he leafed through the stack of single-sheet printouts she kept on her desk and found the listing for a duplex at Silver Bay. It included directions.

After two more tries, two more busy signals, he got his keys and left the house. Part way down the road, he remembered that he'd never called Vivian back.

Too bad. She'd have to wait.

FORTY-FOUR

Passionate account…

Since Linc was blocking the exit to the front door, Diana glanced down a short hallway terminating in a door leading, she assumed, to the garage. If she could get that far and quickly find an electric garage door opener, she could possibly escape. Unfortunately, Linc read her mind and shook his head.

"Don't even think about it, Diana. I won't hurt you, I just want to talk."

She willed her heart to stop racing and concentrated on breathing while she tried to think. She had always trusted and admired this man. Had her instincts been that wrong? All day she'd been kicking herself because her judgment seemed flawed, and her paranoia off the charts, but her mother actually loved Linc. Were they both so wrong?

"What kind of trouble, Linc?"

"The kind that could land me in prison for a very long time."

His statement did nothing to alleviate her fears, but at least Linc's color had returned to normal, and while before he'd been hyper, now he seemed merely nervous. But then her cellphone began ringing from her pocket, and they both jumped.

He held out his hand. "Let it go to message, and then hand me your phone."

She did as she was told, after having only seconds to register that the caller had been Matthew. She watched until the call ended, Matthew hung up, but then Linc did not push "end call," leaving Diana's lifeline to the outside world in a limbo of busy signals. He then pocketed her phone along with the house key.

"Now that we won't be disturbed, let's sit over there." Linc pointed to a group of large unopened boxes that apparently contained new appliances. With some difficulty, Linc leveraged himself onto a dishwasher, while Diana sat much lower on a microwave.

Feeling ridiculous, she stared through a picture window above the kitchen sink, out across the empty back lawn to the golf course and far hillside. No help coming from that direction. As Linc began to talk, she watched a pair of Canada geese waddle up to the neighbor's bird feeder.

"Do you remember when I told you about my first girlfriend, Diana?" he asked in a hoarse voice. "Her name was Kessie Lucas when we first became lovers, but several years later, she became Kessie Koopman."

Hearing the name spoken aloud jarred Diana, but in some deep part of her psyche, it seemed she had already guessed this relationship. As Linc's sad story of doomed love unfolded, the tale of a young carpenter who fell for a child many years his junior, she watched the geese, who mate for life, and wondered why things couldn't work out that well for humans. Kessie had left Linc to marry Henry Koopman, an abusive, disabled war veteran, and Diana was drawn into the passionate account.

"So I helped build that house on Blueberry Lane," Linc said. "But I never should have taken up with Kessie again, because she was a married woman. It was torture seeing her with Koop. He was drunk all the time. He beat her and humiliated her, but she wouldn't leave him."

Tears welled up in Linc's eyes. "Finally, I couldn't take it anymore, so I wrote her a letter and broke off our relationship. I left town, attended law school at UNC Chapel Hill, where I eventually met my wife and started my own family."

Diana was no longer afraid. Instead, her heart was breaking as she listened to Linc bare his soul. At the same time, Linc had not yet explained why he was in trouble, and she sensed he was holding back.

"Then what happened?" she gently pressed, but before he could answer, a loud knocking began at the front door.

Linc panicked, his green eyes once again darting with indecision as the knocking got violent. Diana was shocked when he flipped his small knife open and moved cautiously towards the sound. By the time she screamed out to warn their visitor, it was too late, because Linc had opened the door.

"Matthew?" she gasped, as Linc pulled him inside.

FORTY-FIVE

What really happened...?

Matthew couldn't understand why Linc had yanked him inside, then kick-slammed the door behind them. But then he saw the terror in Diana's eyes and the knife in Linc's hand. Reflexively, Matthew chopped down hard on Linc's right wrist and the knife clattered to the floor. Before the elderly lawyer could recover from the blow, Matthew balled his right fist and slammed it into Linc's face, then he gut-punched him with a left hook.

Diana screamed as Linc stumbled backwards into the kitchen and collapsed against a pile of stacked boxes. The lawyer hugged his ribs and moaned as blood gushed from his nose and spilled onto his white silk tie.

Diana screamed again as Matthew moved towards Linc. "Stop!" she cried. "No more, please, Matthew!"

Breathing hard, Matthew hesitated and noticed that Diana was pleading. She came close to and lifted the handkerchief he habitually carried from his pocket, and then approached Linc. She knelt down and handed Linc the handkerchief, which he pressed to his nose.

"I wasn't going to hurt her, Matthew," the man whimpered.

"You sure could've fooled me." His adrenaline still pumping, Matthew fought an urge to strike again. Non-violent by nature, he struggled to understand why he'd just attacked a man who was supposedly his friend, and he was ashamed.

"I know this looks bad, Matthew, but you need to calm down and hear what Linc has just told me," Diana begged. She patted a small box, then wilted down onto the one beside it. Linc remained half sprawled on the floor.

Matthew kept standing. "I'm listening, but someone better start talking real soon."

"Well, here's what I know so far…" Diana started talking, while Matthew kept an eye on Linc. As she brought him up to date on a story so bizarre it had the ring of truth, Matthew stared at the geese in the yard. The male kept guard while his mate fed. The female was pregnant.

When Linc eventually recovered enough to sit upright and continue where he'd left off with Diana, Matthew began to sympathize with the man's painful declaration of unrequited love for Kessie Koopman, but he also distrusted him. And when Linc told the next part of the saga, he had some serious questions.

"So you beat Koopman within an inch of his life at the juke joint and got warned off by the police, but then you went to his house two nights later. Why would you do that?" Matthew demanded.

"Matthew's right," Diana interrupted. "Why couldn't you leave well enough alone?"

"I really don't want to talk about it."

Matthew and Diana exchanged a look. Linc had told them a cock n' bull story about how Kessie had intended to leave Henry Koopman. Linc claimed she'd finally worked up the courage to ask for a divorce and was taking her little four-year-old daughter, Kristy, to live with an unmarried aunt in Baltimore.

"If Kessie and Kristy had already left for Maryland, then why did you go to Koopman's?' Matthew persisted. 'Were you looking for trouble?"

"Oh God, no!" When Linc threw back his head in despair, Matthew saw that the blood from his nose had soaked his collar and felt guilty all over again. "Didn't you hear me?" Linc continued. "I only went there to make sure they'd really gotten away. I needed to know they were really gone."

"So what *really* happened?" Diana gently coaxed.

The sun went under a cloud and the geese flew away.

"Henry Koopman was dead when I got there," Linc said at last. His hands trembled as he rubbed his face. "It was awful. I tripped over his body in the dark, but then I took out the penlight I used to carry and saw that he'd shot himself."

"Koopman shot himself?" Diana seemed incredulous.

Linc vigorously nodded his head. "Yes, there was blood everywhere. It looked like he'd put the gun in his mouth and pulled the trigger. He was wearing his dress uniform, shoes spit-polished. I saw bits of skull and brain all over the new drywall."

Matthew realized that Lincoln Davis, usually calm and collected as a page from Southern Etiquette, was dissembling before their very eyes. The part about Koopman's dress uniform sounded true, because Bearfoot had told Diana the coroner had found brass buttons and good quality shoes buried with the male skeleton. But as far as Matthew knew, Bearfoot had said nothing about the skull being blown apart, which surely would have occurred during the suicide Linc had described.

Linc opened his long bony fingers in an appeal. "I panicked, you know? I understood why Koop killed himself—because his beloved Kessie had left him—but I knew the police would accuse me of murder, because of what I'd said that night at the bar. Because I'd threatened to kill him."

"They sure enough would have arrested you," Matthew growled. He wasn't buying Linc's story. When the old lawyer began bawling like a baby, Matthew was glad Diana's mother wasn't there to witness it.

"God help me, I'm not proud of what I did, and I've carried that guilt for forty years, but that night I found a shovel and buried the bastard out in the yard. Took me hours to clean the place up, so I didn't get home until almost dawn."

"And if it weren't for me," Diana added with tears in her eyes, "Henry Koopman would have stayed buried."

"That's right." Linc nodded miserably.

"So who buried Kessie and the little girl?" Matthew didn't want to be cruel, but he'd come to believe that Linc was lying through his teeth.

The effect of his words was dramatic and immediate. Linc began shaking his head so hard, Matthew could almost hear it rattle.

"No, no, no!" Linc babbled incoherently. "I read about those other bodies in the newspaper, but they couldn't have been Kessie and Kristy. They got away to Baltimore, I'm sure of it!"

He kept repeating those words as Diana wrapped her arms around his trembling shoulders. Matthew thought, if it weren't so pathetic, it would be comical, because Linc was a man buried deep in denial.

FORTY-SIX

The here and now…

"Did you believe him?" Diana asked as Matthew drove Queen Vic up one of the last steep ascents in the mountains outside Boone.

"I believe he believes himself after all these years."

They had been discussing the mystery of the bodies of Blueberry Lane off and on the whole trip. She realized Matthew was weary of the subject. She also knew they disagreed about Lincoln's guilt or innocence when it came to the death of Henry Koopman. She believed Linc, Matthew was not convinced.

Many inconsistencies and unknowns remained. They'd heard of no forensic evidence proving that Koopman's skull had been shattered by a suicide bullet. What had become of Koopman's truck? Linc said he'd seen it parked at the house that fateful night, but why hadn't someone gotten suspicious when the truck never moved? Did Margie Koopman believe that Henry and his family had moved to Fort Bragg without their truck?

"But you do agree it was Kessie and Kristy buried out there?" she asked Matthew.

"Oh, yeah, it was them." Matthew crested another amazing hill, with fog sleeping in the valleys and rays of brilliant sunlight stretching golden fingers along the mountaintops. "I also agree with you that Linc didn't kill the two of them."

"Do you think he knows in his heart that they're really dead, Matthew?"

245

"Maybe, but that truth will never reach his brain. He can't allow it. Linc needs to believe that his beloved Kessie is alive somewhere in Maryland, that she went on to live a happy life, maybe even got married, like he did."

"Yes, and that little Kristy is all grown up now with kids of her own."

"It would be pretty to think so," Matthew said as the town of Boone appeared before them, nestled in the arms of the distant valley.

Diana snuggled close. "You're pretty smart, for a sentimental old white man. Do you think Linc will tell Mama everything?"

Matthew downshifted as they began a very steep descent. "If they're gonna get married, and it looks like they are, he needs to come clean. He's lived with his guilt too long already, and even if Linc never shared it with his first wife, he's got one last chance with Vivian. If he's not honest with her, I won't be happy about their marriage."

Deep down, Diana agreed. She didn't know how Mama would react if Linc confessed, but she also believed that he needed to take that chance, even if it meant losing her. They had worried that Linc would feel pressured because Matthew and she knew the truth. He might assume that they'd pass it on to Vivian, making him vulnerable unless he made the first move. But no, they'd both assured Linc that it was up to him to reveal his past—both to Mama and the authorities—and only if he chose to do so.

As they entered the Boone city limits, Diana wondered aloud. "Will Linc be in legal trouble if he goes to the police?"

"I'm not a lawyer like he is, so I'm not sure. But I think the Statute of Limitations would prevent prosecuting a crime that old, assuming anyone even believed there was a crime."

Matthew stopped at a red light as a group of rowdy Appalachian State University students laughed and shoved their way across the street. "All these years later, I suspect the cops would have to take Linc's word for what happened, whether they believed him, or not. I don't think they have any concrete evidence to prove otherwise."

"Well, *I* believe him," Diana reaffirmed. "But I also think he needs to tell Wayne Bearfoot. Otherwise how will Margaret Koopman get closure? Whether she cares or not, those bones deserve to be buried properly, in graves with headstones."

"Now who sounds like a sentimental old white woman?" Matthew teased. "You know my opinion. Those bones don't care one way or the other."

"Maybe not, but the living do. At least *I* do. So I hope Linc does the right thing." She poked Matthew in the ribs. "And by the way, neither of us is *old*, so let's cut that out. We're in our prime, and I intend to enjoy every minute of it."

"In that case, stop talking about those bodies and everything else we've left behind," Matthew said. "We came here to have fun, so get with the program, Diana."

"I'm right here with you, Matthew. Nothing exits but the here and now. I promise."

She kissed his cheek and felt almost like a naughty teenager as they turned onto King Street, the main drag in Boone. Maybe it was the high altitude, but as they passed through the tunnel of funky stores, casual eateries and souvenir shops, she was suddenly giddy with the freedom of it all. Folks of all ages—tourists, students and even some locals—climbed up and down the hilly sidewalks with smiles on their faces. Some had a purposeful stride, others had all the time in the world to get where they were going, wherever the spirit moved them.

But oddly, for the past half hour Matthew had seemed in a rush to get here. He'd exceeded the speed limit on the highway and was currently impatiently tapping one finger on the steering wheel after a series of red lights.

"What's your hurry, Matthew?"

He glanced at his watch. "It's almost four o'clock."

Diana did not say "so what?" But she thought it. She knew it took time to decompress, to make that transition from one's busy work schedule to vacation time. But that had never been a problem for Matthew, who was normally so laid back he was half asleep.

In fact, he'd been uncharacteristically uptight planning this vacation, perhaps because he'd done it all on his own. He'd even made suggestions while she was packing her suitcase, urging her to bring something "dressy" along with the ratty stuff they usually wore in the mountains. Strangest of all, Matthew had asked before they went to sleep last night: "Do you want to stay in the Hilltop Inn, or camp out at my uncle's trailer?"

"Your uncle's trailer, of course," she'd told him without hesitation, because while most people would choose the fancier accommodations, the old trailer where she and Matthew had first made love was near and dear to her heart. Even anticipating their upcoming nights together induced a powerful tug of excitement.

"Where are you going, Matthew?" she now asked as they moved deeper into town. Usually they went straight to the camper, unpacked, and then returned to civilization for dinner and groceries.

"You'll see…" he answered mysteriously, and then pulled abruptly to the curb.

They had stopped beside the Watauga County Courthouse for no apparent reason. Diana was completely confused, while Matthew was obviously extremely nervous as he again checked his watch.

"Before we go inside, Diana, I need to ask you something…" His hand shook as he dug into the left pocket of his jacket and removed a small red velvet box. "Go on, open it."

Holding her breath, she gripped the box as firmly as her trembling fingers could manage. The lid made a little click as it opened on its hinge, and inside was the most beautiful diamond engagement ring she'd ever seen. Mounted in an ornate antique silver setting, its tiny facets caught the sunlight coming over the ridge top behind the courthouse, blinding her with tears of joy.

"Will you marry me, Diana Rittenhouse?" Matthew solemnly asked. "Tomorrow?"

FORTY-SEVEN

Two spoons…

After saying *yes* as many times as she could before Matthew smothered her words with his kiss, Diana only came up for air when he reluctantly broke the connection.

"The license bureau closes at 4:30 today and won't open again until Monday, so we better hurry," he warned. "Are you sure you're okay with this, Diana? I know it's short notice, but you always said you wanted your wedding to be sweet and simple."

"It's perfect." She kissed him again. "Very simple, and very, very sweet. Now let's get going before they lock the doors."

Room 119 was empty except for a young male clerk who asked them each to show two forms of identification, collected a fee of sixty dollars, and reassured Diana more than once that no blood test was required and there was no waiting period. They could get hitched tomorrow—no problem. He issued the license and congratulated them, but as they were leaving, he called out:

"Hey, are you sure you're old enough? You have to be eighteen in North Carolina."

"Wise guy!" Matthew growled happily as he snatched Diana's hand, and they left.

Not until dinner that night did Diana get answers to some of the many questions that swirled like a maelstrom in her head. The Dan'l Boone Inn was their favorite restaurant, located on

Hardin Street just off King, not far from the courthouse. For decades the grand old structure had welcomed guests from all over the world with its famous family-style meals. They offered every meat, side dish and dessert typical to southern country cooking. This policy guaranteed everyone left fat and happy. Since early May was still considered the "off season," they were surprised to find they had only a short wait before being admitted to the dining room.

"Penny for your thoughts?" he said as they stood in line in a wood paneled hallway hung with antique photographs. Glass cases filled with old-timey tools, firearms and other memorabilia lined the walls.

"Here you go!" Diana handed him a penny. She knew the routine, because they'd done it many times before. Matthew fed her penny into an ancient machine that looked like a jukebox. It lit up, gobbled the coin, and after passing through an embossing wringer, the penny emerged flattened into an elongated oval bearing the image of a frontiersman holding a rifle and the words: "Dan'l Boone Inn." "Thank you, kind sir," she said.

"For good luck," he said.

Diana knew the good luck must be true, because her change purse was full of these flattened pennies, and here she was with Matthew, still together after five eventful years.

An elderly waitress named Lucy spotted Matthew the moment they entered the dining room and insisted upon taking charge of their table. The woman had known Matthew back when he was with Lynn, his former wife. The first few times he'd brought Diana here, the reminiscences about Lynn had made her uncomfortable, but no more.

"You remember Diana, don't you Lucy?" Matthew asked once they were seated.

"Oh yes, sir, I certainly do." She smiled at Diana.

"Well, as of tomorrow, she'll be Mrs. Troutman—she'll be my wife." He proudly captured Diana's left hand and held it up to the candlelight so Lucy could see her ring.

"Oh my lord!" Lucy squealed, turning many heads in their direction. "Congratulations, you two. What took you so long, Trout?"

Before Lucy bustled away, Matthew caught her hand and sternly whispered," We don't want any fuss over this, you hear?"

"No, sir, I wouldn't dream of it."

"What kind of fuss?" Diana asked when Lucy left.

Matthew seemed shy. "Aw, you know. She might get it into her head that we need a cake, or something."

"Well, that would be embarrassing, wouldn't it?" But secretly, nothing would bother her at this point, because she was in shock—a good, dizzy kind of shock—and she just didn't care what anyone said or did.

She held up her ring again. The dancing flames sparkled on its many tiny faces. "Are you sure Ginny won't mind you giving me this ring?" Matthew had explained it was a Troutman family heirloom, passed down through many generations of Ginny's grandmothers. "By rights, it should be hers."

"Nope, I asked her," Matthew said. "As you know, Trevor has already given her a diamond and she prefers it that way."

Diana had fretted all afternoon about owning this priceless treasure, but she dearly loved its elegant ornate design. Ginny herself had said she favored a more modern style, as had her mother before her, so the ring had skipped two generations to reach Diana. Yet Diana suspected that Ginny's daughter Lissa might feel differently someday, so she'd make sure it passed on to her.

Matthew had taken one of her rings to the jeweler to compare and had the family diamond resized to fit. He had also purchased silver wedding bands for them both. He had arranged everything, and Diana was touched and impressed.

"Ginny did have some concerns…" he said once their table was laden with fried chicken, country fried steak, mashed potatoes, corn, fried okra, beans, and a basket of hot rolls. "She wanted to be here for our wedding, along with Lissa and Trev. She was afraid your mama would be furious, not to mention Liz and Danny. And she wondered if your children, Robby and Amanda, would resent not being invited?"

Suddenly Diana felt a pang of guilt. She didn't want to exclude these people she loved, but she also didn't want to steal anyone's thunder. Ginny, Liz, possibly even Mama were all planning to marry in the near future with much fanfare, while Diana wanted none of it. She wanted Matthew, pure and simple. She'd told him many times about her aversion to big weddings and, thank God, he'd taken her at her word.

"We can host a little party to celebrate with everyone when we get home," she said. "I just want to get it over with."

"Like a tetanus shot?" Matthew grinned.

"No, like we say *I do,* then escape to the trailer alone."

"I can live with that."

He'd her that he'd hired a Wedding Officiant, a woman about Diana's age, to lead them in a simple ceremony which would be less religious, more spiritual. Diana could tell the woman before the service if she wanted anything special—a poem or custom vows.

"Where will it be?" she asked.

"I reserved a little one-room chapel overlooking the mountains, not far from where we're camping. It's very rustic,

Diana, no heat or electricity. But since it faces east, and our service is scheduled just after sunrise, we should have plenty of light."

"Yes. Morning light. A new beginning."

As they quietly finished their meal, both too emotional to eat nearly as much as usual, Diana felt both nervous and calm, because Matthew's plans felt right to her. But then Diana's inner peace was shattered when Lucy, followed by the singing busboys and girls of Dan'l Boone Inn, arrived with a big white cake lit with crackling sparklers.

"Was this your idea?" She accused Matthew.

"Not guilty," he said, a big smile on his face. "I'm sure we can thank Lucy for this."

When they finished singing "Here Comes the Bride" that same phrase over and over about ten times, since it was the only line of the lyrics anyone knew, Diana blew out the sparklers. After Lucy had dished them each an enormous slice, Diana thanked her and asked her to divide the rest of the cake among the other guests. Lucy agreed, served their coffee, and eventually left.

"Wow!" Matthew breathed.

"Wow is right." She dipped her spoon into his cup by mistake at the exact same moment he started to stir his coffee. They both laughed, because this had happened the very first time they'd come to this restaurant. "Do you remember what this means, Matthew?"

He looked deep into her eyes. "Of course, when two people put spoons into a cup at the same time, it means they will someday marry one another."

FORTY-EIGHT

Alone together…

They'd set their travel alarm for six because the service was scheduled to start at eight, and they feared, needlessly, that they would oversleep. After making love, they'd both been so keyed up that slumber hadn't been an option. They had talked, giggled like teenagers, and then lain in silence, holding hands in wonder.

In the morning Matthew cooked their traditional vacation breakfast of biscuits, bacon and fried eggs. Then somehow they managed to get dressed in the cramped quarters.

Matthew wolf whistled. "You look mighty fine, Mrs. Troutman."

Diana, who seldom thought of herself as "Mrs." anyone, but rather an individual in her own right, liked the sound of it anyway. She was also grateful he'd asked her to pack something dressy, even though the longish, soft blue sheath dress with a matching flowing jacket was an outfit he'd seen many times before, right down to the turquoise and silver accessories she always wore with it.

Matthew grumbled a little about putting on his dress shirt and tie, which he seldom wore, but in the end he looked quite handsome in his dark slacks and double-breasted sports coat.

She told him so, then took his arm as they carefully climbed down the steep metal steps from the camper, Diana taking extra care not to catch a high heel.

"I think we'll pass muster, Matthew, but I feel a little overdressed out here in this field.

"Don't worry, we'll shuck these duds as soon as we get back." He winked, then kissed her cheek when they reached Queen Vic, which was inelegantly splashed with red road mud, not the storybook wedding carriage. "Are you ready to go?"

"Let's do it."

It turned out the small chapel Matthew had chosen was less than a mile from their campground, so Diana was surprised she'd never seen it before. It was well hidden by a stand of virgin forest, and as they slowly zigzagged higher up a gravel switchback road, she spotted the rustic stone and log structure clinging to the side of a hill. It faced east, as promised, towards the rising sun, and offered a panoramic view of endless mountains still obscured by a scrim of mist.

"Matthew, it's breathtaking, it's perfect."

As they left the car, he wrapped his arms around her, taking it all in. "Yes, it is," he said.

Matthew had told her the chapel had two parking lots, but in this upper lot they saw only one other vehicle. The traditional army Jeep undoubtedly belonged to Carroll Jennings, the minister Matthew had hired. She was standing beside the oaken back door, arms crossed, waiting for them.

"Welcome!" She gave them each a big hug. Up close, the tall, slim woman with a friendly weather-beaten face seemed like someone Diana had known all her life, yet they had never met. She wore a dark long sleeved, ankle-length linen robe and a small silver cross. She smelled like the outdoors. Her white hair was cropped short, much like Diana's, and the deep laugh lines at the corners of her smiling mouth put them both at ease.

"Well, you two look old enough to know better," Carroll said once they'd dispensed with the introductions. "Usually I feel obliged to counsel the couples I marry in advance, but I'll wager you already understand what you're buying into."

"Yes, ma'am, I do." Matthew grinned.

The minister's words reminded Diana of a thought she'd had several weeks ago: caveat emptor—buyer beware. It pretty much summed up every human endeavor worth taking a chance on, marriage included. "I understand," she told Reverend Jennings. "And I'm ready to go."

"So be it!" Carroll laughed. "Anything special you want me to say when we get inside?"

After assuring her that they just wanted the service short, simple, and legally binding, it seemed they were ready to start.

"But where are your two witnesses?" Carroll asked.

They looked at one another.

"We need two witnesses?" Matthew seemed seriously distressed.

"Of course you do, if you want it legal." Carroll frowned, then shrugged. "But don't worry, I suspect we can work something out."

"Are you sure?" Diana felt they'd gotten this far, so she couldn't abide a last minute screw-up.

"Trust me." Carroll held up one hand. "Now, you wait here for five minutes. Give me that time to set up at the altar, then open the door and walk slowly up to me. Got it?"

"Got it," Matthew answered as Carroll disappeared into the dark interior, then closed the door in their faces.

"Are you sure it will be all right?" Diana gripped his hand.

"I guess we can trust her." They counted off the longest five minutes of their lives. When the time was up, Matthew opened the door and they began walking hand in hand.

In those moments, Diana was hyper aware of many things at once. In the dim cold space that smelled of pine, she sensed the rough-hewn rows of pews on both sides and the uneven planks beneath her feet. Straight ahead, the minister at the pulpit was simply a silhouette before a floor-to-ceiling window that framed the forest and the brilliant blue sky, with the sun burning the mist from the eternal, majestic mountains.

Mostly she was aware of Matthew's warmth beside her.

By the time they reached the pulpit, Diana noticed another external sound—the soft sigh of others breathing in close proximity. Matthew noticed at precisely the same moment that they were not alone, so they turned in unison and saw them:

The others—all of them assembled like quiet smiling ghosts fixed on Matthew and her. She saw Liz and Danny; Ginny, Trev, and Lissa; Mama and Linc. And behind them in the last row sat Diana's own grown children, who now seemed more like intimate strangers—Robby and Amanda Rittenhouse.

Had Matthew not been supporting her, she would have fainted on the spot. "How did you do this?" she whispered as tears flooded her eyes.

Matthew also seemed in shock. "I didn't do it. It must have been Ginny. She was the only other soul who knew."

For many seconds the couple and their audience stared at one another like one organic, mutually dependent entity, until the Reverend Carroll Jennings cleared her throat and rapped the pulpit.

Even as they turned away to face the minister, Diana sensed the loving force at her back. But soon the words, the vows, carried her back to Matthew, until they were alone together. No one else.

"I do," they told one another.

"I love you," she told him.

EPILOG

One week later…

Matthew and Diana cut their honeymoon short to attend a celebration their wedding guests had planned. Since they had banished everyone right after the ceremony, returning to Mooresville early was the least they could do. Also, Diana wanted to spend a few precious days with her children before they scattered back into their own lives—Robby to Philly, Mandy to Sarasota.

Everyone clapped when they emerged hand in hand from the lake house, and then walked to where rented picnic tables that had been set up for a barbeque feast. The meal included an unfortunate whole pig rotating inside a big steel drum. A Pig Pickin' would not have been Diana's choice, but the "boys"—Danny, Trev, and Robby—who had become great friends, were wildly enthusiastic about the idea.

"Pretty cool, right, Mom?" Robby greeted her, gave her a hug, and shook Matthew's hand as delicious smelling smoke from the barrel wafted past them on the breeze.

"Very cool," she said as all the dogs—their Ursie, Juan's Wolf, and Danny's Amazing Grace—sniffed excitedly near the food source.

Amanda was right behind, with Ginny and Lissa in tow. "I suppose you'll have to celebrate all over again for each of the other three weddings," Amanda commented rather snidely.

"Sounds like a plan." Matthew grinned.

While Diana's son Robby had immediately forgiven and forgotten any old animosities between himself and his mom, Mandy would require more work. The years of separation had taken a toll on the mother/daughter relationship, yet Matthew believed any lingering resentments would fade in due time.

Diana's kids had been staying at the lake with Ginny and Lissa all week. In some respects, Mandy and Ginny were bonding like siblings. Dark, brooding Ginny and blond, outspoken Mandy had both been rebellious runaways, and they brought out the wild streaks in one another.

"Diana, we have some great news!" Liz and Danny approached in funny, matching plaid shorts. "They accepted our offer for that 1920's bungalow. We plan to move in and get settled before our wedding."

"Congratulations!" Matthew and Diana said in unison.

"But what about that other business?" Diana eyed Liz meaningfully.

"I don't want to talk about it."

Neither wanted to discuss it at the party, and Liz had only given Diana a few scanty details, but the gist was that the SBI had arrested Jose Nunez and two others on charges of drug trafficking and conspiracy to commit murder.

Diana and Liz would be required to testify for the prosecution about Nunez's link to the drug house on Helms Street—he had already confessed to slashing Diana's tires and chasing her through Mooresville. But since Diana and Liz had nothing material to offer about the pharmacist's murder, they would likely only have to give formal statements, not appear at the trial.

"So we'll put it behind us," Diana said.

"Way far behind," Liz agreed before she and Danny wandered off to help Trev and Robby, who were serving as the chefs.

Ginny, Lissa and Mandy also left to join a lively game of beach volleyball, where Juan Porter and Johnny Sorvino were beating Bobby and Juanita.

"Hard to believe, isn't it?" Matthew gazed out at their lawn, where pretty much everyone who mattered in their lives had assembled to honor their union. He wrapped his arms around her waist and led her to their two special Adirondack chairs, which proved to be already occupied by Vivian and Lincoln.

"Yes, every part of this is hard to believe." Indeed, Diana had been floating in a state of perpetual incredulity ever since they'd said their vows. She was amazed by the warmth of family and friends, the overwhelming gift of Matthew himself, but mostly by the blanket of contentment now wrapped around her life.

As the sun dropped lower in the sky, washing the trees, shrubs and grass in rich orange light and sending long blue shadows across the beach, Matthew and Diana pulled up the resin chairs and joined the older couple.

Once they were settled, Mama got right to the point. "Lincoln told me all about it, you know." Vivian's face was drawn and pale.

"Yes, Linc told us he had decided to tell you," Diana said. "Are you all right, Mama?"

"We're still together, aren't we?"

They were together, hands dangling between the chairs linked by their little fingers. Yet they seemed slumped, resigned, not yet recovered from Linc's admission of what by anyone's standard was a colossal lapse of judgment.

Linc lifted his handsome head of thick white hair and nodded at the dock, where Sheriff Wayne Bearfoot and his family were seated along the edge. Wayne's wife held their infant son in her arms, while their row of daughters splashed bare feet in the lake.

"I told the sheriff everything," Linc admitted.

Matthew and Diana remained silent as he explained. They already knew how Linc's confession had gone, because Bearfoot had told them.

"Why was I so stupid?" Linc groaned. "If I'd just come clean back then and reported Koop's suicide rather than covering it up, the forensic evidence would have supported my story."

This was true, because Wayne had concealed a vital detail from the press: the fact that the back of Koopman's skull had been blown away by a bullet, consistent with suicide.

Regarding the other two bodies, the sheriff's best guess was that Koop had somehow found out that Kessie had been unfaithful and that the child, Kristy, was Linc's. In a drunken rage, Koop had murdered the two, hopefully while they were sleeping in bed. The tiny fabric shards the lab found on the female bones were consistent with fragile nightgown material.

Bearfoot suspected that Koop had then buried their bodies, cleaned up the crime scene, but had ultimately been unable to live with the guilt.

Indeed, Bearfoot had told Diana and Matthew that when he suggested this scenario, Linc had refused to contemplate such a horror and had broken down in tears.

Clearly even now, Linc was in deep denial as the sun set on the lake and he continued his story:

"If I'd given the police the weapon, rather than tossing it off the River Highway Bridge, they'd have determined it was Koop's gun and found the powder burns on his hands," Linc finished miserably.

"Well, you were young and you felt guilty," Mama added sternly. "What was *really* stupid was taking up with that girl in the first place."

Diana glanced at her mother and felt bad for them both. Linc's old girlfriend was ancient history, but now it would be front page news, at least for a little while.

"Did Bearfoot ever find out what became of Koopman's truck?" Matthew asked.

Linc nodded. "When he interviewed Koop's sister, Margie, she told him the truck had been registered to her parents, who died in that ridiculous train accident. When she went to sell the lake property and found the truck just sitting there, she sold it along with the land and made a few extra bucks."

"You'd think she would have asked some questions, or at least wondered why her brother just left the truck there," Diana said.

"You would think so," Linc agreed. "But back when I knew her, Margie was a stone cold bitch. She never cared about anyone but herself and her money. If's Koop's disappearance benefited her in some way, then she didn't want answers, and that was lucky for me. If Margie had bothered to look for Koop, or questioned the truck, or called Fort Bragg, then everything would have come out. Eventually they would have questioned me."

"But that would have been a good thing, Lincoln," Vivian spoke softly. "You'd have gotten it off your chest and not suffered in silence all these years."

"Maybe you're right."

Diana watched them together and sensed that eventually they'd be all right. They'd go to Paris next month, their relationship would survive, and in time, even Linc would heal. He was off the hook as far as the police were concerned, and even Matthew believed Linc's story.

About that time someone rang the old school bell mounted in the yard, calling everyone to dinner. Eager to leave the subject behind, Mama and Linc left at once. Matthew and Diana lingered.

"What do you think?" she asked him.

"Well, I think Linc hasn't told Vivian the whole truth, because she doesn't know about the DNA test done on that little girl's bones."

"Did Wayne tell Linc that Henry Koopman was not the child's father?" Diana held her breath.

"Oh yeah, Wayne told him, all right, and we all suspect who the real father was." Matthew looked to the sun sliding under the horizon across the lake. "Wayne also told Linc that if he allowed them to take a sample of his DNA, they could give him a definitive answer."

"Oh my God, what did Linc say?"

"He said he'd rather let that sleeping dog lie."

Kate Merrill is an art gallery owner, real estate broker, and the author of numerous romantic suspense novels. She lives with her family on a lake in North Carolina, where she enjoys swimming, boating, and allowing her strong-headed Golden Retriever to take her for a walk.

Diana Rittenhouse Mystery Series

A Lethal Listing
Blood Brothers
Crimes of Commission
Dooley is Dead
Buyer Beware

Amanda Rittenhouse Mystery Series

Murder at Metrolina
Homicide in Hatteras
Murder at Midterm
Assault in Asheville
The Mayberry Murders

Mainstream Romance

Northern Lights (as Christie Cole)
Flames of Summer

Non-fiction

MISS ADDIE'S GIFT, Portrait of an American Folk Artist

www.katemerrillbooks.com

www.ingramcontent.com/pod-product-compliance
Lightning Source LLC
Chambersburg PA
CBHW070327260626
47160CB00003B/968